DIAL UP FOR MURDER

DIAL UP FOR MURDER

THE HACKER CHRONICLES BOOK 1

CLEM CHAMBERS

ISBN-13: 9781503179981

CONTENTS

CHAPTER ONE
1984 AND ALL THAT

Peter was worried. The business he had worked so hard for was slipping away. He had given up on his original plans and had turned to desperate measures. 1984 was meant to be the year of the dystopia but instead it was turning out to be the year of his personal financial disaster.

Setting up in business had always been put forward as something faintly heroic. Though it had turned out to be frightening, there was nothing brave about it. To get going Peter had borrowed money from his family but had seen it dwindle quickly. Twelve thousand pounds seemed like a lot of money but it had shrunk to eighteen hundred in a matter of weeks. The adverts he had placed were unsuccessful. The three thousand pounds he had invested in ads had evaporated without a return.

Now he stood in a rundown exhibition hall, packed with market stalls pretending to be computer companies, and felt broke, lost and doomed. Everyone, bar him, seemed to know exactly what they had to do. Their stands were colourfully laid out and stacked high with products. His small table was bare in comparison. He had a pile of brochures and two signs, one of which had been bent in transit.

'Plug into the Future,' said his main banner.

Compared to the flashing lights, balloons and posters of the other exhibitors, he felt it might as well have said, 'For sale, something boring.'

Peter tried hard to look positive. He forced what he thought might look like an affable air onto his face but it slid off the instant he forgot to hold onto it.

Today, the world was populated by a horde of spotty teenagers sporting zipped anoraks and slightly damaged pebble glasses. They thronged, clutching bulging plastic bags, taking his free brochures like shoplifters desperate not to catch the eye of surveillance.

'They cost a quid a copy,' he felt like pointing out as the disinterested brochure collectors disappeared into the melee with his precious literature, 'You bloody better read it!'

Three hours had passed without a sale, when a thick-set man in his mid-thirties stopped at Peter's pitch. The prospect looked out of place amongst the crowd. He wasn't dressed for the sudden downpour the geeks seemed to fear, but as if he was on his way to the golf course.

'Excuse me son,' he began, 'are you Online Data?'

'Yes,' said Peter. 'Can I help you?'

The man gave a huge grin, much too wide to be polite. 'My accountant reckons I could find your service useful. You see I don't know much about computers, but as I get it, I can take a computer, plug it into the phone and talk to your computer, which is also plugged into loads of other people doing the same thing.'

Peter smiled back. At last, someone who knew something about what he was selling.

'As long as you've got a modem, that's absolutely right. You can leave any other subscriber the equivalent of mail, which they can read on their computer. You can even meet them on our electronic chat lines and talk with them. There are games to play and programs to download.'

'Download, what's that?'

'Online Data has programs on its host and you can pull them down onto your computer via the phone line.'

The man nodded dismissively. 'Ah I see, can I join now and get sorted out here?'

Peter beamed. A sale at last; he was beginning to fear he was going to score another duck. 'Of course . . . It's five pounds a month, which is offset against a pound an hour usage charge. We bill you at the end of each month.'

He bent down to get his order form out.

His precious customer scowled, 'Ah that's no good, how much is it to join for good?'

Peter straightened up. 'Pardon?'

'For life? I'm not interested in paying monthly. I'll pay you now and that needs to cover the lot, for good.'

'We don't do an unlimited usage membership.'

The man looked annoyed, his face reddening a little. 'Well if you did what would you charge?'

Peter coughed nervously. 'It's hard to say. No one's ever asked before. I mean, a lifetime can be a long time. You see, we charge by the hour.'

'Well how about a couple of years then?'

Peter began to feel a surge of panic. His voice raised a tone.

'It's difficult to judge.'

The man leant forward. 'Watch my lips,' he said. 'How much?'

Peter flinched back and blurted, 'Two thousand pounds.'

The man pursed his lips in thought and held a mental conversation with himself. He pushed his right hand into his back pocket and pulled out a thick wad of light yellow paper.

Okay,' he said, counting the fifty pound notes, 'You're on. You'll give me an account and a phone number now. Right?' He recounted the money.

'Well actually . . . .' began Peter, about to tell him of the registration procedure. The man paused and leered at him. 'Err . . . Yes of course.' Peter reached down and pulled out a manual. 'I'll write it on the inside of this and set everything up for you tonight.'

The customer folded the notes in half and handed the bundle to him. Peter pushed the money into his pocket and picked up a subscription form.

'Can I have your name, sir?'

The man reached over and took the form from him. 'Look, you don't need one of these, do you?' He showed his teeth again in what might pass for a smile. 'Just give me a book of words and the numbers. If you need to reach me, mail my computer. If I need you, I'll do the same. That's how it works, doesn't it?'

Peter swallowed to clear his throat. He nodded. 'Okay.' He opened the front cover of the ring bound book. 'This is our computer's telephone number.' He wrote it down. 'What ID do you want?'

'What's that?'

'That's the system's name for you . . . '

'Wedge. Will that do?'

'Yes.'

'Fine then, Wedge it is.'

'Okay,' Peter wrote it in, 'that's in capitals. Make sure you type it in in capitals. And this is your password.' He wrote wedge, as the password. 'You can change it to what you want when you log in. Then no one will be able to guess it and get access to your ID, mail and things.' He closed the book and offered it to him.

The man opened the front page again and took a look. 'Right, I've got that. Stay lucky!' He turned abruptly on his heels.

Peter watched Wedge make his way into the throng and disappear. 'Do you want a receipt?' he muttered to himself. He took the money out and pulled a note from the bundle, raising it up to the light and staring at the watermarks. It looked kosher enough. Peter quickly counted the forty of them and then counted them as four lots of ten notes. Whichever way he did it, it came out at two grand.

An anoraked figure stopped. Looking directly away from the table to some point in infinity, it went to take a brochure, trying to locate a folder by touch with a groping hand.

Peter pushed his arm away. 'Fuck off Kid! These things cost money.'

The Anorak pretended not to notice his invective and trundled on.

Throughout the afternoon, he continued to pat the bundle in his pocket, reassuring himself of the cash's whereabouts. The one-day show had cost him one hundred pounds for a table top and two hundred for brochures. The profit seemed as miraculous as the sale itself.

Three normal subscriptions were sold late in the day. The buyers were committed for three months with an automatic monthly continuation if they didn't cancel. His subscriber base had just risen to twenty-six. Of the millions of computer users in the UK he had convinced twenty-six to join Online Data. If only he could convince one per cent of the remainder.

If he was careful, the two thousand pounds would buy him another two month's operation. He now had about three more months to start bringing in some more money. The cold blasts of the harsh world had been dulled by one man with more money than sense. If only everyone would be as free with their cash.

As he loaded his beat-up car with a box of his show things, he felt good. Tonight he was rich. Tomorrow the takings would be in the bank and just numbers on a page but for now, it was real money in his hand.

He slammed the boot down, wondering how many others at the show had made that sort of money; not many, he was sure. Today, the powers that be must like him.

———

The next morning he felt the resolve of a man with liquid funds. His office was above a tailor's shop which didn't open until ten o'clock. To one side of the protected entrance, behind a display window that jutted out, was a battered brown door. He pulled the security shutter back down behind him and went in. The stairs were a steep thin corridor, unevenly rising in a spiral up two floors. The first floor, which he wasn't using, was strewn with cardboard boxes. It could be entered from the first landing by a single creaking door. He continued on up to the second floor where his embryonic and embattled business empire lay.

The building's owner, the despotic ruler of the shop below, had shown him around when he had first viewed it.

'The whole place is on a tilt,' said the ancient Jewish man bluntly. 'Hit by a bomb during the last war. This is only the front half. We never rebuilt the rest. I've worked here since 1918.'

That didn't seem particularly surprising as pretty much everything in the place seemed to have been there for sixty-five years too.

A door on the second floor landing testified to the blitz. It opened onto a twenty foot drop to a yard that once must have been part of the larger whole.

He had hung two pictures on the bare walls. Both looked unhappily crooked, however set, but the bleak office was in desperate need of something to brighten it up.

His modern, but second hand desk looked good amongst all the shabby gloom. On top of it sat the crowning glory, his XT PC. This state of the art computer was going to revolutionize everything, but it seemed the world was not going to catch on to what it could do quite as quickly as he had expected.

He dropped his post down unopened and sat in front of the computer. As long as he was looking at the screen his surroundings need not impinge.

WEDGE had already been on and Peter's logs said his password was changed. He had sent Peter an email.

'THIS IS A TEST,' it said. 'MAIL ME BACK. WEDGE'

Peter answered it.

'Dear Wedge,
Message received.
Regards,
PeterT
Sysop'

He loved email; it had all the pleasure of normal post without any of the drawbacks. When you sent it, you didn't need to go out to a post box, you just typed SEND. You could tell if the receiver had read it, you could tell when a letter was written. As it was just data in a computer, a desk wouldn't fill up with paper, it just sat on the machine as a record you could keep for as long you liked.

He had plans to link Online Data into other computer mail systems for international link up, but for the time being, the company was too broke for that kind of dream. There had been sixteen accesses the previous night and seven hours of usage on the clock. He stared vacantly at the filing cabinet, the other major piece of office furniture, and strained for inspiration.

'More ads,' he thought. 'Ones that work this time.'

Below him he could hear the rattle of the shutters going up as the shop opened. He walked out into the tiny kitchen with its toilet cubicle and made himself a tea. If he had the money, he would hire an advertising agency to do the job properly. He thought about the two thousand and thirty pounds now in his top drawer. That wouldn't go far, but a few calls couldn't hurt.

The door intercom buzzed. He walked slowly over to it, trying not to spill his drink.

'Online Data,' he said.

'I've come to join,' said a muffled voice accompanied by metallic traffic noise.

Peter pressed the entry button on the phone. It buzzed angrily as it opened the lock below. The door creaked and banged shut with a rattle. He made a dash for the desk, pivoting around the hot splashing drink, put the tea down with an annoying spill and headed for the stairs. He saw an old thin man hesitantly looking into the deserted floor below. He started when he saw Peter.

'Ahhh . . . Online Data?'

Peter smiled down at him. 'We are up here at the top.' This wasn't strictly true; there was another floor above him, derelict and barely watertight. A door in his office led up to it. He had explored once, but that was enough. It led to what the Victorians had called a fire escape. The whole setup looked more dangerous than a leap from a window onto the street.

His caller looked like a van driver; the type of man too old to put up with the rigors of driving a mini cab who had therefore pastured himself off to do small deliveries. As he entered the office, the visitor pulled an envelope from his jacket pocket.

'I want an unlimited usage account,' he said reading off the back of the letter. He squinted at some scrawling. 'A book of words, with all the details in it.' He corrected himself, 'Written in it, it says here.' He looked questioningly at Peter and held the envelope half out to him.

Peter took it and tore it open. It was a large amount of money. Then it dawned on him, it was another two thousand pounds. In fact, it suddenly looked just like the budget for an advertising campaign.

'Yes, yes, of course,' he said, snapping himself out of his revelry. 'Sit down.' He pointed to a chair in front of his desk. 'Would you like a coffee?'

The man looked regretful. 'No, mustn't hang around.'

Peter sat down and got out a manual.

'What ID do you want?' he asked. 'Sorry I didn't catch your name.'

'Smith,' he said, 'Henry Smith.' He shook his head and looked confused, 'Give us whatever is easy.'

Peter quickly filled out the inside of the manual and gave it to Smith. 'Do you want a receipt?'

'No,' came the reply, 'I must be off.'

Peter shook his hand. 'Thanks for calling in.'

Smith nodded nervously, 'Goodbye.'

The door banged closed below and Peter stuck his head around the stairwell to make sure Smith had gone. He rushed back into his office and snatched up the envelope. He pulled the money out and counted it.

'Another two grand,' he said to himself in amazement. 'Fantastic!' Wedge must have told a friend.

———

Colin woke up hot and uncomfortably sticky. It was four in the morning. The room he worked in was heated by an electric blower which he wouldn't switch off, except when it looked like it might catch fire. He squinted through bleary eyes at the mess of empty coke bottles and fast food cartons spread around him.

It was time to get back to work. His project, a Sinclair Spectrum computer game, was nine months late, but they couldn't fire him because it would be ready by Friday.

Which Friday he wouldn't say and they had so much money tied up in promotion, his bosses couldn't gird themselves up to throw him out. It had to be finished soon, or so they told him. He marvelled at how promises would always buy him more time, no matter how often he broke them.

Working late had pushed his work pattern further into the night until he had to sleep into the day to maintain the night hours. The best thing about working at night was that he didn't get disturbed by constant interruptions from marketing men wanting demos for customers and press. It was a pity they wouldn't let him take the work home, as then he could get on with other things untroubled. He kept telling them, all he needed was to be left alone.

On the positive side, since he was working in the office, he could hack computers on the company's phone bill. Hours on the line to the States were just swallowed up in the overall telephone costs. An extra thousand pounds on the quarter's total made the sales department look busy; the company would never know it was him trying to crack computer systems around the globe.

He hauled himself into his chair, lit a cigarette and took a swig of flat coke from a can that stood on his monitor. His computer was on but the screen was dead. He powered the monitor up and waited to see the results of the night's work.

'WEEEEEEEEeeee,' he cried at the top of his voice, as the picture resolved. There was a message from his program waiting for him:

MASTER I HAVE ENTRY TO THE BOX OFFICE
VIDEO HOST ON
ID: MASTER
PASSWORD: SECRET

'Lu . . . uv IT!' He rattled the keyboard with a furious burst of typing. His modem bleeped and the screen flashed up the communications software. 'Let's have a dig.' He began to chuckle to himself.

———

Roberts' phone buzzed. It was the intercom. He snatched up the handset.

'I'm in a meeting, damn it.'

'It's a Mr Zorro on the line, he says it's important.'

He looked up at the company accountant sat at the other side of his desk.

'It's that bastard hacker.' He spoke into the phone again, 'Okay, I'll take him.' He jabbed a flashing button. 'Roberts speaking.'

'Hello,' said Colin. 'You don't know me but I believe that you received a message from my machine on your mainframe this morning. As you may well be aware, you have a security problem with your system.'

'Yes,' snapped Roberts. 'What do you want?' He clicked the phone onto speaker.

'I haven't done any harm,' Colin's tinny voice echoed around the room. 'My interest is little more than academic, you see? It's just that I like to test security on systems relying on the phone network for access. When I find one that is vulnerable I like to inform the owners and offer my services to help them make their systems secure. Not all hackers are ethical like me, you see.'

Roberts put on his calming voice. 'I see. And what exactly are your services?'

'Well, it is pretty open, but for a small retainer I will tell you how to watertight your setup. Then every month I can monitor it remotely and test it to make sure it's okay. Also I can tell your computer department of anything new that happens on the security front to make sure they are always up to date.'

'How much will this cost?'

Colin hesitated, 'A thousand pounds a month.'

'That's agreed. Now my manager needs to come and see you, to find out how to close the loophole.'

'I'll send you a contract and then I'll visit,' said Colin.

'Fine, I look forward to getting it. Make sure you send it for my attention. That's Mark Roberts.'

'Mark Roberts,' Colin muttered.

'Got it?'

'Yes got it.'

'Okay, bye.'

'Bye.'

Roberts hung up. 'Get me that fucking idiot Swartz, in here, now!'

The accountant leapt up and wheeled out of the office. Roberts opened a drawer and pulled out a packet of mints. He pried one out and began crunching on it like a dog gnawing on a bone.

The accountant reappeared with the Data Processing Manager.

'The little fucker that got into our system has just been on the blower. He wants a grand a month for time immemorial, to tell you how to keep bastards like him out of my system. I don't know how much we've spent on this fucking computer.' He glared at the accountant, 'Well how much . . . '

'Err six hundred thousand pounds, approximately.'

'. . . But I know one thing, I ain't having some little shit crawling all over it and then telling me I've got to pay him. I suppose he could have flushed it all down the karzi if he'd wanted to . . . ' He stared at the DP manager. 'WELL?'

'Yes he could have,' said Swartz awkwardly.

'Yes he could have, YES HE COULD HAVE,' Roberts yelled, spraying particles of white mint. 'What the FUCK ARE YOU DOING? My warehouse men don't leave the fucking gates open at night. If they did, their fucking feet wouldn't fucking touch the fucking ground.' He stared into Swartz's eyes. 'What have you done about it?'

Swartz took a deep breath and straightened himself. 'Well, we've found how he got in and we have plugged the hole. It was a stupid mistake, but it was left by the installation engineers. It's standard practice to close it, I would have thought Tomkins would have sorted it.

Roberts looked at him. 'He didn't get the fucking sack for being Einstein, did he? You better watch you don't follow in his bloody footsteps, because if this little bastard gets back in, you'll be going out the same fucking window. Geddit?'

'Yes sir.'

'Now, you are sure he can't get back?'

'Yes.'

'Abso-bloody-lutely certain that you've blocked him?'

Swartz shifted from side to side. 'Yes.'

Roberts didn't like the way Swartz shimmied. 'Because if you're not, you'd better do everything you need to do, because I'm not having it happen again. No way.'

'I'll double check everything, again, myself.'

Roberts snarled, 'Well, get cracking then.'

Swartz left quickly.

'This could prove to be a big problem,' said the accountant darkly.

Roberts reached for his desk diary. 'I'll sort it out. Meanwhile you come back to me with a report on how we can protect ourselves in the meantime. You can't trust fucking computer wallies for anything but fuck ups.'

'I will have it on your desk tomorrow morning.'

'And Ravi, while you are at it, keep your eyes out for a new propeller-head.'

'Will do.'

———

Roberts dialled.

'Special floral services,' replied a gruff-voiced man.

'Hello, I haven't used you for a bit. What have you got on offer these days?'

'Well sir, we are presently specializing in hospital deliveries,' the voice wheezed rhythmically.

'That's fine, just what I want.'

'What sort of arrangement had you in mind?'

Roberts pondered momentarily. 'Nothing outlandish, just something that will last a long time in a ward. Quite a large display, something that will be remembered for years to come.'

'Certainly.'

'How much will that cost?'

'Our standard charge is twenty,' croaked the reply.

Roberts narrowed his eyes, 'Let's say twenty-five.'

The voice creaked slowly, 'That will certainly add to the overall effect. Perhaps sir might at some point consider our funeral service. We can cater for all sorts of small private occasions, should the sad need arise.'

'I didn't realize you did funerals.' Roberts was taken aback. 'How much does that come in at?'

'It's a new addition for established customers and a tasteful wreath costs five hundred.'

'That's quite a bit, but even so, that's good to know.' He smirked to himself. 'I can think of a few times where I could have used that, even at that price. I better take a mental note.'

'It's most discrete.'

'Look, I'll send someone around to the shop in the next couple of days with the details and twenty-five.'

'Is it for immediate delivery?'

'Yes.'

'Thank you.'

'Goodbye.'

Roberts hung up. He popped another mint into his mouth and ground it into a paste.

———

A punk rocker with a pink Mohican shook Colin awake. 'Hey man, it's four. IT'S FOUR, IT'S FOUR.'

'Yeah, yeah, yeah,' he murmured, waking slowly. He hated the afternoon part of his artificial shift.

The punk jumped over to a small CO_2 fire extinguisher lying in the corner of the room. 'I'm gonna get you man, I'm gonna get ya.' He waved the nozzle threateningly.

Colin stuck his head under the cushion he used as a pillow. 'Sod off,' he moaned.

The punk stuck the nozzle under the cushion. 'Time . . . to . . . . wakey wakey.'

Colin sat up sharply, his arms thrashing. 'Sod off! Sod off! Sod off!' he screamed.

The punk jumped back and fired a huge white cloud. 'Yeah . . . bullseye . . . yeah, yeah,' he cried, pogoing on the spot.

'Shit, shit, shit.' Colin threw his pillow at the punk, who ducked.

The door opened and Graham, the Development Manager, came in. 'Jesus guys, can't you pretend to be humans? What are you going to do if we ever have a fire in here? Piss it out?'

The punk looked faintly sheepish. 'Just letting off steam.'

Graham eyed him. 'I need those graphics tomorrow morning, Ralph.'

'Easy man, easy.'

Graham grimaced. 'Just make sure they are good man, good. Okay?'

The punk shrugged. Meanwhile Colin had slipped on his unspeakably dirty jeans.

Graham turned his attention to Colin. 'How's Anthrax going?'

'Okay,' he muttered.

'Got the graphics in?'

'Yeah, almost.'

Graham smiled; maybe at last things might be getting somewhere. 'Can I see them?'

'No, they're all in but I haven't linked them yet.'

Graham sighed, 'When can you show them to me?'

Colin looked away, 'Dunno, maybe soon . . . . by Friday.'

Graham threw his hands into the air. 'I'm getting a lot of stick over this. The press want it, the distributors want it, shops are ringing up, it's advertised, the posters are out and I can't even show the sales people a few moving graphics. Come on Col, you've got to get it done. I mean, it's going to be a big hit.'

Colin smiled. 'It's nearly there, all the numbers are in, they are just in the wrong order. Just a few more routines and a few more bugs and it'll be ready.'

'Are you sure?'

Colin knew this was the end of their futile resistance. He had won long ago, they were over a barrel. 'Yeah, it's close, it's very close. If I didn't get so many distractions it would be finished by now. I mean if I could work from home, it might be only a week.'

Graham had visions of Colin taking his hardware and disappearing. 'Work at home?' He gave Colin his best stern look, 'That would be impossible. It's out of the question.'

Colin looked depressed. 'Okey dokey . . .'

'Soon!' said Graham, as if it had to be true.

'Yeah, yeah, soon.'

———

Roberts buzzed an extension as he thumbed through the flimsy contract Colin had sent him.

'Accounts,' said an Asian voice.

'Roberts here. Send me up two and a half grand in petty cash.'

Forty minutes passed before Ravi appeared with the money. He put it down on the desk with a blank form. Roberts signed the sheet at the bottom.

'Did you have to go to the bank?' he asked.

The accountant nodded. 'What shall I put it down as?'

'Sales incentives or something.' He pushed the form away.

Ravi nodded, took the chit and left.

Roberts counted the money quickly, then took out a blank sheet of paper and wrote on it:

Colin Fordham,
39 Cardington Crescent,
Leytonstone,
London.

He folded the sheet around the money and placed it in an envelope which he addressed.

He buzzed his secretary. 'I've got a package that needs a bike.'

'Yes Mr Roberts, I'll get on to Nodel right away.'

———

On a back street road of a shabby area, in a little pebble-dashed terrace house, a tiny bathroom's shower was on full blast. The doorbell rang.

'Oh hell,' she cursed; why did it always go when she was washing her hair? She stepped out, dried herself hurriedly, slung on her dressing gown and wrapped her head in a towel.

One day soon, she promised herself, she would move out of this bedsit and get a flat all of her own. Peering through the peep hole at a little man dressed in a suit, she put on the chain and opened the door slightly.

'Does Colin Fordham live here?' he asked.

'Yes but he's out.'

The man smiled. 'Do you know when he'll be back?'

'No, he spends most of his time at work, he's hardly ever here.'

The man smiled again. 'Could you tell me where that is? You see, I'm from the Readers Digest and I have a prize. I have to deliver it to him today, personally. He's got the third prize in this month's lucky draw.'

'Oh,' she said. 'How exciting.' She thought for a moment. 'He works off the Mile End Road, I think, now what are they called? Oh yes, Excalibur Games, they'll be in the book. What's he won?'

The man shook his head happily. 'Sorry, I'm not allowed to say, you will have to ask him. Company policy, I'm afraid. Thanks a lot. Goodbye.' The man turned his back and marched sharply away.

She closed the door. 'Lucky swine,' she thought. 'I didn't think anyone really won those things. There's no justice.'

———

With a bucket of take away fried chicken in one hand and a litre of Coca-Cola in the other, Colin was set up for the night. As he strolled down the Whitechapel Road, between the alcoholics content with their drinking, he pondered the idea of doing some work on the game. He decided to make his mind up when he had eaten. Perhaps some progress might be in order to keep the bosses a bit less unhappy. Up ahead, just before the Underground station was an alley where Jack the Ripper had committed one of his heinous murders.

'What a bastard,' he thought as he passed it.

A figure stepped out from the gloom. 'Got the time, mate?'

'No, mate,' he replied, halting. 'No watch.' He displayed an empty wrist.

The figure reached forward and grabbed him by his coat and threw him into the darkness.

Colin sensed two figures. A massive blow to his stomach shot the air from his lungs. Everything blurred as he was pinned, struck and struck again. His bowels emptied and he urinated with the shock. He went limp, then passed out.

Chapter Two

ATOT

The hazy world was blue and white; harsh, acrid smells wafted around him. Colin's tongue clicked against his throat as he tried to speak. His jaw was frozen.

He opened his eyes to see a blue nylon curtain. The slightest movement sent waves of pain through him. He tried to move his right arm but it was bound, he tried to call but his mouth wouldn't move. He gained more consciousness. He moved his left arm, quacking a strangled groan of pain. Most of his head was covered with something. His hand flopped down and he fell asleep.

———

The noise of the curtain being pulled woke him again.

The nurse noticed the movement. 'Hello Colin, how are you feeling today? Don't try to move much, just relax. I'll get a doctor to come along and see you in a minute.'

———

Time passed. The police had been to see him twice in the fortnight. He had seven fractured ribs, a broken collarbone and jaw. Having his mouth wired up was nightmarish, he often felt he might choke. He could write now without too much pain, but that was little consolation.

'No,' he had written on a pad, he didn't know who had done it.

'No,' he didn't know why.

'No,' he didn't get a good look at them.

'No,' nobody had a grudge against him.

'No,' he couldn't understand why anyone would do it.

'No,' he didn't realize it looked like a professional job.

'Yes,' he would tell them if anything occurred to him.

It was all so messy. Words like hacking and extortion kept going through his head. 'Maybe,' thought Colin, 'I should have asked Box Office Video for less money?'

———

Graham looked at the ghost of his former programmer. He found the drawn scared figure even more repulsive than its former dishevelled self. What was worse, the little snert was going to walk out on the project.

'Look Colin,' he pleaded,' I know you've been through a lot, but you can't quit. I mean, we've just got to have Anthrax; you can't just leave us hanging out to dry. It could, it will be such a big hit. If you don't finish it, it'll be just one big write off for everyone.'

'I'll finish it freelance,' he muttered painfully.

'No way,' said Graham firmly.

'Give me a grand now, a grand on playable demo and a grand on completion.'

'You know we can't do that, it's against policy.'

'Take it or leave it,' said Colin, turning to go.

'Look, hold on,' said Graham desperately. 'I'll check with Mike.'

'I want my hardware too,' said Colin, carefully moving his mouth.

'Give me an hour. I'll see what I can do.'

———

He had moved into a hotel, then into a new bedsit in Brixton. He had paid cash and used a false name. One good thing about working all night was that he had saved quite a bit of money. Excalibur had capitulated to his demands as he had expected, so he felt even happier about his finances.

'One thousand pounds for nothing,' he had thought, walking across the car park with a boxful of hardware held carefully in his arms.

He stopped by a call box and dialled a number. The phone was answered with a whine of a modem. He placed a small tape recorder to the mouthpiece and answered it with a pre-recorded computer dialog. The digital message finished and he hung up. He flagged a cab and headed to his new home.

———

Roberts was red with fury. 'Get out of my fucking building and don't fucking come fucking back.'

Swartz looked up from his monitor, the sweat running down his face. 'But . . .'

'Don't fucking BUT me . . . ' he screamed, 'get fucking gone. Now!'

'But . . .'

Roberts lurched forward, just restraining himself from hitting Swartz. 'NOW,' he hollered, spraying him with saliva.

Swartz grabbed his jacket and stumbled for the door in a panic. All the monitors in the building were flashing; everything had been wiped out by a tremendous crash.

'My things . . . ' he said weakly, as Roberts pursued.

'I'll send you your fucking things in a fucking bin liner.'

Swartz bowled out into the forecourt feeling his pockets, 'My keys,' he said looking at Roberts astride the door.

'If you think you're taking the company car home,' Roberts bellowed, 'you're even more fucking stupid than I think you are. You can fucking walk, you fucking incompetent bastard.' He turned around and tried to slam the office door behind him.

The mechanism resisted so he shook it violently until it closed with a shudder. Swartz retreated and ran out onto the road. Robert stormed up to his office and grabbed the phone.

'Special services,' said a crackly voice.

Roberts took a deep breath. 'I want funerals.'

———

Peter stared out of the window at the rumpus outside. His office overlooked a crossroads guarded by a set of lights. Over the short period since he had moved into the office, cars had smashed into the central beacon on three separate occasions. There seemed no good reason; perhaps they were on a ley line intersection and filled with enough cosmic power to attract cars to swerve at them.

Today's uproar was different. A tramp on crutches had sat down in front of a lorry waiting at a red light and now refused to move. The truck inched its imposing bulk forward, trying with gusts of frustrated airbrake sighs, to persuade the bedraggled man out of the way. Instead, the derelict banged on its grill with his crutch and swore incomprehensibly at everything.

A crowd of people formed. Two sympathetic onlookers approached to try to coax the grey ball of rags out of the road, but he swung at them, keeping them at bay with circular thrashes. The tramp stared around triumphantly and bellowed invective. Cars began to blow their horns in annoyance. The driver of the wagon climbed down from his cab and ran to a callbox. A few minutes passed and a large police van appeared with four stout constables. They restrained the tramp with expertise, manoeuvring, then tussling, manoeuvring again then tussling once more.

They dragged him onto the pavement and thence into their vehicle. Peter wondered if a warm police cell was the tramp's goal as he watched the twisting body being manhandled through the barred back doors of the van. He had certainly gone out of his way to earn one.

Over the last four days a motley crew of delivery men and dispatch riders had been turning up with the tariff of two thousand pounds. He had banked £21,000, bought himself an expensive leather jacket and had a nice roll of cash in his pocket. He felt on top of the world.

The phone rang.

'Online Data.'

'This is the manager's secretary, Lloyds Bank, Whitechapel. I have a call for Peter Talbot.'

'Speaking.'

'Putting you through,' she said. The phone clicked.

'Hello, Mr Talbot, it's Steven McDonald. I thought I would give you a call and make sure everything was running smoothly with your account.'

'Yes, great, thank you.'

'Can I take this opportunity to invite you to lunch to discuss your banking requirements?'

'Eh, that's very nice of you.'

'Are you free tomorrow?'

'Yes.'

'Shall we say twelve o'clock?'

'That's okay.'

'At your office? It is always a pleasure to get an idea of our customer's business.'

'Fine.'

'I look forward to seeing you tomorrow.'

'Yes, see you then. Bye.'

He hung up, feeling confused. He had never been invited out by anyone, let alone a bank manager. When he opened the account, he had to give so many details and references it had made him feel like a desperado. Now they wanted to entertain him. With a little money life seemed very different.

The door buzzer rasped. He got up and pressed the intercom button. 'Online Data.'

'Is this the computer place?' said a female voice.

'Yes,' he said, unlocking the door. He heard it slam. 'We're at the top,' he called down before going back to his desk.

'Hiya, I'm Jay Jay,' said a young women, stabbing in on high heels. 'I want to find out about being on the line.' Her leather mini skirt squeaked and an enormous bead necklace clicked as she moved.

'Online,' he corrected.

'Online,' she repeated with a giggle.

'What would you like to know?'

She sat on the edge of his desk and swung her black hair back with a flick. 'Everything.' Her chest heaved under a red T-shirt and as she leant back her small embroidered jacket slipped away.

Peter swallowed. 'Where shall I begin?'

She lifted her right leg onto the desk and dangled it over the far corner. 'At the beginning.'

He turned uncomfortably in his chair. 'Would you like a coffee?'

'Later,' she said quietly, looking across at him mysteriously. 'Tell me everything.'

'Well, you need a computer and you need a modem.'

'A modem?'

'That's a gadget that talks with another computer. You would use it to speak to mine.' He pointed to the box on his desk. 'You use the computer and modem to log in via your telephone line. So basically your computer rings up mine for a chat.'

'I love intelligent men,' said Jay Jay, dangling a shoe from her toes. 'So I've logged on,' she said distantly, 'what then?'

'Well, you can send and receive electronic mail. You can chat in real time with up to sixteen people at once, by just typing a message which they all get instantly. You can chat privately to someone; even make your own room which you can let other people into.'

'No one else can hear me?'

'No, not if you don't want them to. That way you can have a private party. You can join conferences on subjects and leave comments on them; you can start your own special interest area.'

'Any subject?'

'Yes, whatever you are into to.'

Jay Jay's shoe fell to the ground. 'Science makes me randy.' She rubbed her toes together.

Peter bent down and picked up the court shoe. 'Ah,' he said, trying to break the silence. He hung it carefully back on her foot.

'Oooh,' she giggled. 'That's nice.'

He sat back with a start, 'Then there are the databases you can use, they're like encyclopaedias really.'

'Being computerized is such a bother,' she sighed, letting a small long-strapped clutch bag slip off her arm to the floor, 'and so expensive.' She moaned and rolled so that she lay on her side across the desk top.

His trousers were becoming tight and very uncomfortable. 'Yes quite.' He rolled his chair under the desk a bit more.

'I don't really have two thousand pounds,' she said, as if it hurt. She pouted at him. 'I don't know what to do.'

Peter grimaced. 'That's a tough one.'

She twisted and rolled up, kneeling on his desk, her jacket falling off as if it was just laid on her back. She looked down at her left shoulder, which had a bee tattooed on it. 'Maybe if we were friends you could give me one.'

Peter flushed and his mind went horribly blank. 'Argh,' he gurgled in a strangled gulp. 'We can be friends, but . . . '

'Do you like butterflies?' she purred, stripping off her top to reveal her breasts. She arched her back to accentuate them and twisted to display two Red Admirals perched daintily on the incline. 'They are my pets,' she said, running her fingers over them.

The buzzer sounded and Peter leapt up like a sprinter and bounded across the room. 'Online Data,' he reported rather loudly.

'I want an account,' came the reply.

He spun round. 'I've got another customer,' he said apologetically. 'I'm sorry.'

With amazing speed she was fully dressed again. She walked up to him at the door and pressed her palm against his crotch.

'You're a hard man,' she said. 'I'll drop by another time.'

He grinned shakily, 'Okay.'

The door buzzed.

She kissed him on the cheek and sidled out.

The door buzzed again.

He pushed the entry button. 'Sorry,' he called into the intercom,' this things a bit dickey.'

It was another delivery man with an envelope of money.

———

The morning brought him a nasty surprise.

'HELLO YOU HAVE BEEN HACKED,' read the mail from an unknown new account called hedgehog. 'I WILL BE CALLING YOU TO STRAIGHTEN OUT YOUR SECURITY.'

Peter swore and started to trace back the loophole. He soon found it. His setup came with a number of accounts standard to the software he was running. They had passwords which needed to be changed from day one. He had missed two of them and the hacker had crawled through. He changed them. As these accounts had powers granted them, not given to a normal user, the hacker had had an opportunity to get up to more mischief than simply giving himself a free account.

Peter began to check for other new accounts that the hacker might have put in place. He found one called ZORRO. He deleted it and the Hedgehog ID. He checked for trojans, destructive programs which the hacker could have installed on the machine for later use.

He found three and erased them. Then he checked the password file but it was untouched. He had programs running all the time that monitored the comings and goings on the system but he hadn't been quite paranoid enough.

As he double-checked that he had closed the hacker out, the phone rang.

'Hello, this is the Hedgehog,' the voice said nervously.

'Hi hacker, have fun last night?' said Peter curtly.

'My interest is purely academic,' said the voice. 'I like to test the security of people's systems.'

'Well, you succeeded. What do you want?'

'Other hackers less scrupulous than me could have caused you a lot of damage.'

'True.'

'I wondered if you would like me to do some consultancy to help make your system watertight?'

'Not particularly.'

Hedgehog seemed unperturbed. 'It's just that something really nasty might happen if you remain as wide open as you are.'

Peter laughed. 'You mean one of your logic bombs might go off?'

There was a moment of silence. 'Oh, I'm glad you found it, I was about to tell you.'

Peter laughed again. 'IT . . . you mean them, don't you?'

'Yes them. They are merely an example of what can happen,' said Hedgehog indignantly.

'Are you looking for work or trouble?'

'Neither . . . well I'm always interested in work.'

Peter rocked back in his chair. 'Well I might need someone who knows what he's doing, sometime in the future, but you've hardly shown yourself to be the sort of person worth trusting, have you?'

'I can be trusted.'

'If you make some useful suggestions then I might give you an account. How's that sound?'

'Any chance of any cash for it?'

'No. If you can find another loophole and tell me about it properly, I will be impressed. Then there might be money in it. Interested?'

'Alright, I'll give it a whirl.'

'What's your name?'

There was a pause. 'Colin.'

'I didn't catch your full name.'

There was another pause, 'Colin Fordham.'

'Okay Colin, impress me and I might put some work your way.'

He hung up without further ado. The phone rang again. It was the hacker.

'I'll bring you round a report on your system in a few days, with some of your security lapses.'

'Thanks. Bye.'

'Bye.'

He wasn't sure whether he had done the right thing, but having a tame hacker was better than having an untamed one. Maybe getting the guy to give him the once over might be a good thing. He didn't want foxes breaking into the farm now he had a golden goose.

At twelve o'clock sharp the bank manager arrived. He had a dense toothbrush moustache and a chubby face that made him look like an overweight Hitler. Peering around inquisitively, he greeted Peter.

'This is where it all happens,' said Peter, ushering him in

McDonald sat down. 'Excuse my ignorance, but my files say you are an online service provider. What exactly is that?' He smiled genially. 'I know practically nothing about computers. I tell a lie, my boy has one and he plays games on it.'

'We are a little different to that, let me show you.' Peter pointed to the machine on his desk. 'This is the heart of Online Data. People subscribe to be able to connect with this and we provide them with various services like mail, databases, conferencing, which the computer operates.' He passed him a manual. 'This will give you an in-depth overview.'

McDonald looked at the diminutive, humming box of electronics. 'What happens if the computer has an accident?'

Peter smiled confidently. 'I fix it. It's not a big deal. It's the subscribers that are the valuable item. They are the real assets of the company.'

'How much does a system like this cost?'

'Six to seven thousand pounds.'

'That's not a lot of money for the income it generates.' For an instant McDonald looked uneasy. 'You must have lots of customers.'

The momentary uneasiness spread to Peter. 'Just over three thousand,' he lied furiously. He couldn't bring himself to start an explanation of how a few people with large amounts of cash kept turning up. 'A few adverts have brought in a huge response. It's been hard keeping up with it all.'

McDonald nodded reassuringly. 'It sounds like an exciting business. Do you have much competition?'

Peter felt relieved that the manager didn't quiz him on why there were no cheques. 'Yes, but we seem to have got our marketing right. That makes all the difference in hi-tech.'

'Yes, I'm sure it does.' McDonald put the manual in his brief case. 'Shall we go to lunch?'

'Yes, great.'

The manager eyed the office like a security camera as they left. 'What are the rents like here?' he queried as they made their way out.

'Cheap, four hundred a month.'

'That's good. Keeps the overheads low, that's for sure.'

Throughout lunch, McDonald quizzed him about the business in a sort of relaxed interrogation. Did he plan to expand, how was he insured, had he thought of starting a pension, what car did he drive?

He broke up the questions by bemoaning how badly banks were treated by their customers and further interspersed them by saying what a fascinating business Peter had set up. Peter for his part made long enthusiastic speeches about how the future belonged to online systems and how they would make the world a global village. The waiters fawned and bantered. When the head waiter was out of earshot, McDonald explained how the restaurant was a customer of the bank.

'Sometimes I think we keep them afloat,' he said in a hushed voice. 'Tricky business, catering.'

By the time the dessert arrived, the bank manager was waxing lyrical about golf. The effects of two glasses of wine and a total indifference to the sport made Peter glaze over. He found himself staring at the wall thinking about computers and when the bill arrived he felt relieved. On the way back to the office, McDonald began to tell him how it was good to see young people doing well. Peter wasn't sure if he should be flattered or patronized.

Would he have been so popular if he had approached the bank for a loan a month earlier? As they parted, not for the first time, a question nagged him. Why the hell were people giving him all this money? The change in his fortunes had been enough to catch the bank's attention and the change had been so fast that it had swept him up in a wave of pleasure and relief. He believed in the idea of Online Data, he believed in his product. He was sure that he was doing well because the world believed in the idea enough to pay for it. He didn't want to think any deeper about it; success was beautiful.

———

He did not get to see much of his flat. Leaving the office very late, it was generally time to go straight up to bed by the time he arrived home and in the morning he was barely awake until he was sat at his desk in the office and starting on his second mug of tea. Benign neglect kept it in a better state of order than he deserved. The amount of use was neatly matched by the amount of attention it received; otherwise he would be living in a pigsty.

The morning brought another two accounts. System usage was building. The logging programs were showing a consistent increase in activity and the money received was turning into usage. He had promised himself a new car when the bank account had fifty thousand pounds in it. He hankered for something better than the little runabout he flogged mercilessly around town. His ideas for the replacement swung between splashing out on a flashy sports car and getting something practical. The cash was pouring in and soon he would be able to make the actual choice.

The whole area was scattered with pubs. They all seemed marked by a clientele that considered drinking a very serious activity, rather than part of a bigger picture. Next to the tailors stood The Queens Head, a tatty, rough establishment frequented by tatty, rough drinkers. When, as now, the mood took him, he would drop in and get a sandwich and a coke. An old man, stubby and thick, his robust frame like an over-stuffed pillow, began to talk to him.

'I bus about London usually,' he said, nurturing his pint of Guinness. 'I think I'd kill myself if I couldn't travel around on a ticket all day. I know all the routes. You see there's nothing for an old soldier like me to do otherwise. I'm no farking good at sitting at home looking at the wall. It would drive me bonkers. Just because you're old, people think you're useless. Me, I'm full of energy, I can get around as well as I ever could. Only carry a stick to get a good seat.'

He paused to look disgusted. 'During the war I was a paratrooper.' He pressed two fingers on his upper arm. 'They didn't tell you, when they threw you out over Arnhem, that they'd want to scrap you as soon as you was too old to die for your country. I used to work for a dry cleaners, till they went skint. What sort of job is that? Mind you it's better than none at all. You try getting a job and they say, over sixty, fark off, we need young men. Young men, they don't know the meaning of the word work, too busy chasing pussy.'

Peter turned slightly from the old man as a figure approached him.

A mean-looking stranger leant forward over the table to say something to Peter. His sharp features held an evil intent. 'That's a nice jacket,' he said menacingly in a low voice.

Peter looked up at the man, whose jeans, jumper and short straight brown hair fitted a typical police description. 'Thanks. I just got it.'

'Let me try it on,' he said putting one leg up on a stool.

'No, I don't think so.'

'I'll give you ten quid for it.'

'No thanks.' Peter looked up into his deep-set eyes and smiled. 'You can buy one up the road in Brick Lane.'

The stranger clenched his fists. 'Are you gonna sell it to me or am I gonna have to give you a good kicking?' He started to crouch menacingly.

Peter prepared to jump to his feet but as he was about to respond, the stranger collapsed to the floor. The old man had sent his would-be attacker sprawling with the crook of his stick and was up standing over the sprawled figure in an instant.

'Farking yobbos!' he gurgled. 'Can't you see we're busy?'

The stranger scrambled to his feet, then fell again with a frightful yelp, felled by a knee to the groin which the old man had raised with slow but deadly precision.

'Thatch, Thatch,' screamed the bar lady in panic. Over the counter jumped a massive blue Great Dane. With two huge bounds the dog stood over the writhing body and began to growl with a slobbery resonance.

'Chuck him out, chuck him out,' cried the bar lady.

The dog reared up and barked. The stranger began to flee, paddling backwards with one hand, still holding his groin with the other.

'Fuck off . . . fuck off,' he cried desperately. He turned onto all fours and sprinted up, careering towards the door. The pony-sized dog loped after him, rumbling evil growls. Crashing onto the door, he threw it open and disappeared. The hound stopped, turned around and padded slowly back to the drunken applause of the pub's customers.

'You all right George?' called the bar lady.

'Yes my darling,' he called back. He looked at Peter and then at his glass.

Peter took the hint. 'What will you have?'

'It's a pint and a whisky chaser.'

Peter went to the bar and brought a round, with a brandy for himself. 'Thanks,' he said, putting the drinks on the table. Pulling a fifty pound note from his pocket he handed it to George. 'Here's something for later.'

George stopped stroking the Great Dane and unfolded the money, 'Blimey, a dry Sir Christopher Wren,' he said, looking a bit shocked. He patted the dog firmly in merriment. 'You're a soft bitch, aren't ya,' he said, rubbing the dog's head happily.

'I've got a proposition for you,' said Peter. 'How would you like to do some part time work for me? I need someone to look after the phones, take orders, you know? Someone to keep an eye on things when I have to go out for an afternoon or the day. Do you fancy it?'

George sunk the whiskey in one. 'Ahhhh!' he exclaimed happily, licking his lip. 'Sounds like a runner to me.' He banged the glass down on the table and beamed. 'You give me twenty a day and I'll look after the shop for you.'

Peter held his hand out. 'Deal!'

———

When they left the pub, they saw the stranger fifty yards down the road, stood in the doorway of an empty shop. He stiffened when he saw them and swaggered towards them with a purpose.

Peter stepped forward to meet him. He put his fists up and began to bob from side to side on his toes.

'OK then, let's see you take it,' he taunted, waving him on with one hand. 'Come on, let's see you.'

The man hesitated as Peter waited, poised and confident. The stranger stopped, dithered, turned and began to run off.

Peter dropped onto his heels and looked at George. 'He's no stomach for more.'

'You're a farking con artist,' said George with a grin.

Peter shrugged. 'You'll never know.'

———

Colin was doing the rounds of the games software houses. He rung them up, told them he was finishing a game on the PC and asked whether they were interested in what he was doing. He would say that a number of other companies had been chasing him to sign it and that he would come in and demo the product to them, to show what he could do.

He then explained that as it was very nearly finished he would probably sign it over the course of the week to another company, but perhaps they might talk about the next game.

They invited him around and he showed them the demo. In it, a fat man with a big nose and a bulky laser-rifle walked across a scrolling background of attractive graphics. The character jumped, fired, crouched and fell over and died. Various abstract shapes representing hideous aliens moved across the screen. Meanwhile, Colin told the development people about the special bonus levels that were going in, the many different types of weapons that the little fellow was going to have.

He explained the elaborate story behind the game and detailed how he could have more moving graphics on the screen than there had ever been because of a new technique he was using. They knew he had worked for Excalibur Games and the magazines had been raving about what they had seen of the project he had written for them. The demo looked primitive but they knew how hard it was to show anything polished until the bitter end.

Colin told them that Excalibur was holding Anthrax back for Christmas. He told them that they were an even more impressive company than his previous employers who he had left because they would not let him produce the kind of top quality product he was completing now. They on the other hand seemed like good people to work with.

The software house always tried to convince him to sign the nearly finished game. He demurred but they cajoled. A good game could easily gross sixty to a hundred thousand pounds and it would either fill a gap in their plans or work out as an added bonus to their sales. A first rate game from a proven author was a rare and precious thing indeed.

When they reached the right price, he was always convinced. Three thousand pounds for signing on the spot, another three thousand pounds promised on play-test version and four thousand on completion was the usual offer. Sometimes they would give him four or five thousand upfront and the advance was all he was interested in.

As he collected his cheque, they didn't know Excalibur had tried to restart Anthrax from scratch with a new programmer. Nor did they know that he had disappeared without trace and didn't live at the address he gave them. They thought they had pulled off a coup and signed a sure-fire winner. When it was too late, they would realize that even if they could find him, he wasn't worth suing.

Colin reckoned he could hit another six software houses for advances with his demo. It only took him a couple of days to change it about. He thought it best to make them look different just to cover his trail a little. Sometimes he thought he might write a complete game. Software houses would kill for a hot finished product, wherever it came from. He had never written a finished game but he told himself that as it was pretty easy, it was probably too mundane for his special talents.

———

Amongst the scanty morning post was an invitation to a day of power-boat racing on the Royal Docks. For some reason, British Telecom had invited him to their hospitality suite to enjoy a prime view of the action. Somewhere, from deep within the heart of their marketing computers, he had fitted the correct criteria. The rest of the process had been automated. As the virtual world of data crossed into the real world of paper, an RSVP had spanned its journey from algorithm to acceptance. He rung the number on the card and told the voice at the other end he would be there. The confirmation was keyed into another machine and the cycle of information was complete. The tiny flaw to all this technology was that they had simply selected the wrong guy to ask along.

Earlier, when he was unlocking his office door, the assistant manager of the shop had come out to greet him. Maurice took out a letter from an envelope and offered it for Peter to read. A man in his early fifties, he had always genuflected politely through the shop window whenever he saw Peter coming or going. He had won that month's £250,000 premium bond lottery.

'I've handed in my notice and I'm leaving,' he said. 'I thought you'd like to know.'

'Congratulations,' said Peter, shaking his hand. 'That's amazing.'

'It's a bolt out of the blue,' reflected Maurice.

Peter wished him more good fortune. He knew how he felt. One minute you're poor and downtrodden, the next you're a hero and free. It seemed the most important factor in life was outrageous luck.

The race meeting was a paradox. Amazing, aerodynamic boats hurtled with a complete lack of sanity around a boring but potentially watery grave. It seemed that not one of the races passed without a hideous accident where miraculously no one was killed. Watching from the hospitality quay was a crowd of dignitaries, representatives of large telecom customers, whose restraint was incalculable. They looked on, detached, like decadent Romans witnessing carnage in the Circus Maximus. He raided the finger buffet before it had officially opened, loading up his plate well past the point of decency. He hadn't eaten on the Friday night, the opportunity had not arisen.

The boat races had very quickly become extremely similar. There didn't seem much skill involved in bouncing round in circles for ten minutes. The first away invariably held his ground and, barring collision, won by denying anyone else enough room to pass. Who smashed into who was the main excitement, but Peter felt a bit depressed at the prospect of deriving pleasure from such a mean spectatorship.

Having caught up with his nutritional needs, he started to scan the throng for women. Work had deleted his love life and trapped him into a cell of money-making. He had determined this might be a window of opportunity to break out.

Everyone seemed so old. He wondered whether the computer would have cancelled his invite if it had known that he was twenty-two. He was just about to give up hope of finding an eligible female, when a family party appeared.

From a marquee, carrying paper plates, a late middle aged couple with their two daughters headed for a water-side vantage point. Peter worked out their trajectory, arrival point and the best route to get there before them. He headed there with haste. Both girls were quite pretty, the tallest of the two looking about his age. The younger seemed, perhaps, a little bit too young. Here might be the opportunity he was looking for. If not it would be back to making money and celibacy.

His navigation worked like magic. He stood nonchalantly looking out towards the race when the party moved in next to him. To his right stood his primary target, a brown haired female with a blue jumper and a striped skirt. She browsed around and began to watch the race in progress. Everything had fallen into place, but now he lacked the opportunity to actually make contact.

The months of solid work had left him out of practice with any kind of socializing. Peter felt like a car that had been left in a damp garage for too long. It would just take the right spark for ignition then the rest would follow. All he needed was an ice breaker, but his mind was a blank. He was watching the boats too intently; he needed an excuse to turn away and a reason to utter a hello. He couldn't be too obvious, he needed to be suave, and somehow the slavering wolf needed a mask. Every opening line he had ever heard churned past but failed to gel as the right thing to say. He had a sinking feeling that he had already lost his opportunity.

'Do you come here often?' she said, leaning forward on the railing and catching his eye.

Peter nearly started in surprise. 'Eh no. I've never been to one of these things before.'

'Nor have I,' she said, laughing notionally.

Like a lock when the water level finally equalizes, his mind opened. 'My name's Peter.'

'I'm Mary,' she said demurely.

They shook hands.

'What do you think of the boats?'

She leant forward on the railing, plate in hand, and studied the scene for a moment. 'I can't really see the point. It's fun when they smash into each other and bits fly everywhere but they are too far off to get a good look.'

Without warning the contents of her paper platter slipped across the tilt of its resting place on the rail, dropping into the inky water below. 'Oh damn,' she complained, 'there goes lunch.'

Peter tried not to chortle at the food's graceful escape. As he was restraining himself, Mary saw him grin and started to grin back. They smiled at each other, a smile that widened until the laughter broke.

'It's not fair, it's not as if I'm on a diet.'

'Let's go and get some more, I'm peckish,' suggested Peter, lying.

She turned to her parents. 'Mum, Dad I'm going for some more food. This is Peter.'

The father grumbled something and glared at Peter. The mother likewise turned a scornful look on him.

'Hi, nice to meet you,' he said.

The father nodded and the mother ignored him.

———

The food tent had been denuded by the time they got back to it. They rummaged like scavengers, winkling out the dainties from among the leftovers. Peter played the gentleman and handed her his best finds. It was a fraud backed by a full stomach. By the tent, the speakers of the commentary drowned out their conversation, forcing them to shout short messages at the top of their voices.

'Why don't we go somewhere quiet?' she screamed, 'This racket is killing me.'

Peter nodded and then, cupping his mouth with his hand, 'How about the Isle of Wight?'

She turned to him and put her lips his ear. 'Perfect!'

————

At the back of the race compound was a hamlet of tents. It was deserted, now the exhibitors and customers had spread out around the water's edge and become caught up in the competition. They moved inside a small blue bivouac that seemed to have been cleared and sat on two white plastic folding chairs, amongst the fast food litter of wrappers, cups and beverage stirrers.

They talked and ate. Mary was studying acting at drama college and taught art at a secondary school. She was vivacious, bright, sparkling with a wildness that almost shocked him. She told him lewd jokes, apologized after each one for the bad taste, then challenged him to tell her a worst one. He was soon struggling to keep up.

'Come on,' she said, pushing him provocatively.

Peter held her arms away and they tussled. 'No, I can't remember any more.'

She stood up and smiled wickedly at him.

'Well then, we will have to do something else.'

She stepped over to the entrance of the tent, untied the door and zipped it down. Peter looked at her questioningly, a tingle running down his spine.

'Open your mouth and shut yours eyes, if you want a nice surprise,' she sang, walking back towards him.

'It better be a nice surprise,' he said, obeying.

He could sense her in front of him.

'You must keep your eyes closed,' she said.

He felt her hair on his face and then his shirt. Warm soft lips touched his. He reached out to touch her and there was no resistance. As he touched her back, she straightened slowly, his hands sliding down to her bottom. She moved closer to him as he held her buttocks.

'No peeking now.'

He hooked one hand underneath her skirt and then, encountering no complaint, followed it with the other. He slipped his fingers under the fabric of her panties and continued the caress. She pressed forward again, lifted her skirt and dropped it over his head.

'You can open your eyes now.'

'It's dark in here,' he said.

She folded onto his back and laughed.

He wrapped an arm around her legs and stood up, lifting her onto his shoulder.

She squealed with surprise.

'I'm taking you home, to bed,' he said.

'No, no, spin me round first, spin me round.'

He began to turn. 'Like this?'

'Yes, faster, faster.'

Around and around he whirled with small stamping paces. Mary giggled uncontrollably. He started to feel giddy and began to slow down but with a slap she urged him on.

'Don't stop,' she slapped. 'You are not allowed.'

He quickened again but lost his balance, sagging to his knees rather than dump them both onto the hard ground. Mary rolled off onto her back and lay looking at him. Her lips were wet, her eyes liquid with tears.

'Now,' she rose with a growl and grabbed his shoulder. She tugged him forward onto her. 'Now!'

———

The next afternoon, he decided to head back home at five. He had felt utterly drained and exhausted from the moment he woke. There had only been a brief interlude between Mary leaving at dawn and his normal rising time and he could not function with so little sleep.

The day had been a long haul, a dull monotony where everything hummed, especially his head. He began to yearn for sleep. At lunch time he lay down by his desk and used his raffia waste paper basket as a pillow. Sleep came easily, but the phone rang every time he drifted off and he gave up trying to get any peace.

George had told him to, 'Fark off home and have a kip.'

The idea of leaving the office to George, for no better reason than rest, seemed too wimpy. He wasn't prepared to admit being completely defeated by the results of his over-indulgence.

He drank coffee until it made him shake, then started on tea. Why was it, while everyone else his age seemed able to stay up all night dancing, having sex and getting stoned or drunk with impunity, for him it incurred a terrible retribution?

The appointed hour arrived.

'Okay George, let's wrap it up!'

The phone rang. George picked it up. 'Online Data, night security speaking.'

'Hello,' said an American voice with the whispering echo of satellite linkage, 'is Mr Peter Talbot there?'

'He's probably gone home sir, but I'll try his line for you.' He jabbed the hold button with a stubby finger and turned to Peter. 'It's a yank and I think he's calling from America.' Peter rubbed his eyes in hesitation. George reconnected himself, 'I'm afraid there's no answer, can I take a message?' George hung up; the reply was obviously negative.

Peter picked up his keys. 'Probably important.' He yawned as if to excuse himself.

'If it was, he'll call again. You just mind yourself on your drive back. I don't want to get the push 'cause you topped yourself at the wheel.'

———

The traffic was hellish. In his stupor he hadn't calculated for the rush hour. At nine o'clock at night it was a twenty-five minute ride, tonight an hour after he left the office he was still on his way.

He had forgotten what a mess they had left the bedroom in. The sheets were in a hill in the middle of the bed and the mattress was half off its base. He wearily rebuilt the bed to make it habitable again. The phone rang downstairs and when he answered it, there was a long silence.

' Hello . . .' There was silence. 'Hello . . . If you're there I can't hear you. I'm afraid you've got a dud line.'

'Ahhhh . . . ummmm,' said a female voice.

'Who's that?' he said, feeling stupid. 'Mary, is that you?' Having said her name he hoped it was.

'Ooooohhhh . . . ' The voice went breathy.

'Hello?' It sounded like it could be Mary, but then again it was hard to exactly attribute such primitive utterances to anyone.

'Ummmm . . .'

'Mary?'

The panting and groaning continued.

'Look, come on, don't play games.' He wanted to say, 'Bloody hell Mary, at least say it's you,' but what if it wasn't?

'Ahhh . . . um . . . ummmmm.'

'Look, if you don't say who you are, I'm hanging up in five seconds. Five,' he said firmly.

'Ummm.'

'Four.'

'Ummmm,' the voice was more intense.

'Three.'

The voice gasped.

'Two.'

'Oh yes, oh yes.'

He hung up and took the phone off the hook.

Peter thought he should count himself lucky to get a heavy breathing phone call from any woman, but he was too exhausted to appreciate it at that moment. Most men had to pay good money for that sort of thing.

As he slid into bed he felt he had achieved a day-long goal. Like a prophesy, a parental cliché was fulfilled. He was asleep before his head touched the pillow.

In a dream, his doorbell rang. He answered it and no one was there, then in an instant he was back in bed. It rang out again. He got up and went downstairs and answered it once more. Under the porch floated his old maths teacher hovering like a phantom.

'Think boy think!' said the mathematical ghost, glaring piercingly at him.

'I don't understand?'

'Use your God-given brain.'

Peter slammed the door in his face and was returned to his bed.

The doorbell rang again.

'Oh what?' he muttered. He twisted his head and peered at his alarm clock. His vision resolved; it was seven in the morning. He pulled on his dressing gown and went to the door. Who the hell was it at this time?

Through the misted glass of the door and his barely open eyes, it looked like Mary.

He opened the door. 'Mary? What's going on?' he mumbled.

She pushed in and grabbed him by the arm. 'I just have to have you.' She pulled him into the lounge.

He hopped, off balance, just managing to push the door shut with his foot.

'Was that you last night?' he asked, trying to wake himself fully.

Mary sunk to her knees, clasped his waist and pulled him down onto the ground until she was kneeling over him. She pushed his dressing gown back and took his penis in her mouth. She looked up impishly at his expression.

Momentary concepts of protest melted away like butter on hot toast. Words that formed in his mind never made it to his lips. As soon as his body responded, she rose up, lifted her skirt slightly and impaled herself on him. She tilted her head backwards and swished her hair from side to side, riding him like a horse at full gallop. She smiled to herself and groaned and murmured, throwing herself up and down with worrying abandon. She began to rub herself beneath her skirt and concentrate on an impending orgasm.

Peter's dressing gown had risen up to his waist and his buttocks were friction-burning on the carpet. The pleasure was being more than negated by the pain, but at least it had woken him up.

Mary cried sharply and instantly fell forward on him. He used the moment to lift up and pull his dressing gown back under his exposed flesh. As she looked up, her hair curtained his face. She grinned at him through cat-like squinting eyes.

'Surprise!' She squeezed him tightly with her muscles and began to push and stretch him. She rested forward on his chest.

'I'm being bad today,' she said, 'very bad.' She gripped him like a vice and pulled up.

He moved his hips up with hers.

'No knickers,' she sighed, lowering herself pneumatically.

Peter was lost in the moment as his body began surging under the ruthless manipulation. He moved to the conducted rhythm, cadenzaed and then crescendoed.

She stood up and looked down at him. 'I've got to be off in a minute,' she said running upstairs to the bathroom.

Peter composed himself and got up shakily. He flopped into a chair and waited until she came down again.

They kissed. Her kiss said, 'See you later.'

As he went with her to the door she pinched his bottom. 'I'll call you at work.'

———

George had a huge smirk on his face as he showed a well-dressed, middle aged woman into the room.

'Mrs Davenport,' he announced, 'this is Mr Talbot, the boss.' He reversed out and disappeared.

'Hello,' said Peter standing up.

The first thing that struck him about his visitor was her hair. Designed on heroic proportions, an imposing masterpiece of precision, it was like a decoy, masses of sculptured golden locks distracting the viewer from a face that had once, a long time ago, launched a thousand ships.

His attention was next drawn to her clear piercing eyes that seemed like the viewing screens of a hard calculating mind.

A huge coat of some exotic animal extraction hushed about her frame like a living thing. The fur flowed as though it might detach itself without notice and maul him. A low rift of scent began to pervade the air with a sweet odour like chocolate.

'So you're the new kid on the block.' Mrs Davenport held out a limp, bejewelled hand. Buttressed somewhere between the loss of youth and a surrender to the inevitable, she seemed ageless.

'Yes,' he said, shaking it unsatisfactorily. 'I suppose you could say that.'

She sat down. 'Now then, to business. As I have had it explained, your computer can help me. Please correct me if I am mistaken. I can be contacted by anyone with a connection to you. I can buy a one off membership for two years. I can deposit money into my account and transfer it to any other account for a ten percent handling charge.'

Peter shook his head. 'No, if you put money into your account and keep a credit balance, you can use it to buy other user's uploads. Uploads are things like programs, perhaps specialist advice another user might offer or, for example, a mailing list. We take ten percent of the price of the sale.'

Mrs Davenport waved a long fingered hand. 'Someone buys a download thing from me for a hundred pounds, I get ninety pounds. That's correct?'

'Yes.'

'Someone puts money into his account, buys my service, you debit him. I ask for a cheque, and you remit.'

Peter shrugged, 'Yes, you can certainly look at it like that if you like.'

'That's fine, that's what I want.'

She produced a tortoise-shell cigarette case and a gold lighter.

'Call me Glenda.' She lit up, then blew a long thin trail at an invisible point of aim. 'I have a lot of agency work. Foreign customers from all over the world, all with different tastes. I want to work towards coordinating it all under one umbrella. Big customers can open an account with you and we can run the transactions through your system. If everything works out smoothly we can expand from there. We can try it out and then take things in measured stages.'

Peter smiled. 'What kind of agency business are you in?'

She raised a dismissive eyebrow. 'Temping.'

'Do you employ many people?'

'About a hundred girls. Roughly forty full-time, sixty part-time.'

'That's a lot.'

She batted her eyelashes and looked for an ashtray. He tipped the paperclips out of his and pushed it towards her.

'Thank you.' She paused and looked seductively at him. 'You come highly recommended. You're quite the buzz of the moment. Computerization, automation, it's the coming thing. So many businessmen these days go everywhere with their computers. We have to move with the times.' She pulled out a thick envelope from an inside pocket and placed in on the desk. 'Is it okay if I send around a girl now and again for a bit of training? I won't always be the one operating the instrument.'

'Certainly.'

'Thank you.' She passed him a card with her name and a portable phone number on it. 'You should come around and see us sometime.' She winked.

————

As soon as she left, George bounced into the office.

'What a darling!' he exclaimed.

Peter looked worried. 'I think I've just made an error.'

George looked indignant, 'What you mean, didn't you give her one or something?'

Peter scowled, 'She's got to be a Madam and I think she wants to use us for her business.'

George laughed. 'Leave it out, don't look gift horses in the mouth. She ain't doing no harm.'

Peter grunted to himself. 'Yeah well, tell that to the judge'

George laughed again. 'You're a bleeding head case, that's your problem. You're onto a winner here. It's raining money. Fill your boots; you're never going to get another chance like this.'

Peter stood up. 'I'm gonna buy a new car.'

George grinned. 'That's more like it. You only go round once.'

As Peter walked towards the tube he wished he had said, 'Yes, but it's how you go round,' but it was too late.

Chapter Three
THE TIDE

The instant Peter got back to the office the skies opened and the rain began pouring down in sheets.

'What have you bought yourself?' asked George, bringing in a mug of tea.

Peter stared out of the window at the grey street blurred by the downpour. He shrugged. 'I didn't. Every time I fancied something I couldn't bear to part with the money.'

George put his hands on his hips and looked disgusted. 'Go on with you, you've got loads. Sod the money, you need a decent motor.' His pudgy nose seemed to redden. 'You're up and coming. You're a man about town. Don't leave it till you're too old to enjoy it. How many times have you seen a fat, bald, old geezer, like me, in a Ferrari, driving around like he wished he was a youngster? It's a joke.'

Peter was a man with a phobia.

'You're right, it's not as if I'm mean, but I can't pull the trigger. It's such a bloody large amount of cash to buy a car worth having. I mean, if you go for a car that's not just four wheels to get you from A to B, you're talking silly money.'

'Look, I open the post,' said George. 'I see the bank statements. One hundred and sixty eight grand, that's how much you've got in the bank. It's not as if you've got debts, that's real clean lucre and it's all yours. It's coming out of your ears. I got another six grand while you were out. If you can't afford a nice set of wheels now, when will you?'

Peter glared with frustration. 'I know, but I just think of all the things that could be done with twenty thousand. I read the car magazines and examine all the pros and cons, then decide on what I fancy. Whatever it is, it's always more than I feel it's worth. This time I made up my mind to get a low mileage, second hand BMW. I got into the showroom, ready to buy, then, wham, I don't want to part with my money. I promised myself that I'd buy a decent car. I've passed all the targets I set myself, a month ago, but all I can think of are the alternatives. Do you realize how many wells you could get dug in African villages for that? Alright, I'd never give that sort of money to charity, but even so, it's an unnerving perspective.

'Look at it this way; it's a significant down payment on a house. It's a couple of grand a year of interest, if I put it in the bank. What's worse, 20K doesn't exactly buy a Rolls-Royce. The trouble is the further away I get from buying, the more I fancy changing my mind and turning around. I'm a bit like those metal balls that float in mid-air between two magnets.' He grinned. 'You should have seen those cars, you could eat your lunch off the engine compartments.'

George put his hand over his mouth and squashed his face up in thought. 'Why don't you pick one out and I'll go and sort it for you. That way you won't have second thoughts.'

Peter slurped his tea considerately. 'I'll tell you what? It can't cost more than twenty K, taxed and insured, it's got to have below thirty thousand miles on the clock and be less than three years old. The rest is up to you.

George saluted. 'Monsieur, consider it done.'

———

Peter felt like a warrior riding back from battle on his trusty but fading steed. It would soon be time for a fresher mount. The base model Ford was small, noisy but totally practical.

The car was rather battered. For a start, the left side had been gouged by the wheel nuts of an armoured security lorry that had run him off the road. The lorry driver, seeing a tractor pull out in front, had mistaken Peter, overtaking at his side, for part of a heist and had manoeuvred accordingly.

Peter hadn't had time to react and had overtaken the truck on the grass verge on the wrong side of the road, his adrenaline taking control of the car rather than his brain.

Unlike him, the lorry didn't stop further up the road to check the damage. It had taken Peter a few minutes to realize he was lucky to have not wrapped himself around a tree, but by then the moment had passed.

In general, everyone seemed to consider a small car open season. Most drivers of bigger vehicles behaved appallingly towards him, as if he might be intimidated by their superior bulk. Peter always retaliated, secure in the knowledge that size also equalled value. It cheered him to note how easy the bullies were deflated by confrontation.

He swept home on a sort of auto-pilot. When the traffic was light, whole stretches of the route seemed to be edited out of his mind.

He lay on a fake leather settee, his head on a yellow patterned pillow. He held the remote control of the TV in one hand, staring unfocused at the muted picture. In the other hand he held the phone.

'What about tomorrow night then?'

Mary tutted, 'Not tomorrow, I've got a workshop.'

'Wednesday?'

'Nope, I've got to go to a play with a friend, it's a must.'

'Friend?'

She laughed. 'Are you getting jealous?'

'When girls say friend, they mean boyfriend,' he said indignantly, 'they say Sarah or Tracy when it's a friend-friend.'

'It's Nigel and he's gay, so there.'

'Can I come then?'

'No, it's work, you know, study. You wouldn't like it, it's an experimental piece. I'm only going because I have to.'

'I don't mind, I'll put up with it.'

Mary snorted. 'No, everyone will be there, everyone from the academy.'

'So what's the problem, you could introduce me. I'm not Quasimodo.'

'They're all very stuck up. If you're not an actor, they're not interested.'

'I'll pretend I'm a film producer, I'll get by.'

'No and that's final. You wouldn't like me to invite myself to your business meetings, I don't see why you should invite yourself to mine.'

'Thursday then,' he said, adding a heavy tone of exasperation.

'I can make it around nine, is that okay?'

'That's fine by me, we can pop out for something to eat.'

———

The next morning he drove over to Earls Court for a computer show. Hardware, the actual machinery behind Online Data, was forever leap-frogging the previous technological advance announced a few months before. He felt he had to try and keep up with change. The trade day was a civilized, hushed affair, quiet doldrums before the maelstrom of the public opening at the weekend. It was a time for the attendees to reflect on how purchases a year earlier were now on sale at half the price.

For Peter so much had happened in the last three months that a year seemed a lifetime. He was apart from it all; his users weren't into the technology, they were into communicating. He wondered sometimes what they were communicating about and he had begun to fear the contents.

Now all the dream equipment on display was within his financial grasp. He felt like a rich kid in a giant toy shop. It was a feeling he liked.

One stand had a large photograph of a mobster holding a Thompson machine gun in one hand and a bundle in the other. For a second, the handheld computer clasped in his palm looked like an envelope of money. The slogan read, 'We're going to make you an offer you can't refuse.'

'We're going to make you an offer you can't refuse,' he muttered. It seemed familiar.

———

He parked in a back street near the office and clamped the steering wheel with an anti-theft device. The car didn't have a radio so he didn't mind putting it out of sight. There was nothing inside to steal. He thought it highly unlikely anyone would 'borrow' such unexciting transport for a joy ride. The wing damage would dissuade anyone from stealing it for profit, but he took the extra precaution anyway; after all, someone might want to pinch the anti-theft device. It was, after all, a very dodgy area.

Nearby was a large derelict lot that had been appropriated by a freelance parking company. Large, violent looking men patrolled the uneven ground with hungry-looking Dobermans that eyed everyone as if they were a side of beef. From their mean expressions it was obvious they were only waiting for permission to begin the feast. Peter had parked there at first but had decided against what he judged to be a three pound daily insurance premium.

Walking up the stairs to his office, he caught the sound of quiet, breathless panting. As his eye line cleared the top step, he stopped in his tracks. Sat on his desk was a girl. In front, his trousers round his ankles and her legs around his waist, stood George.

Peter turned around and went into the disused office below. Amongst the discarded boxes was an old, half broken, paint splattered chair. He sat down on the creaky seat and waited. It was a tatty room that obviously hadn't had any positive attention for many years. In each corner was a white carton of vermin poison, a rectangular, lethal cache of card with an obvious warning in red printed down the side, and a single rodent-sized hole at one end. Peter thought about the power of knowledge and considered the ramification on the rat population if they ever learnt to read the wrappers on their food. After a few minutes the shuffling and muted thumping stopped. Peter rummaged through his pockets for something to pass a little more time but was rewarded with nothing but receipts. He heard footsteps on the stairs and the main door opening then closing. He counted to one hundred and went up.

'Hello boss,' said George when he entered, 'cup of tea?'

Peter pointed at the computer on his desk.

'See that? That's got what is called a hard disk in it. It spins like a record but really, really fast.' He walked over to the machine. 'The disk has got a head, in fact several. Like the needle on a record player, except that they fly over the disk at a height of a fraction of the thickness of one of your hairs.' He scowled. 'If you bang the drive enough, its head dives into the disk and damages it by carving the surface up and spreading debris all over the place. The heads then crash into that debris, nose dive again and so on until the whole thing doesn't work anymore. Now if you bang my desk hard enough, then you will bang the drive. Bingo, no Online Data. This is why we take back-ups of the hard disk just in case someone gives it a good knocking.'

George blushed. 'I didn't know.' He held out the palms of his hands. 'She took advantage of me, she found me irresistible.' He grinned. 'I showed her the computer and how it works. She was very grateful.'

Peter sighed, 'You hardly know anything about the computer.'

George laughed, 'I know a bloody sight more than her. Switching a computer on is a lesson in itself.' He looked plaintively at Peter. 'You don't mind if she comes back do you?'

'I should be more concerned about whether I'm going to sack you. Was that one of Davenport's girls?'

George nodded.

'How old are you George?'

'Seventy.'

Peter started, 'Seventy! I thought you were in your early sixties.'

George looked very uncomfortable, 'Not for a few years.'

Peter turned away and went to his seat. He stared at the computer in thought then turned to George. 'You are meant to be here to take care of business. Make sure you do that. Before you teach the girls, eh people, how to use the system, you'd better get expert with it first. I certainly don't expect you to use this place as a knocking shop, especially when I might be expected back, eh, or even at all for that matter. Is that understood?'

George nodded. 'Right you are . . . cup of tea?'

Peter sighed, 'Yeah go on. Any calls?'

'The Yank called again, he wouldn't leave his number.' He appeared with two mugs. 'I've done the banking, there was one new customer, first thing.'

————

Peter had taken Mary to a bistro close to his flat. It was an unusual lively place, about as trendy as the suburbs of London could manage. It was decorated like the overflowing storage area of an antiques market. A canvas canoe hung from the ceiling, a traffic light flashed the changes on the far wall. Random artefacts inhabited every nook and cranny of the interior, decorating the place to an even more eclectic extent than the customer who graced the tables. It was an ambiance the locals appreciated and two unconvincing bouncers asserted its popularity at the door. Instead of the usual inert background muzak, taped Californian radio shows were played, rambling on, disembodied in time and space, selling the American dream to the foreign savages. This surreal background lulled Peter into an eerie dreamlike state of mind, where anything might happen and be acceptable. Happily, beyond the mesmerism, the real world was firmly in control. The food was average, the bar was slow, the drink was the same as everywhere else, but however thin the magic, the place was always full.

————

Mary took a diary from her bag. 'How about Monday night?'

'Monday night?' He worked it out to be absolutely certain. 'That's five days from now.'

'I know but I've got so much on.'

Peter looked annoyed. He snatched the diary out of her hand. 'Let's have a look at this.'

Mary folded her arms and glared at him. 'If you must.'

Peter found the page. 'You've nothing down here between now and then.' He flicked back a few pages and noted that most of the entries were single capital letters. 'So how come you can't see me before Monday?'

'I was just making sure that I had remembered all my appointments. I only write in the ones I might forget.'

Peter leafed through the telephone number sections. Again there was nothing but initials. He looked around for P and found himself under the right dates. 'You mean like me?'

'Exactly,' said Mary with a degree of satisfaction.

'Thanks,' he said indignantly. 'And why do you use initials?'

She leant forward and took the diary. 'So I can remember. Initials are all I need bother with, you should try it.'

Peter finished off the last of his mud-pie. 'Here is a question for you. Why don't your parents like me? Whenever I come over to pick you up, you could cut the atmosphere with a knife.'

She brushed her hair over her shoulder. 'They just haven't got to know you yet. Mum and Dad are very shy.'

'I can't say I have ever got that sort of reaction before.'

A bare foot appeared between his legs. 'Stop jabbering and tickle me,' she said, 'and don't stop until I tell you to.'

He tickled her sole lightly. 'Like this?'

'Yes.'

As he drummed his fingers lightly over the flat of her foot, she bit her bottom lip. He could feel her shaking with tiny tremors, tugging at his other hand which held her ankle.

Her face creased into a tormented twisted smile and tears began to roll down her cheeks.

'Shall I stop?' he whispered.

She shook her head. As he continued to run his fingers in small motions over the balls of her feet her shivers grew into shaking as she pulled against him. Suddenly she tore herself away, rattling the table as she grasped it. Peter sat back with an uncontrolled jerk, trying not to turn to see if anyone was looking.

Mary mopped her eyes with her napkin. 'RRRrrrr . . . ' she growled, leaning forward with a hungry grin.

Peter smiled. 'However it felt, don't do it to me.'

She pouted. 'Shall we get back?'

Peter waved at a waitress and settled the bill.

She led him by the hand, out of the restaurant and over the road to his flat. She hummed a tune which he didn'trecognize.

———

Peter answered the phone.

'Peter Talbot, please,' said a male voice.

'Who's calling?'

'Malcolm Collins from Uridium Investments.'

'Peter Talbot speaking.'

'Ah . . . Mr Talbot, let me introduce myself. I'm Malcolm Collins from Uridium. We are investment brokers.'

Peter grimaced. 'I've got all the pensions I need thank you.'

'Oh no no, we are not pension brokers, we are investment brokers.'

Peter wasn't convinced. 'I must say I have heard that one before. I get a couple of calls a week offering me policies and plans.' He hated jousting with telesales men but could never just hang up on them. They were usually very well prepared and he could tell from their intensity that they were under a lot of pressure to perform.

'I'm not selling, or advising or suggesting schemes,' said the baritone voice, 'I'm buying.'

Peter was relieved. 'Buying, oh good, what can I sell you?'

'Well, it's your company I'm calling about.'

'Ah . . . I see, or rather I don't.'

'You see, we are investment brokers and we act on behalf of clients who are interested in making an acquisition of part or all of a company. Our role is to help them match up with the sort of business they want to invest in, by finding them the right kind of opportunities which fit into their strategies.'

'Okay, I've got that. Does that mean that I end up paying you any money?'

'No. We take a commission on any transaction, but that comes from our client. Without further ado, we have a client that wishes to be in a position to make an offer to buy Online Data.'

'Oh yes . . . ' Peter was shocked.

'He has substantial resources and is looking to make investments in a number of high technology opportunities.'

Peter felt defensive. 'To be honest I don't really consider us for sale.'

'I understand, but I hope that you would be open to proposals.'

Peter picked up a pen and prepared to jot down notes. 'So what kind of offer are we looking at?'

Collins continued, 'My client is looking to invest around £250,000 in the right company, for which he is looking for seventy-five per cent of the equity.'

Peter scrawled a big cross over the page. 'Well, that's not even in the ballpark I'm afraid, we will make more cash than that in year one.'

There was silence. 'Well, my client has substantial funds, as I have said. Obviously he would be able to invest more for an interest in a bigger operation. May I suggest a meeting?'

'Okay.'

'Shall we say next Tuesday?'

'Let's make that the Friday after.'

'I'll have to come back to you and confirm, but I will pencil it in, at say twelve at our office.'

'Okay.' Peter wrote the information on his pad. 'I'll see you Friday week.'

George puffed into the office in grubby overalls. 'I've got the bulk of the rubbish out down there. I'll start painting tomorrow.'

Peter hung up and looked at George's red face. 'Good, but don't strain yourself.'

George took out a sheaf of paper from his inside pocket and pushed it in front of Peter. He had folded their tops under and pinned the documents down with his hand. 'Sign here!'

'What's this?'

'The papers on your motor, HP, insurance, the works.'

Peter tugged at the agreement, 'What have you got me then?'

'You'll see, just sign.'

Peter scrawled his moniker in a box at the bottom that had been crossed in pencil. 'It's done.'

'Tomorrow, I'll need a bank draft for five grand for the down-payment. I thought, why spend it when you can borrow it?' He passed Peter a grubby envelope with writing on it. 'That's the details for who it should be made out to.'

'I hope the car's not too flash!'

George blew a kiss with his hand. 'It's lovely. You wait and see.'

'Just to keep you up to date, someone wants to buy us out and I'm seeing him next week.'

George looked disapproving. 'Is that why I'm painting downstairs?'

Peter laughed. 'No. Anyway, you don't need to worry, they won't be able to afford us.'

George stood to attention. 'Right you are sir. I'll be on my way home now then.

Peter ringed the address on his pad. He didn't like the idea of selling out; he hadn't stopped enjoying himself yet.

The phone rang and Peter answered it. The line hissed and echoed. It was the American. Randy Meyer introduced himself as the Vice President of Overseas Developments of a New York based online service called MonoLog.

It was hard to hold a conversation, because of a delay of a second caused by the satellite; pauses were lengthened and replies clashed.

He was calling Peter, he said, 'To open up a protocol for communication between the two companies.' Peter marvelled at the way Meyer talked without hesitation, repetition or deviation for minutes at a time. When he interjected, there was a gap, followed by a continuation of what seemed like the output of a pre-recorded tape.

'So what sort of service do you supply?'

The lag passed. 'Distribution services.'

The lag passed again, then real silence took its place.

'Right, I see. We are mainly a mail and bulletin based service with database access.'

'We consider that network services are the communication nexus of the future. We appreciate the benefits that we can offer the consumer who needs to have access to a pool of supply. We have heard a lot of good things about your system and its positioning in the UK. I understand that you have a common mission with similar aims and concepts to our own. We are interested in developing a synergy and would like to explore some convergences.

MonoLog feels that the customer bases of your system and ours are complimentary and that our corporate goals address the same needs and the same section of the marketplace. Naturally as there is a broad landscape of international ramification and opportunity to be exploited, we are keen to get familiar with all players, especially in the European and Pacific Rim theatres. What we would like to do is invite you over to our operation and show you how we do business over here. There are several issues we would like to discuss with you. I would like to be able to meet with you head to head. Can you make it over? We will look after your ticket and your accommodation, all you need to do is tell us when you can come.'

Peter had never been to the US before. 'Yes, well, that would be very nice. I can't make it next week but I can come out on the Monday after.'

'That's fine. I'll FedEx the items to you with a provisional itinerary. Peter, it's been a pleasure talking with you. I look forward to meeting up.'

'Thanks, I look forward to that too.' He hung up. 'I'm flavour of the month,' he thought, 'maybe I'll get an OBE in the next post.'

———

When it suited her purpose Mary seemed to be free at the drop of a hat. That night, Peter's spur of the moment idea of spending a weekend in Margate was immediately accepted. As luck would have it, the weather was going to be terrific. On Friday evening they made the long, tedious journey to the coast. The roads were choked with commuters returning home from London, some of which lived as far away as Herne Bay, nearly sixty miles from London.

The hotel was grand; a huge remnant of the age before airliners swept holidaymakers to sun-bleached haunts in the Mediterranean. Their room overlooked the sea front and the grey blue waters of the north sea. Mary stood by the window and watched a ship pass on the far horizon.

Peter put his arms around her and kissed her neck. She tilted her head so her hair fell from her shoulder. 'I wonder what's happening on that boat?' she said distantly.

Peter unzipped the side of her skirt and unfastened the button holding the waistband in place. 'Beats me,' he said, as it fell to the ground.

———

They ate sumptuously in the Victorian restaurant. On the high painted ceiling above, a goddess and accompanying cherubs sat on a cloud and showered the diners with fresco fruit. They spoke little; it seemed as if there was nothing to say.

In the morning, Mary wanted to sunbathe on the beach and after an exploration of the town Peter could think of no good excuse to counter the suggestion.

Returning to the hotel, they changed, leaving their things in the room. Covered in beach towels, they walked the two hundred yards to the sea. Even when the sun was so hot, he hated sunbathing. Messing about with suncream and lying like a washed up porpoise gave him no feelings of pleasure at all. The whole process seemed utterly pointless.

Watching her from a worm's eye view made him feel exposed and paranoid. The massive blue horizon, underlined with a strip of yellow sand, amplified her nakedness. Oiled and shiny, lying bare save for scraps of cloth, her body aroused and unsettled him. Giant figures rolled around them, there were shouts and cries. He sat up and surveyed the scene. From this different perspective the world was more reassuring, full of nothing but harmless fun and frolics. The tide was up, people paddled and bobbed in the water.

He stood. 'Let's go for a swim.'

She moved her head an inch. 'You go. I'm just getting warmed up.' She smiled inscrutably from behind her dark glasses.

'Come on, we've got all day to get brown.'

'No, every second counts.'

He bent down, picked up an armful of sand and dropped it onto her. 'Come on, before the tide starts going out.'

'You beast,' she cried, jumping up. She brushed her front, but enough stuck to the cream.

'Come on, a swim will wash it off.'

She put her hands on her hips. 'That's not fair.'

'Come on, let's go.'

As they waded in, the water was cool but not biting.

He lifted his knees and sunk up to his neck, watching her pick a way towards him, between the friendly swell of the waves. Reaching his position, she gave him a salty kiss before turning around.

'See you later,' she said walking away.

'Spoilsport,' he called, to no response.

He had swum a lot when he was young. At the age of ten he had gained all kinds of certificates for distance and technique. That seemed like only yesterday and he felt at home in water. He lay on his back and paddled, watching people on the beach from a greater distance. The sandy bottom rose up in bars he could touch with his feet. A few feet back and they sank away again.

He followed the ridges out until they were gone. Further away still, an athletic man was powering back to shore with an impressive display of Australian crawl. He watched him plough through the water with the aid of flippers. As he turned his attention away, he realized he was now much further out than anyone else. He turned to begin his swim back, feeling a cool undertow pull against him. He tilted onto his front and began a slow deliberate breast-stroke. With every moment he felt himself being sucked a little further out. Every action merely retarded the current's effect. He began to feel out of his element.

For the first time he felt at the complete mercy of something that was without feeling or intellect. The two and a half inches between the waterline of his chin and the air intake of his nose was all that kept him from drowning. Below the surface he would be dead in 180 seconds. He switched onto his back and tried a backstroke, but when he turned over the beach seemed yet further off.

He attempted the butterfly but immediately knew he couldn't maintain it. He felt the impulse to shout for help, but as he couldn't hear the beach with all its noise, so he was sure they would not be able to hear him. Lifting up to yell would make him sink and he needed to stay calm.

He doggy paddled and watching the sea front recede and tried not to worry. He concentrated on the idea of challenge, trying to work through every option and its permutations. He knew fear was a greater enemy than the water, but that if fear came, then no amount of logic would chase it away.

The tide had turned and caught him, a current was dragging him somewhere and he was unable to resist.

As he paddled he could see the people as distant dots of colour mingling on a yellow canvas. They were happy and safe, unaware of his difficulties; life was carefree for them while he was in mortal peril. Though he could see them and they might see him, he was unable to communicate his distress. Soon, he thought, Mary would raise the alarm and a boat or helicopter would pick him up.

Ultimately this moment of drama would turn into a moment of gratitude. How embarrassing it would be, how welcome. All he had to do was wait.

Time passed and he was too far out to see people. He could tell that he was being slowly pulled up the coast. He turned onto his side and began to pull for land at a pace he felt he could strike indefinitely. The sun had passed its zenith and was falling.

He guessed at his distance from land, a mile, perhaps as much as three? Where were his rescuers? How long had he been in the water?

He tried to work it through. Mary would get worried enough within an hour to call the authorities. Surely, they would take no more than another hour to get their act together, even allowing for problems at Mary's end.

How long would it take to find him? Surely, at most, half an hour after setting out. So how long had he been in the water? Was time passing slowly because of his mental state? It felt as if more than the theoretical two and a half hours had passed.

The water beat warm then cool. It felt as if the coast was coming slowly towards him but he wasn't sure. The heat of the day was dying, the sun arcing down lower. He was sure he had been adrift for hours, but if he had, it seemed that his chances of being rescued had been missed. His mind wandered and he talked to himself in repeating mantras.

'Where is the fucking lifeboat, where is the fucking helicopter?' he repeated to himself.

He kept paddling, hoping the coastline was getting closer. Perhaps the tide had turned, perhaps he was out of the current or it now led him to the shore. He wondered if he was drifting off to sleep as he muttered to himself. The world was getting blurred and distorted.

The authorities must be looking in the wrong place; maybe there was a disaster that had called them away. He counted his strokes, each one bringing him he hoped a little closer in to land.

He felt thirsty, his arms leaden. They waved in the water as his feet moved slowly from side to side. On the horizon he could see lone figures walking down the sand. At first just black points, they started to resolve into men with metal detectors. He felt exhilarated; he was indeed coming in to shore.

'It must be early evening,' he thought with amazement, realizing for the first time just how long he had been adrift. Soon he would be on the beach; his goal was growing visibly closer with every effort now that his target was no longer an abstract horizontal line. Soon the seafront of Edwardian boarding houses grew large and focused. More and more detail proved his progress.

'Not far now, nearly there,' he repeated in his head with every languid stroke. The mid ground was now sand, his foreground a shrinking band of blue-green. His knees hit the bottom and he tried to stand.

He fell, a small wave pushing him forward, ducking him into frothy water that poured into his nose. Spluttering, he hauled himself up and tumbled out onto the sand. He lay exhausted, the final arc of the waves washing around him. Where were the people now, where were the men with their detectors? Rolling over, he watched them, too far away to call, encapsulated in their headphone cocoons.

Clambering up and barely able to support his weight, he stumbled forwards. His legs shook; his leaden body uncoordinated and useless. Collapsing onto his hands and knees, he looked towards the stairs, a hundred yards ahead, which led up to the road.

It was so warm in the evening summer air, he hadn't realized just how cold he had become, floating for hours in the sea. He kneeled, rested and then forced himself on. The warm friendly sand sapped his little strength, yielding beneath him as he fought to make each step towards the solid stairway.

On the steps he felt even heavier, but he used the railings to help himself up. His mouth was dry, his throat sore and hard but now at least he was in his own element. Leaning heavily against the thick black iron balustrades of the promenade, he guessed this was Westgate-on-Sea, a quiet adjunct town a couple of miles from Margate. There was a line of boarding houses across from him and fixing on the nearest door, he crossed the empty road and rang the bell.

A small lady in her late sixties answered.

'Can you help me?' he said in a painful whisper, 'I've had an accident.'

She looked at him with a mixture of concern and worry. 'You had better come in.'

She led him down a thin corridor to the kitchen where she sat Peter down in a wooden chair. She introduced herself as Ethel.

'I'll just be a moment,' she said, leaving him to return with a blanket. 'This will keep you warm,' she said, wrapping it around him.

'Can I have some water?' Peter asked with difficulty.

She put a pitcher and a long glass in front of him.

'Thanks.' Peter drank.

'Shall I call the doctor out for you?' she suggested.

Peter finished the glass. 'No, I'll be okay, I just need to get my breath back.' He smiled, catching sight of the clock over the cooker. 'I've been in the water for five hours. Got caught by the tide.' He poured another glass.

'Oh, you poor thing.'

'Well, no harm down.' Peter looked down at his feet. 'Sorry about all the sand.'

'Now don't you worry yourself about that.'

'Can I borrow your phone in a minute, I need to ring my hotel and get my girlfriend to pick me up. Do you have the number for the Metropole?'

'I'll run you there,' Ethel offered, stripping off her pinafore, 'it's only just round the corner really.'

Peter accepted. The thought of standing by the pay phone in the hall and waiting for the hotel reception to answer was too much for him.

———

Ethel owned an Austin Mini, more of a contraption than a car, which she drove indecently slowly. Peter fell asleep during the short ride. The keys were not at the front desk, and still wearing the blanket he went to his room, Ethel fussing behind him as if she, a little old lady, could catch him should he topple over. He banged on the door and Mary answered.

'Where have you been?' she said, looking out of the brightness of the room into the darkness of the corridor. She started, realizing the state he was in.

'Where are my trousers?' he asked, stepping into the room.

Mary turned and came back with them. He took them and stuffed his hand into the right pocket. He found his fold of cash and awkwardly pulled out a random number of large denomination bank notes.

'Here you are, this is a little thank you,' he said, pushing it clumsily into Ethel's hand, 'and thank you.'

She looked at it. 'Oh no, I can't take this, this is far too much.'

He pulled the blanket from his shoulders. 'I insist.' He handed her the blanket. 'Thanks,' he smiled weakly, 'now I just must lie down.'

'You take care now,' said Ethel gently.

He nodded, 'Bye,' and closed the door.

Mary looked at him from across the room. She was flushed.

He let himself fall onto the bed.

'Are you okay?' he heard her saying as he fell asleep, hoping in the back of his mind that he wasn't in reality still just floating in the sea.

———

He woke with a terrible pain in his leg. He stretched his foot up against the cramp and his eyes focused as the agony subsided. Peter looked at Mary who sat by the window reading a book.

'What time is it?' he asked, his voice hoarse. He lifted up stiffly, his body aching.

'Eleven.'

He swung his legs off the bed and onto the floor. He felt bruised all over. He hobbled gingerly into the bathroom, drank, then showered. He was sunburnt and the red patches stung furiously.

'What are we doing today?' asked Mary, as he came back into the bedroom.

'Going back,' he answered, heading for his clothes still in their suitcase.

She got up from her chair as he passed and put her hand on his shoulder. He stopped. 'Ouch!' he grimaced.

'I'm sorry about yesterday,' she said, sliding her hand across his towel.

He caught her wrist and gripped it. Letting her go again, he turned. 'Okay, you're sorry, that's fine. There are some things that sorry is no good for.' He turned away.

She hugged him around the waist. 'I'm sorry.'

He unwrapped her arms. 'I was in deep trouble out there and you let me down. Alright, it wasn't your fault that it happened, but it wouldn't have taken much thought about me to get me out of it. The chances are, I should be dead.'

'I thought you had gone off.'

'Where? Why? I didn't go off, I just nearly drowned. I don't care what you thought or why you thought it. You just failed.'

'Failed you?'

He paused for a moment in thought, looking at his feet, trying to encapsulate how he felt into a short logical statement. 'It's just something fundamental. How can you share yourself with someone who you can't rely on when you're in trouble? I mean, there's no future to it. In the end you were just another day tripper on the beach.'

She slapped his scarlet face and stormed to the door. 'You're being horrible,' she shouted, her eyes full of tears.

The door slammed.

He regretted his outburst but within moments felt the dull anger return.

———

The drive back was a sullen affair. The car buzzed and rattled, flat out on the motorway. Peter wanted to drive recklessly but restrained himself to appear in control of his feelings. Mary began sobbing to herself intermittently which made him feel rotten. There was something dreadfully appealing about a weeping woman, something that demanded consolation and forgiveness.

Arrival came at last. The house where she lived with her family was big and daunting. Set in a cramped street, too small for the grey carcasses it set apart.

She took her case from the back seat and stood holding the door open.

'I love you,' she said tearfully, and slammed it shut. She ran to the front door.

He accelerated away, tyres squealing, muttering random thoughts under his breath. A black cat wandered into the road and he was an impulse away from not veering around it.

'Bloody cat.'

———

The phone rang. It was George.

'Is that Online Data?' he said through a crackly haze.

'Yes, George, it is.'

'In that case I've got a delivery for you outside.'

Peter heard a horn blow in the street and through the phone earpiece. 'Where are you calling from?'

'From the wheelie blower. Are you coming down or what?'

Peter looked out of the window down onto a large red Mercedes.

George was wearing a black peaked cap and a suit. As Peter came onto the pavement and crossed the road, he powered down the window. 'Where to, m'lud?'

'What did I sign up for?'

'Look at the front first, then I'll tell you.'

Peter read the number plate: ODL 856. He asked, 'And how much did that cost?'

'Sit at the wheel, then you can Gestapo me.'

George got out and into the front passenger seat. Peter climbed in. Leather and wood. Lights and buttons. He found the switch and put the window up. He put his belt on and noticed 29,000 miles on the clock. He rolled forwards to the lights which were red, then pulled gingerly away on green.

'Okay, what's the damage?'

'23K including tax, insurance and plate. Trust me, I'm a doctor.'

Peter felt relieved; he had thought for a moment that he had let himself in for a nasty shock.

'That's a little over budget.'

'It's cheap, it's quality. On top of that, you won't need to keep getting a new model to keep the number plate up to date. You can run a motor like this until hell freezes over and it will still be an eye catcher.'

'Sold.' Somehow all the money in the bank had failed to make Peter feel successful. The fact he had more money coming in than most people could imagine hadn't made much of an emotional impact. This was different; it made him feel big and strong. It was like a diploma after his name. 'I could get to enjoy this.'

'Mind you, you're a bastard to get insured.'

Peter grinned. 'What happens if you do this?' he said, slamming his foot down on the accelerator.

'Eeeesh!' emitted George, pushed back by the rush. 'I crap myself for a start.'

Peter put his hands in his jacket pocket and pulled out his old car keys. 'You'll be needing these.' He threw them in George's lap.

'I'm not sure I'll get much for it,' he said disparagingly.

Peter smiled to himself. 'Well, if you want to sell it, by all means do. I thought you might like a company car.'

George beamed, 'That's real decent of you sir, real decent.' He clasped the keys tightly in his hands. 'You're a gent.'

———

Peter took a cab to Uridium Investments. It turned out that Uridium didn't have an office but shared an accommodation address in the heart of Shepherd's Market, a louche part of the salubrious Mayfair area.

The offices were time-shared by a host of small consultant and accountancy practices who used them by the hour like the lady professionals who walked the streets above looking for rich clients to soothe.

The reception hall felt like a cross between a hotel foyer and a station waiting room. The tiny area was decked out in designer decorations, tired by the prolonged friction of the transient residents. He listened to the high pitched receptionist answering the flow of calls on the switchboard with a never repeating list of firm names.

'Wilkins Partnership,' she whined at the phone system's prompting, as the glass fronted door clunked open.

A balding man in his early thirties entered and eyed him up.

'Peter?' he inquired with a hesitant half smile.

Peter replied, 'Yes, that's me.'

'Malcolm Collins. I hope I haven't kept you waiting too long. I'm expecting my client any minute; in fact, I thought you'd probably get to meet before I got here.'

He sat down and opened a black leather briefcase. He pulled out a presentation file. 'This is some information on Uridium.' He put it onto the low coffee table.

Peter picked it up and began to read. He scanned the pages which seemed to contain a great deal of writing with very little content.

'Yes, I'll read this later.' He put it back on the table. 'What made you ring me in the first place?'

Collins sat forward in his chair. 'We draw up a list of interesting companies for our clients, based on a set of criteria. We do some research and then make recommendations. Online Data came out as one of a shortlist, so as is our practice, we called you for talks.'

The door opened and a large stocky man barrelled in. Collins turned to him rising. 'Howard, meet Peter Talbot.'

Peter got up and they shook hands.

'Howard Kendal,' said the man in a heavy aggressive East End accent.

Collins went to the reception desk and garnered a set of keys. 'Let's go to the boardroom.'

He led them down some tight stairs into what had been the cellar. It was a dark low space, made even more claustrophobic by panelling that had been applied to achieve an atmosphere of snug wealth. The boardroom itself was a long thin area with a whispering extractor fan. A white board hid behind wood shutters left slightly ajar. Rustic eighteenth century etchings of lovers courting hung around the walls. The room hummed with the smell of tobacco, which reinforced the feeling that this was a financial sweatbox where business Sumo-wrestled deals to the ground.

They sat at the far end of the room. Collins took more papers from his case while Kendal lit a cigarette. From his large right wrist sagged an even larger gold Rolex. The packet of Players No 6 cigarettes sat incongruously in front of him as he waited with muted impatience for the broker.

Collins pushed a document over to Peter. 'This is a non-disclosure agreement, can you please read it then sign.'

Peter looked at Kendal who was eyeing him intently. Instinctively, he didn't like Kendal or Collins and he didn't like the idea of selling. He pushed the document back. 'I won't sign anything that's not reciprocated. If you sign one for me I'll sign one for you.'

Collins looked fazed. 'I'm sorry, is this a problem for you? It's common practice.'

Peter grimaced, 'It might be common practice, but if you want to take something from me you've got to give something in return.'

'Let's cut the crap,' interrupted Kendal abruptly. 'I want to buy you. I've got the money, you've got the company. You show me your figures and I'll make my offer. Okay?'

Peter shook his head. 'Not really. If you want to buy from me, we've got to do a few other things first. One, we've got to agree conditions and a formula for the price. Two, we establish an exact price from the formula. Three, you show me you've got that kind of money. Four, an independent accountant verifies the variables in the formula to confirm it for you. Then you buy the company.' He smiled, he felt rather proud of himself that he had come up with such an impressive scheme off the top of his head. 'Fuck them,' he thought, 'how could they ever buy the business in any event and why would he sell it?'

Kendal stubbed his cigarette out. 'Doesn't sound like what I've got in mind.'

Peter stood up. He leant forward and shook both men's hands. 'If you feel any different, call me.' He turned and left them where they sat.

He flagged a cab and headed for the American Embassy in Grovesnor Square. His ticket for the States had arrived and his passport needed a visa. 'Why are you even thinking about selling?' he asked himself. 'How could you possibly have more fun doing anything else?'

A Vauxhall Cavalier cut up the taxi. 'Bleeding lunatic,' shouted the cabbie, blowing his horn. 'Why don't they give people a chance?'

'Maybe they're in a hurry?' offered Peter.

The grey haired head of the driver turned a trifle to show the merest hint of a profile. 'The trouble with people nowadays is they believe in Darwin. You know, Charles Darwin. They think just because they are descended from animals they have to carry on acting like them.'

————

Peter arrived at the airport at seven in the morning feeling dazed and confused. He had risen at half past five and felt the worse for it. It suddenly struck him just how ill-prepared he was. He had packed a small case with a couple of changes of shirt and underwear, a single pair of trousers, a toothbrush and a razor. This seemed as if it might be below the bare minimum needed for the short stay booked by his new American friends, but it was too late now. A small feeling of nervousness was replaced by the realization that he could always get what he lacked while he was there. He was going to the city where, apparently, everything was available at a price and his pockets were stuffed with money.

Things hadn't run to plan the evening before. Mary had turned up unexpectedly at his door. She had made a special effort to look alluring and was all demure smiles as she stood before him.

Peter tried not to be too frosty but stood awkwardly trying not to invite her in. Then without warning she burst into tears. His defences crumbled and she breached the gates. The crying stopped as abruptly as it had begun. She stood in the space that passed for a hall, her face shining with tears. She smiled girlishly at him, her head cocked.

'Let's make up,' she said. 'I need you.'

'I don't think . . . '

She took a step towards him, 'Please.'

He backed off. 'No, I don't think so.'

'Please . . . ' She moved forward, putting her arms on his shoulders as he moved back into the lounge.

He braced her away from him by her forearms. 'No!' he said sternly. She grinned at him devilishly, the sparkle in her eye breaking his mask with a smile of his own.

'Please,' she said quietly, his arms bending as she leant forward. She kissed a dancing kiss, her tongue passing into his mouth. She had a physical heat he could feel, a live energy that made the hair along his spine stand to attention. She kissed his cheek, then his ear, teasing it for a time before kissing down his neck. She touched his reciprocating groin and caressed it. As he kissed her shoulder she sprang back and turned from him.

'I win,' she cried, striding towards the door. It slammed behind her, rattling the frosted glass with a brittle vibration.

'Shit,' he muttered. Competing feelings of relief, rejection, anger and lust flowed through him. The logic and reasoning he held so dear were swamped in a torrent of emotion. The turmoil broke his rhythm. He watched television, his mind churning away, trying to sedate himself with the constant input of images. Distracted, midnight came and passed. At ten to one he finally summoned up the motivation to go to bed.

———

Heathrow was an unfriendly jungle of nomads. Herds of travellers jostled for position within a system that enforced a uniformity of passage. Peter hadn't flown much before, except during holidays as a child, so he enjoyed the novelty of the experience. His passport was crisp and new, his American visa freshly stamped.

He leafed through a copy of Byte magazine and waited for the boarding call to summon him to his gate. The periodical's thick body seemed designed to be read on long journeys, there being no way of digesting it completely without many hours of study.

MonoLog Inc had booked him in club class and he felt very happy about having the red carpet treatment. When they took off he had felt a pang of terror. It was a fear unlike any he had felt before. It was a deep anxiety, oozing from something buried deep within him. He started to perspire a sticky sweat; his mouth dried and his tongue seemed to swell. As the plane levelled he began to relax again. It seemed that somehow, he had picked up a phobia and he wondered if he would feel the same during landing.

Angst was soon replaced by annoyance. People who were scared of ordinary things like spiders and needles always infuriated him. Peter had, up to that point, always prided himself on being free of such irrelevancies.

He determined to take flying lessons when he returned. That would get him straightened out.

The plane was half empty and he noticed that during the flight people in the economy class lay across the empty rows, sleeping. Horizontal was obviously the best way to fly. A little extra seat space seemed a poor deal in comparison, but with a few contortions he managed to manoeuvre himself to a position where he could slip into unconsciousness, in a semi-reclined position.

He hated the meals, they came when he wasn't hungry and he felt that with one false move, he would send one of the courses into his lap. He decided the jet set life was a drag.

When it came to the landing, the anxiety returned. The airframe lurched forwards and jigged from side to side in small sharp movements. The engine pitch changed and through a parting in the clouds he saw the ground. He directed his attention away from the descent, trying instead to control his breathing. Rather than worry about the process of a large heavy object meeting the ground at great speed he thought about the system back in London. Unhappily no amount of thinking about computer hardware could drown out the sensation of descent. With a profound jolt the plane touched down and the passengers clapped as the engines screamed in reverse thrust. The routine landing was over and he was extremely relieved.

The travellers queued, waiting for the doors to open. He watched them from his seat, knowing from his little experience as a child, that he would catch up with them as they waited for their baggage. As it was, he met up with them waiting to get through passport control.

Newark was not an easy-going place; the skies might be friendly, but the airport was not. Immigration seemed to hold an attitude that if you weren't an American citizen, then you were to be punished. The whole process was housed in a dark windowless room blocked at the exit end by glass partitioned cubicles inhabited by glum, surly officials. Every visitor was treated with the disdain and slowness of pace Peter thought better suited to a third world police state. An hour and fifteen minutes later he stood behind the yellow line and waited to be next. He moved forward and handed his passport and two forms to the fat uniformed clerk. The official studied his passport with an expression stolen from a comic-book Nazi storm trooper. He looked at Peter's face piercingly.

'How long do you plan to stay?'

'Just till after the weekend.'

Hershall, as it said on the badge clipped to his shirt, ticked the forms. 'You here on business or pleasure?'

'Business.'

'What business are you in?' CRUNCH, he marked the papers with a metal machine.

'Computers.'

'Computers, huh.' He tore off the end of the immigration form and stapled it onto a page near the visa. He lifted his stamp again and ran amok with it. He pushed the passport back.

'Have a nice stay,' he snarled.

Peter smiled, 'Thanks.'

He took his papers and walked into the land of the free.

The luggage had been pulled off the moving circulators and piled into a hill of irregular rectangular boxes to one side of the conveyor system. His small case was in the middle and he grabbed it by balancing on one leg and tilting forward. Jerking his balance back he plucked it away. He passed by the customs desk where a stout woman asked him if he had any goods to declare.

'No, nothing,' he replied.

She marked the form and he handed it in by the exit door.

Amongst the waiting crowd outside the baggage hall stood a tall man in a black suit holding a sign saying, 'TALBOT ONLINE DATA.' The black peaked hat gave away his occupation. Peter wasn't expecting someone to meet him, but planned to improvise his way into New York and grab a hotel there.

He walked over to his driver. 'Hi, I'm Peter Talbot.'

'Hi, I'm Zeke,' said the chauffeur in a slow friendly tone. 'How are you today? May I take your bag?' He pushed his hand forward like an offer of friendship to a dwarf.

'Fine, thanks.' Peter's instinctive response was to carry his own luggage but he handed the case over as if required to do so. 'Cheers.'

'If you would care to follow me to the car, it's this way.' Peter followed him. 'Is this your first time to the Big Apple?'

'Yes.'

'Are you staying long?'

'I'm going back on Monday night.'

'Monday huh, that's not a lot of time.'

Peter looked around at the enormous airport foyer as they walked. 'It is, if you're a mayfly.'

Howard seemed to lose the next sentence as though it had evaporated off his tongue. 'What part of England are you from?'

'London.'

'London, I have a cousin in London. I went there when I was at college. I love England.'

'It has its moments.' Peter smiled

They stepped through the automatic sliding doors onto the 'sidewalk'. Peter always hoped they would go 'Phhhhiiiistttt' like in Star Trek, but they never did.

A huge jet black stretch Cadillac lay docked before them. Zeke opened the rear passenger door.

'Thanks,' said Peter, climbing aboard. The bulkhead closed with a satisfying clunk; life was cool and dark inside. The driver put his case in the huge boot and Peter heard the muffled sound of it closing. A stream of white light illuminated the padded womb, as Zeke got into the driving seat. Peter toyed with the idea of turning on the small TV, but he got easily car sick as a passenger, so thought better of it.

'I have instructions to take you to the Hilton on 5th Avenue, is that okay?'

'Yes, fine.'

Howard adjusted his hat as the thick window rose.

They didn't so much drive away as cast off. The airport was a jagged place, bristling with hustle and bustle of a most un-European nature. Queues of cabs lined up in front of marshals, who shouted like market hawkers, impenetrable cries of slogans long since corrupted beyond recognition.

Peter felt very happy to forego all the troubles of a tired traveller on the final leg of a trip. The limo was for him an adjunct of his destination. Everything would run automatically until he reached his room.

Through the black paned windows he watched his trip out of the confines of the Airport, a ghostly distant grey silent movie. Newark was also not a nice place. Back home he had occasion to watch videos and often, more through lack of choice, he ended up watching science fiction action. The story was generally the same. In an apocalyptic future when law and order had broken down, a hero goes on a quest and saves a maiden along the way. The cities are derelict; the people live in a concrete jungle of post-industrial collapse. It was a fittingly violent backdrop for a pessimistic SF blood and thunder story. Yet Peter looked out onto the slums of Newark and saw from his insulated cocoon what he had thought was only a future-fantasy.

The car weaved along potholed roads, little more than a succession of great craters covered with iron sheets. The adverts were in Spanish, the windows covered in bars. Everything was broken down, breaking down or broken up.

Even immovable walls and freeway steel, which might withstand the mightiest blow, were marred, covered on every available surface by the defacing hieroglyphics of graffiti. This indeed was Peter's idea of hell. They passed on, ploughing along a freeway to Manhattan. In the distance above a large hill, a great circling flock of birds billowed and whirled like a storm cloud. Set on a flat featureless expanse of land, its scale was hard to grasp. Tiny dots moved over its surface working the hill like hungry insects, scratching for food. On the far horizon lay the dark ranges of Manhattan, an inky smudge between the grey land and the dark sky. The dots resolved, they were Bulldozers pushing refuse up a mountain of garbage, as if there was always somewhere higher for it to go.

Peter began to feel melancholic. The smoked luxury made a bitter kind of sense. The limo was like a hearse for the living. It was a symbol of respect for a body that had not had detachment forced upon it, but nonetheless wished for and purchased it.

They traversed a great bridge that reared up and soared across the sky. He looked down onto the buildings, black sharp crystals packed together by a great natural force that had pushed them from the strata. They glittered with a savage energy. The towers of the citadel loomed ahead and they entered. Soon they were part of it, amongst the choke of the traffic. The road detoured around the Orwellian Central Station, like a pass snaking through an ominous pass to a valley beyond. This was the future, this was the nightmare, this was the nemesis of humanity.

A Doorman opened his casket. 'Welcome to New York.'

———

Even in the confines of his room he could feel the heavy pulse of the city. Over the quiet rush of the air conditioning, he could hear the distant hiss of noise from the stifled pandemonium.

He lay on the bed absorbing the experience. The phone rang on the side table, the red light flashing frantically.

He answered, 'Hi, Peter Talbot.'

'This is Randy Meyer and how are you?'

'A little weary.'

'I just thought I'd call and make sure everything was to your liking.'

'It's great, thanks, except you might like to make the city a bit softer.'

'Don't you like New York?' Meyer laughed, 'It's just the greatest, most exciting, shit heap in the world.'

'I don't think I'm going to get used to it.'

'You've gotta either tough up or chill out.' He laughed again. 'I wondered, if you feel up to it, how would you like to do dinner?'

'That's really kind of you,' Peter hesitated, 'on condition if I suddenly cave in, you won't hold it against me. I suspect the travelling might catch up with me.'

'Sure, I know what it's like. I'll meet you at seven, nice and early, for sure.'

'See you then.'

Peter took the portable computer from his bag and plugged its modem into the phone socket. He called the computer at the office and logged on. Everything was running smoothly. He mailed George a message.

'Dear George,
got here in one piece.
The weather is lovely, wish you were here.
And not me!
Regards,
Peter'

———

The lift door opened. The marble foyer beyond was lit by golden chandeliers. A dark suited man and two suited women stood centrally on the polished floor and looked towards him. It was his host and two companions.

Randy Meyer was a tall gaunt man in his late thirties. His face was mottled, cratered by the ravages of past acne, his skin a leathery reptilian flesh. He smiled a taut smile.

'This is Sandy my assistant and this is Cherie from Customer Services. When they found out an Englishman was coming to town they blackmailed me to let them meet you.'

Cherie was a small thin woman, starved for beauty, with long yellow straight hair framing a feline angular face. Her suit was red, studded with gold buttons; her blouse, even to Peter's untrained eye, an expensive silk billowy concoction.

He shook her hand. 'It's nice to meet you.'

Sandy was tall, at Peter's eye level. Her black dress suit matched Meyer's black outfit. Whereas Cherie was a drawn beauty, Sandy was a sculpted one. She curved, arched and bowed. Her face was full and round, topped by short cropped dark hair.

'You know you have a wonderful voice,' she said, her hand warm in his.

'Eh, thanks,' he replied, 'I'm not sure they'd agree at the BBC.'

Randy interjected, 'Let's get going before Peter starts getting drowsy.'

Outside the doorman waved to a limo and Meyer tipped him.

'Sabine's,' he told the driver as he sat back. A quarter of a mile later they pulled up in front of an anonymous skyscraper on the edge of Central Park. The restaurant was on the thirty-second floor and had sweeping panoramas of the cityscape.

'Isn't it just an amazing view here?' said Cherie, smiling two octaves.

Peter ordered a Martini cocktail, hoping for the opportunity to say, shaken not stirred. 'Someone should pull the curtains,' he said trying to be amusing. The Americans looked blankly at him. 'It's a joke,' he said, shrugging.

Randy nodded. 'English humour, that's a tough area. You've got to understand we find it hard. The ridiculous, that's funny, but not the absurd.' He smiled reassuringly. 'We absolutely don't have a sense of irony like you Brits, but hell, Monty Python, that's different.'

'I love Monty Python,' said Sandy.

A waiter approached and whispered into Meyer's ear. He got up, 'I have to make a call.'

Minutes spent studying an exhaustive menu passed. Meyer returned but didn't sit down. 'I'm sorry, but I can't stay,' he said.

Cherie and Sandy protested.

Randy shrugged, 'we have an occurrence back at the facility. I have left you an open tab, so enjoy.' He held his hand out and Peter stood and shook it. 'I'll see you tomorrow at about noon.'

'See you then.'

'That's typical, ' said Sandy to Peter, 'he never settles down.'

'That's sad,' added Cherie, 'he's such a fun guy.'

Sandy snapped her menu closed. 'That's decided then, we are having the Beluga Caviar as compensation.'

Peter raised an eyebrow, 'That sounds like a career decision to me.'

'We'll put the blame on you,' quipped Sandy with a pout.

———

'Blame, blame on me,' he muttered. His consciousness rose from a pit of utter blackness, yet he was moving and active. His mind separated from his body, then returned briefly before drifting again. He felt light and unworldly, floating on a warm sea. Behind him lay a presence, resting against him, smooth and undulant.

In front was the rolling penumbra of another. He reached out and touched a breast, firm and round. He squeezed it in his hand. The form moved to him, a leg covered his, rising to his hip. Where had the hours gone that had brought him here, where was here? A plate of caviar was the last moment that connected to this. She, behind, pulled him onto his back and rolled up to kiss. Tongues searched him, her hands on his face. Cherie straddled him on all fours as another mouth took his. He reached out to Sandy and up to Cherie. Cherie moved back and forth, Sandy stroking them, moaning softly as Peter drifted in and out of a waking trance.

———

The room's harsh light burnt his eyes, the smell of scent and sex hung heavily around him. The sheets lay crumpled and detached in a rumpled area on which he lay.

Stumbling into the bathroom, the floor alien, his head concussed, he stepped into the shower and turned it on oblivious to the temperature setting. Cold water shook him and then the flow warmed to soothe. He felt drunk, then sober, unbearably sleepy then awake. The parameters of his world moved on all indices. He sat down in the bathtub and held his head. Moments passed as he tried to compose himself.

Desperately, he crawled out and got up unevenly. He stood naked by the sink and drank a glass of water. Wiping the fog from the mirror he tried to focus on his face. He couldn't.

The unfamiliarity of the room layout made his stagger back to the bed even harder. Head spinning he lay down, then slept.

———

The phone rang and he awoke. He lifted the handset.

'Urgh,' he said, trying to form hello.

'Peter? Is that you? This is Randy.'

'Hi,' he croaked.

'Are you okay?'

'No. I think I must have got food poisoning. I don't think I'm going to make it today.'

'Is there anything I can get you?' asked Meyer.

'No, I'll be okay. I'll call you first thing tomorrow.'

'Well, okay, but you call me if you need anything.'

'Yer, sure, thanks.' He hung up and went back to sleep.

——

It was three in the afternoon. He rose and hobbled to the door. Opening it a couple of inches, he checked. Someone had hung the Do Not Disturb sign on the handle. He dressed slowly, turned the sign round and went down to the lobby.

A bad hangover was not new to him, but this felt different as well as noticeably worse. He sat down by a bar and ordered coffee. Maybe it was jetlag. He imagined legs around his waist, hands and arms caressing him, heaving hips, breasts pressed against his chest, smooth thighs and arched necks. Fingers squeezed, nails scoring.

——

'Hi,' said the pretty waitress, making him jump. She filled his cup. 'Can I get you anything else?'

'No, that's fine.'

Whatever had happened the night before was mostly a loss to him. The full story, in which he was the central character, eluded his mind, while the small fragments recalled were too dream-like to be trusted.

Then the oppression seemed to lift and his faculties started clearing themselves of impediment, but his memory was not restored. He paid the bill and returned to his room to find it miraculously reconstructed. Laid out on the bed, he watched TV. Had he slept with Sandy and Cherie? How had he managed that? What would he say to them tomorrow? He ordered sandwiches in his room, then went back to bed.

In the morning he felt recovered. He woke early, his natural body clock rousing him at six. He showered and had breakfast. At nine, he called Meyer, then caught a yellow cab to MonoLog. The company was situated in the ninth floor of a tower in the middle of the financial district. The imposing ground floor, or first floor as the Americans called it, was populated by monumental bronze abstract sculptures, too heavy to be removed even by robbers armed with forklifts. Going up only nine floors in such a high building seemed a bit of an anti-climax, but nonetheless Peter was beginning to feel slightly intimidated by the scale of everything.

The happenings of the night before last had taken on a mythical feeling. Had it really happened at all? He would have felt surer of himself if he had remembered only one of the women. Two seemed more likely to be a delusion than a reality.

It didn't matter how many bike riders turned up with their envelopes of money, George always felt nervous about handling cash. Before working for Peter he had never seen so much money in one place. The chances were, if Peter didn't put so much trust in him, he would have done a runner with some of it by now.

The thing was, he couldn't do the dirty on such a diamond geezer.

'Sticky money,' he'd mutter to himself, counting it before filling out the bank book, 'sticky money.'

Peter had looked at him questioningly when he had called it 'sticky'. For a smart boy, he sometimes thought, Peter knew bugger all.

Then again, maybe he was just playing stupid. Everyone knows you don't get nothing for nothing. Peter treated him like a gent. The world was full of young bastards, acting like an old man like him didn't have the right to breathe the same air.

So it was good to be with a proper boss, someone that showed some common decency. No one else would even consider giving him a job at his age and the work was the only thing that kept him going.

So what if it was a dodgy lark, what had he got to lose? A knock or a fall, a bad dose of flu or a nasty winter might tip him over the edge anyway. Pensioner to 'brown bread' was a short journey and one he would be taking soon enough anyway.

So bollocks! Peter gave him that touch of ginger, a zest he remembered from his army days. Then, he hadn't known whether he was going to get out alive; now, it was just a trivial question of legality. Most of his friends were killed at 'Market Garden' in Holland and he had lived for the day ever since.

One thing he was certain of, 'happy hour' had a finite span.

George felt particularly important when he was in his suit. Somehow doing the business in his overalls didn't carry the same prestige. He sat at Peter's desk minding his Ps and Qs with a foreign punter and his interpreter.

The small Spanish-looking man sported a thick moustache and chained smoked. His face was rat-like and sullen and he mumbled in Spanish to his pretty Latin assistant as if he didn't want to be overheard.

'Senior Hernandez, says he is very happy to open fifty accounts and also deposit one hundred and twenty thousand pounds with you.'

George's mental arithmetic ground slowly. 'Fine,' he said. He gave up the sums; sure it was a lot of money. Getting up, he smiled politely. 'I'll get the papers for you.' He went downstairs to retrieve a box of fifty manuals prepared before Peter went away.

'Handy Andy,' he thought.

He puffed upstairs and put the cardboard container on the table. Hernandez handed him his briefcase. George opened it. It was packed with piles of different denomination used notes.

'I don't need to count this,' he said. 'If there are any problems we will email you.'

He closed the case. He had drilled himself over and over on the procedure for multiple accounts, as he didn't quite understand what the mumbo-jumbo actually meant. 'When you have chosen the main account, confirm it to us.'

The translator translated. Hernandez nodded and spoke.

'Senior Hernandez, say, it will be a pleasure doing business with you and hopes that this equipment will smooth the waters on all our lives.'

'Yes, mutual I'm sure.'

Hernandez stood.'Cood dai' said the Latin throatily. His black ringed eyes looked soulfully at the old man.

George smiled heartily, 'Sayonara.'

George looked inside the briefcase, deciding to pay it into the bank in stages. Smaller lumps might help to avoid awkward questions. The whole load would be bound to cause a stir. He thought it was amazing that such a tin-pot operation could pay in large amounts of cash without attracting attention. As it was, he always made sure the banking amounts were not round numbers to forestall any unwelcome interest. There were a lot of market traders in the area and therefore a lot of cash business, but what did they think Online Data was, the East End's most successful jellied eel stall? One day they'd get hot on cash banking, but by then they'd be long gone.

He worked out the total money in the briefcase on a scrap of paper.

'Farkin 'ell,' he muttered, underlining the result, £220,000. 'A lot of very sticky money!'

Chapter Four
MONOLOG

Peter walked from the lift onto a small landing.

The hall area was an ochre coloured, artificially lit rectangle with four doors. An engraved plate across the door directly in front announced MonoLog in jagged black letters. The three other doors were unmarked, save for electronic touchpads for code-key entry.

He walked through the appointed entrance to the front desk. A young blonde with a headset looked at him with a blank gaze.

'Can I help you?'

'Randy Meyer, please.'

'May I have your name?'

'Peter Talbot.'

She turned a book on the counter around. 'Would you fill the log in please?'

'No problem.' Peter scribbled illegibly as she phoned through.

'If you would care to take a seat, Mr Meyer's assistant will be with you in a minute.'

He picked up a copy of The Wall Street Journal and began to read.

Sandy entered the reception area. She was wearing a mustard yellow outfit, trimmed with black and highlighted with red piping. The jacket was trimmed to the waist, the skirt split at the front with a slash and overlap. He glanced up and caught the spark of an impish, knowing look. He cursed his amnesia.

He stood and greeted her, 'Hi there.'

'Hi Peter, I hope you're feeling better.'

'Much, I hope you and Cherie were okay.'

'We were just fine.'

'That was some party.'

Sandy mouth dropped slightly open, her eyes veiling for a moment like the beat of a butterfly's wing. 'Wasn't it,' she drawled putting her hand on his shoulder. 'Randy has asked me to show you around the facility. He'll catch up with us as soon as he can.'

'Fine. Lead on.'

She turned on a high heel. 'Walk this way.'

Peter stopped himself from cracking the oldest joke in the world and followed.

Behind the wall that flanked the receptionist was an expanse of open-planned office space. Broken into little cubicles of fawn sound-inhibiting dividers, the area was a maze of work booths. Cartoons and notes were pinned around, defining someone's territory within the bland, brown forest, like feral droppings.

Absolutely quiet, the space had a scent; a bland, faint, sickly sweet aroma of candy. Most of the work capsules were empty, deserted as if the workers had been suddenly evacuated.

'This is administration. We look after our accounts function here.'

She pointed to a big glass walled area. 'We hold our staff meetings there and generally take care of the knotty stuff.' She pointed to an arch to the far right.

'That is the VP's offices. It's to one side so they can hang out and do their thing. Offices are offices, not interesting, right.'

She winked at him. 'Let's go see the neat stuff.'

Peter followed her to the lift.

'How long has MonoLog been going?'

'Eight years. It was originally set up by a group of Nevada businessmen as a shared computing resource. After a while they realized that they had a great deal of spare processor time and that they could release it to interested parties for worldwide transactions and communication.'

She punched some numerals into the door directly left of the lift.

'This is the programming centre.' She opened the door.

'How many programmers have you got?' asked Peter.

'Only four in development right now.'

Peter looked down the long corridor. 'You've got a lot of room for four people.'

'We're between phases. Our code is stable and maintenance is low, so we just have a core. We got up to eighty at one point and I guess those times will come again if we upgrade the system. It ain't broke, so we don't need to fix much.' She smiled enigmatically.

'How long have you been with MonoLog?'

'Two years.'

'What did you do before this?'

She flexed her long fingers like a magician about to perform a magic trick. 'I worked in Vegas.'

'Vegas. Sounds exciting.'

She smiled. 'Not really, business communications are pretty much the same anywhere. I guess Vegas is pretty unique but you get used to it. Let me show you the hardware.'

In the hallway again, she typed in another code. Entering a corridor they walked a short way to another door where a security camera looked down on them.

She pressed a buzzer. 'It's Sandy.' She typed a code and they went through into a small area containing a guard sat behind a rostrum.

'Hi Bill, how are you today?'

'I'm fine.'

'This is Peter from London, England.'

'Hi Peter.' He bent down and opened a drawer. 'These are your badges, please wear them.'

Sandy clipped Peter's onto his top pocket and patted it down. The guard pressed a hidden switch in a recess and a further door clicked open. They walked into a large windowless hall filled with row upon row of equipment. The air hummed to the vibration of cooling fans.

'This is the computing centre.' Her voice was muffled by the soft interfering drone of the machines. She raised her voice a trifle. 'We have two clusters of eight mainframes. They were initially used for large batch processing, running payroll and accounting, but as Monlog's network business expanded that side has been reduced and relocated.'

Peter gazed at the machinery with a mixture of awe and disbelief. 'You must have a few million dollars of kit here.' He thought of how many of his set-ups he could buy for a small fraction of the cost of what was before him.

She smiled. 'Sure, and then some more. It's probably all obsolete, but it works. That's what matters. We pay top dollar for that one per cent between ninety-nine per cent and a hundred. We have four guys in here around the clock to make sure nothing disrupts the smooth running of the system. Being online is like being a radio station, you've gotta be there 24 hours of the day, 365 nights and days of the year.'

'Absolutely.'

'I see you are into the technology,' she said, watching him stare at the huge machines.

'Yeah, it has a strange fascination.'

'If I told you I hated computers would you hold it against me?'

He looked away from the computers. 'It can be arranged.'

She laughed. 'Now let me show you something really interesting.' A little pager clipped to her belt bleeped. She read a message from it and smiled, 'That's good, that's real good. The CEO's gonna drop by in half an hour.'

Leaving was almost as difficult as getting in. After buzzing the guard to let them out into his antechamber they signed a book to leave. Then negotiating the next door they were finally back in the main hallway.

Sandy typed a code into the fourth door and it clicked open. In front of them was a dark entrance lit only by yellow pin lights. Ahead was a stairway with illuminated steps, surrounded on both sides by ornamental rock pools fed by cascading trickles of water.

'This is the hospitality suite,' said Sandy, as the door closed itself behind them. 'As such a lot of our business is with corporates, we need a facility to counterbalance the "rocket science". We try and make them as comfortable as possible with us.' She took him by the hand and led him up.

'Amazing!' said Peter as they reached the top of the stairs. In a great room lay a swimming pool, curved irregularly like a natural pond. At the far end was a bar, surrounded by heavy leather chairs and low tables. Around the elaborately mirrored walls were shelves stacked with books. Along one side, heavily tinted windows covered by thin-slatted Venetian blinds faced out onto the city. The lighting was subdued. Like a plush restaurant, the atmosphere was intimate and reassuring.

'It's really something, isn't it?' She walked up to the poolside and stepped out of her shoes. She started to undress. 'Come swimming with me?'

'I never swim before lunch.'

She stood naked before him. 'We've a full twenty minutes,' she said smiling. 'I don't like to get wet on my own.' With that, she dived in.

He unbuckled his belt; it seemed a little late to be coy.

Sandy's pager beeped as Peter rubbed her hair dry with a towel from the heated poolside lockers.

'Perfect timing,' she said rising. 'Mr Andretti will be here in three minutes.'

Peter straightened his tie. He looked at himself in one of the mirrors and combed his wet hair. Sandy was behind the bar pouring a drink. 'What will you have, Peter?'

'Whatever's going.'

'Okay.'

Peter noticed movement in the corner of his eye. He turned to see his host approaching. Andretti was a heavy man in his early fifties. He had jet black hair swept back like Peter's, but held with oil not water. He had a swarthy shadow around his slightly flabby face which carried a sour expression hardened into a mask by many years.

'It's a pleasure to meet you,' he said, holding his hand out before he reached Peter.

Peter stepped forward to meet him. Andretti's grip was like iron, a crushing hold that would hurt. Automatically, Peter pressed down on the base joint of Andretti's thumb, disabling the squeeze at the root of the pressure.

'It's nice to meet you, Mr Andretti. Thank you for all your hospitality.'

Andretti looked at him curiously. 'Call me Frank. It's not so often we have foreign visitors. A few gooks now and again, you understand, but not so many people from Europe.' He moved a little closer. 'Have you got everything you need?'

'Absolutely.'

Sandy brought two large brandies and set them down on a table.

'Just holler if you need me,' she said, disappearing through a side door.

They sat down by their drinks.

Andretti pulled out a large cigar and waved it at him. 'You don't mind do you?' Peter shook his head. 'It's just that some people are so Goddamned sensitive these days.'

He nipped the end off with his teeth and, turning his head away, picked the leaf from his lips and tossed it aside. He began lighting up with a heavy gold lighter. 'It's just sometimes I can't think the right thoughts without some tobacco.'

He puffed. 'So it's a fine thing we're doing.' He paused.

Peter realized Andretti was awaiting a response so he nodded.

'We bring people together and they give us a shit load of money for a simple service.'

'It's certainly a good business,' said Peter.

Andretti sat back, his glass in the other hand. 'You know it's gratifying to be involved with something that lets people have what they want. In the Prohibition days, guys made millions, and that's when a million was a million, just by giving normal people what they had always had, but which the politicians had decided to take away. We're talking freedom here, not alcohol. What people were paying for was not booze but the right to drink booze. Consumption actually went up. They were making a state-ment and they were paying a premium for liberty. That's why history is on the side of the bootleggers, because they were on the side of the people.'

'I hadn't really thought about it that way.'

'It's the American Dream. The way I see it, there's no crime, just things Government say you can or can't do. Take narcotics for instance. Let's look at who gets damaged. The user. Okay, so when has suicide been illegal?' He paused again.

'In the UK, well not since the sixties.'

'Right. So what happens, they make it illegal, the price goes up, the dosage gets more concentrated and unreliable, you get hopeless addicts and death. Then what happens, people get AIDS because clean equipment is hard to get, billions of dollars' worth of crime gets perpetrated to fund artificially expensive habits, people take risks trafficking, prisons fill up with people. And what's the result? You can still buy it on every street corner. Why?' He shrugged.

'The people want it and people get what they want. Now if they made it legit, they could tax it and make a bunch of money. Hell, save a bunch of money too. I mean, there wasn't a drugs problem before they banned it.'

He leant forward. 'You see, we're liberators, we allow things to happen, we help people coordinate projects which there is a need for. We give people the freedom to do, get,' he waved his cigar again, 'buy, sell, order what they like, with impunity. We sell freedom.'

Peter looked impassively at Andretti. He recognized the feeling; without knowing he had been sucked out by the current and was adrift far from the shore.

'Yes, exactly,' he said calmly. He took a swig of brandy. 'Of course,' he thought, 'I knew this. How could I miss it? Simply not wanting to see the obvious is not plausible. What the fuck was I thinking?' He smiled at Andretti and nodded. 'Exactly how far in the shit am I?' he wondered to himself.

'We facilitate,' said Andretti. 'We've gone under the barriers thrown up by Governments and people pay us for the luxury of total unaccountability. You and I are beyond the law, we don't break it. Nothing can touch us.'

Peter laid back and let the tide take him. 'So how can we do business together?' He sat forwards and pretended to listen intently. 'Pretty much up to my fucking neck in the shit it seems,' he answered himself.

Andretti's ash fell onto the table. 'We want to run a link into you. The UK is an important node for a lot of our customers and we want them to be able to talk to your clients. The way I see it, a lot of your users are going to be happy about this. Direct US-UK email has got to be a major benefit.'

'We've had no feedback asking for a US link.'

'I think a link will be mutually beneficial.'

Peter shrugged. 'I'm not going to get into a negotiation with you about this. I'll agree to a link, you pay me what you think it's worth and we'll take it from there.'

'That's not a very solid arrangement.'

Peter looked glumly at Andretti. 'It's as solid as you make me happy.'

Andretti pointed his cigar at him. 'Now that's not such a crazy idea. Yeah, that's got a lot of style. I like that.'

———

Peter sat in his hotel room looking through the window at the street life far below. The horror swept back over him after periods of calm. How had he been so stupid? How could he forgive himself? Could he survive the situation?

He had worried about having a madam on his system, but a whole system full of criminals was more than he could grasp. It was obvious to him now that he had taken a lot of money from a lot of very shady people. Now he was in, how could he get out? He thought about Uridium and their offer. Had he burnt his boats? Would they work out the score and get him in further trouble? Could he sell even if they didn't initially work out what was really going on? Did they already know?

The phone rang. It was Sandy.

'Hi, I wondered what you were doing tonight.'

His dark thoughts had shaken his composure. 'You drugged me, didn't you?'

There was a silence, 'I'm sorry?'

'I said, you drugged me, didn't you?'

'I just wanted you to have a good time. I didn't think it would hit you so hard.'

'I don't really go for people that put poison in my food.'

'Hey look,' she said quietly, 'I'm real sorry.'

'You know, you make me feel very foolish.'

'I'm sorry, I thought it might pep you up after the flight.'

'Do you drug all the men you take out or did I get special treatment?'

'Special treatment.'

'I'm flattered.'

'Don't be like that. You're cool, I like you a lot.'

He sighed. 'Yeah, I like you too.'

'So how's about dinner?'

He was hungry. He had to eat. 'Dinner but no drugs.'

'Sure, I promise. Can Cherie come too?'

——

He looked into the blackness of his coffee. Now he knew what he was into, his options seemed limited. Once on the rollercoaster there was no easy way off. He had to go for the whole ride or try to get off at a safe port along the way.

Whatever he did, he had to retain a front. He looked at Sandy and Cherie. Would an underworld figure say goodnight after the meal, or goodbye in the morning? Some parts of the journey would be fun.

——

The MonoLog limousine arrived at the airport. On the back seat next to him was a lead crystal set of decanters, necked in gold and engraved with the MonoLog logo. It had been left there for him in its walnut box with a message from Meyer.

'Peter,
It was great to have you over to see our operation.
I'm glad to hear you got on so well with Frank.
I look forward to coming over to visit you sometime in the future and I'll be in touch about the link up.
I would just like to say you have made a big impression on everyone and I look forward to a long and fulfilling relationship.
Your friend,
Randy'

Waiting in the airport, he bought himself a pocket computer to play with. He looked at his ticket; by the time he got back it would be morning. He sat at the gate and picked over the manual for his gadget. It was incomprehensible garbage.

———

The flight back was full, but being one of the first to check in, he got a window seat. He threw his coat over himself and was asleep before they took off. A blonde in her mid-thirties sat in the next seat, but he ignored her, intent on being asleep before the take-off and, with luck, for the whole journey back. The acceleration of lift-off made him dream of his new car dashing away from the lights, outrunning an evil black Porsche that continued to hunt him.

A hostess woke him for the meals but he refused them. Every hour or so the arm on which he rested would go numb, the pins and needles rousing him. He turned over and rearranged his jacket, slipping away until once more the cold prickly sensation buzzing in his forearm pushed him out of slumber.

Halfway through the journey he awoke to find himself lying askew, his head firmly resting on his neighbour's shoulder.

'I'm sorry,' he muttered sleepily.

'That's okay.'

'You're the only comfortable spot around.' He turned away and curled up in another position, not awake enough to feel embarrassed.

Long duration travel was a slow torture. A car trip had entertainment value, at least when he was the one in control of the vehicle. Flying was like watching a wall for hours, in a cramped seat, in a stuffy room.

Happily, every time he woke the clock had moved significantly forward. Sometimes it was a pleasant surprise to see how much time had elapsed, sometimes it was a disappointment. So the truncated night of time-zone crossings passed with a few brief interludes.

The sun shone into his eyes. 'Are we nearly back?' he said, squinting at his anonymous neighbour who was now eating her breakfast.

'About another hour,' she said looking at him inquisitively through huge horn-rimmed glasses.

'Great,' he said, trying to mask a shaking, orgasmic yawn. 'Bbbbrrr.'

He smiled at her, noting how her angular fringe had taken the brunt of the trip and become broken and wispy. 'Sorry I haven't been much fun. I'm Peter.' He punched the service button above. 'I hope they've got some of that coffee left. I think I need a jump start.'

'Hello there, I'm Laura. Don't be sorry, I wish I could sleep on planes like you, but I can't. You're so lucky.'

'I could sleep during the three minute warning. Buses, trains, cabs, parties with loud discos, no problem, I just close my eyes and pass out. Easy-peasy.'

'If I close my eyes, I just stay awake with my eyes closed.'

'That must be really boring. I remember as a kid going to Norwich in a coach from London. It stopped at every little town you could imagine. It was terrible. I've hated coaches ever since.'

'Coach, is that like a Greyhound bus?'

'Yes, but probably not as nice.'

'I've never been on a Greyhound, but some people swear by them. See the country, you know.'

'Don't walk when you can ride, don't ride when you can fly. Don't fly when you can stay at home and do it by the telephone.'

'Do you work for the phone company?' she asked ironically.

'You could say that, it feels like it sometimes.'

A hostess appeared, looking untroubled by the unrelenting hours. 'Can I help you?'

'Yes, can I have a coffee?'

'Certainly, I'll be right back.'

'You coming to England for work or fun?' he asked.

'Business, sort of, pleasure too. I work for an art gallery and I'm on a buying trip.'

'Is that an art gallery as in museum, or as in shop?'

'Museum.'

'That sounds interesting, what do you buy?'

'Modern sculpture.'

'Ah right. Statues and things.'

'Statues, mobiles and stuff. I work at the Lakes Institute. Do you enjoy art?'

'Well I'm not sure, I suppose so. The trouble is, most of it is a bit too mystifying. I like things that tell me what they mean. It's hard to rate a piece of communication when the message has to be explained by an expert.'

'I agree with you, but that is the difference between art and great art. Like anything, a piece that will touch everyone is as rare as it is precious. That's why I have to fly round the world looking out for an object like that.'

'How do you know if you've found it?'

She smiled. 'I don't. If it looks good, I buy it. Sometimes, when the crates get opened back at the ranch, it doesn't look so good. Other pieces, when you get to see them again just radiate; before they didn't look like much, I might have bought them just because I liked the artist, but in a different setting it can be another story.'

'It's all a bit too close to the supernatural to me. I can scan the Mona Lisa into my PC, print it out on a colour printer and it's worth a pound. Somewhere down the line I've lost fifty million quid in value.'

'I hate the money side. I've got a budget on this trip of a heap of money. It doesn't make me happy, one bit. Think, I can pay sixty thousand, seventy-five thousand dollars for a piece by a second-rater, just because we have to have an example of his work in the collection. I don't get paid that much in a year. Not that that worries me, but this guy's just slapped some junk together. He's got an infinite supply of Japanese businessmen wanting to buy a part of his reputation for their rice paper penthouses and I have to acquire a piece of it too.' She ran her finger along her fringe, which refused to conform. 'And he knows it.'

'That's a lot of money.'

'Not really. That's just for starters. It's all bizarre. You know, some rich guy dies sixty years ago, with a few dead ranchers on his conscience. He was worried about the history books, so he starts a foundation with two hundred million dollars of his dirty money for a Museum of Art. Now he is too old to enjoy spending it, he wants to repay his debt to society. The foundation invests most of it and before you know, they've got more money for art then they have art to buy and they ain't the only ones with legacies. Prices can only rise, and they do. Once you've bought up all the old works and locked them in your vaults, what do you spend the rest on? They are all falling over each other to get at pieces and the supply of quality, at any price, is always limited.'

The hostess returned with the coffee that Peter had forgotten was coming. 'Thanks.'

'You're welcome.'

Peter tore the sugar into the black liquid. 'How long are you in London for?'

'Five days. Then I'm off to Venice and Rome.' She paused for thought. 'Then Paris, then London again.'

'All business?'

'And pleasure. I like Europe. Compared to Europe, New York State is a wilderness. It's nice and green,' she almost sang the words, 'lots of trees and clean air, but no culture, no history.'

'I've only been to New York City.'

'Oh God, it's not a good example. It's nice in small bursts, like adrenaline, but it's not an environment to live in. Not if you prize your sanity.'

'I had got that impression. Though enough people live there.'

'I go for weekends to shop, but that's it for me. Things are too fast. Now, London I like. The idea of going out at night for a walk and not having to care what turn I take, that's nice. No muggers, no guns, that's unbelievably civilized.'

'Do you know London well?'

'Not really, I've been twice, but I've only really done the tourist things like Harrods and the Tate. It's a bit of a rut. You know, carefully worn by all my other fellow Americans. Follow the trail of the Waldorf salad. You know, I mean, you don't have that in England normally, right? It's an American thing. Well, it doesn't matter where you're told to go in England by the guides; they'll serve you Waldorf salad. I'm always pleased when I make it to a place that doesn't have it on the menu. Then I know I've escaped and broken out of a process.'

'I'll show you around if you like.' Peter pulled out his card and handed it to her. 'Call me if you fancy it. Don't say yes now, just ring if the idea gets appealing.'

'Online Data, that sounds like computers.'

Peter looked puzzled. 'No, commuters sounds like computers, Online Data sounds like mash potata.'

Laura looked blankly at him.

'It's a joke.'

She screwed up her face. 'Okay, I can see that that could be funny. So are you a computer whizz-kid or not?'

'I suppose so, but sadly, computers are crushingly boring and there is very little whiz to it. Say you're in computers at a party and you can clear the room.'

The plane began to incline and there was a bonging noise from hidden speakers. 'Good morning Ladies and Gentlemen, we have started our decent into London Heathrow . . . '

'Here we go,' she said.

Peter swallowed hard. 'Yup.'

———

He had never thought of London as home before, it was just a city in which his home was located. Returning from such a strikingly different place had given birth to a notion of belonging somewhere else. He looked around the road outside the terminal's entrance doors. It was ugly but it was British.

He got a taxi from the rank, rather than slog it in on the tube. A drained feeling had come over him.

When he said, 'Whitechapel, please,' the cabby's manner perked up.

'Have a long journey, have ya?'

'Pretty much.'

'The traffic's murder, best if we go down the Embankment. I can take you through the centre, but it's bumper to bumper.'

'Whatever.'

'You got jetlag guvnor?'

'Probably.'

'They say you should put brown paper in the sole of your shoe.'

'Yeah? I'll remember that next time'

He pulled the dividing window closed.

As they drove along, he watched the cityscape. London seemed somehow more respectable than the Big

Apple. The weight of money showed in New York, the City was merely a growth that supported its manufacture. It was the Queen Ant of Dollars. London's visage seemed to suggest an amiable lack of drive and purpose. It seemed to have a better attitude or at least a less focused one.

The stairs of the office smelt of dust. Wires were painted into the walls like ivy vines embedded into the wood of a tree. A blouse was draped on the first floor landing, a skirt on the stairs leading up. He stopped by the downstairs door and listened hard. Faintly he could hear the intermittent sound of heavy breathing.

He swore under his breath and went into the bare office. The room was spotless, bereft of furniture save for the old bedraggled chair set in its middle.

Seconds after the main door swung closed with a hollow slam, Peter entered the main office.

George gauged his scowl. 'I never touched your hard disk. You don't have to tell George anything twice.'

Peter put his case down and rubbed his eyes. 'Bloody hell, you're the limit.'

'Tea?'

'Tea!' he snorted. 'Tea!' He pulled a face. 'Oh bloody hell, go on then.'

'Coming right up.' George headed for the kettle.

'How much have we got in?'

'Total, two hundred and ninety four thousand including deposits.'

'Two hundred and ninety four?'

'Yer, most of it from a Spanish gentleman.'

Peter slumped into his chair. 'Knowing my luck he's probably a Colombian drug baron.'

'Could be,' called George, the kettle clicking off as the water boiled.

'Have you banked it?'

'Kind of.'

'What's that mean?'

'Hold on a mo.'

Peter waited, listening to the stirring of spoons. George appeared with two mugs. 'Well what's kind of, mean?'

'I banked a bit of it. Then I took the liberty of opening a safe deposit box. Most of it's in there.'

Peter took the tea. 'Why?'

'Well I thought, you might not want to pay tax on it. I mean there's no tracing any of this dosh is there? A bunch of dodgy geezers turn up with cash, the tax man aint gonna know, is he? Most of it's moody, anyway. Why attract attention to yourself?'

'Dodgy geezers, moody, what are you saying?'

'You know?'

'Let's say I don't.'

'HA! Don't pull my plonker. Look, I just reckoned, all this money turns up unannounced, you might thank me if I put it somewhere safe, so you could work out what to do with it at your leisure. It's alright, I know I'm working for a firm, even if it is just you. I've been there, I've done that. In the fifties I used to run with the Richardsons, until they got put away. I know what's what.'

'I see.'

'No you don't. The thing is, it's good to be alive again. If we get caught, what can anyone do to me?' He slurped his tea. 'I look at it this way. As far as the law goes, they wish I was dead. If I keeled over tomorrow they'd be happy that there was one less farking old git to look after. I paid my stamp all those years, never been ill, never claimed until I retired and what do I get back? Nothing, nada. Just enough to stop me starving, enough to keep me in rags. No reward, no respect, no employment. So this is my lucky break, see? My final fling. Anyway, if we get nicked I'll claim senility; I don't know nuffin about computers. I just make tea.'

Peter leant back in his chair and looked at George's smiling face. 'Yes well, now we know, aye. I suppose the penny had to drop sometime. You did well with the money, it was good thinking. What have you done with the box key?'

'It's in your top drawer.'

Peter opened it and took it out. 'A quarter of a million. Not bad considering I've been away.'

George smiled. 'Tidy, I'd say.'

'It's about time I gave you a pay rise too. How does five hundred a week sound to you?'

'Sounds good, sounds very good.'

'For the time being anyway. If things keep going well I think some bonuses might be in order. Now you can afford to take your ladyies to a hotel or something.'

'How can I teach them about computers in a hotel?'

'I'm sure you'll manage.'

Chapter Five
DEEPER

For Peter, the idea of learning to pilot an aircraft was exciting, even though the actual idea of being airborne had become a terror.

As he stood on the forecourt outside of a flying school, waiting for the instructor, he wasn't sure which of the competing emotions was strongest.

Whenever Peter didn't like something without good reason, he went out of his way to conquer the fear by tackling the problem head on. If he didn't like a food, he ate it at every opportunity until he developed a taste for the flavour. He was sure that learning to control a small plane would be a good platform to start sorting out his fear of flying in a big jet. By his reckoning, flight in a Cessna would be significantly more hair-raising and once he had mastered flying one, being a passenger in a huge airliner would hold no fears.

The airfield was a large green rhomboidal expanse of roughly cut grass. On the side edged by a road was a row of large corrugated sheds of which the flying club consisted, surrounded by aircraft hangers and miscellaneous tatty buildings. In the far distance, on three irregular sides were great expanses of wheat, disappearing down the slopes that surrounded the airfield.

A thin man in a white shirt approached him, carrying a clipboard. Peter instinctively knew who he was. The flying instructor didn't look very healthy. His skin was a shiny translucent white, his eyes sunken and ringed by brown circles.

He greeted Peter. 'Hi there, call me Kevin, you ready to go up?'

'Yes, sure.'

Kevin looked hunted; his relaxed chattiness seemed to be underpinned by something. Perhaps the stress of the job had got to him. He looked at the roster on his clipboard and found the name. 'Well Peter, we've got a nice day for it. Follow me.'

They made their way over to a single engine plane. It was a fragile-looking craft that increased Peter's trepidation. Kevin took him around the outside of the plane.

'First off, you always make ground checks. You have got to make sure your machine is air-worthy. Initially I always check that the flaps are okay, but you don't have to go in any particular order.' He moved them slightly with his hand. 'Check the rudder.' He pushed and pulled the tail flap. They moved to the weak-looking fixed undercarriage. 'Check the tyres and, see that?' He pointed at the brake discs. 'Make sure they're okay and that the pads are in good order.' He pointed out the leading edges of the wing. 'Make sure the wings are fine, no cracks, that sort of thing.' They moved onto the propeller. 'Check the prop, check it's not going to fall off.' He moved it. 'Right, let's get on and get going.'

Peter strapped himself in and listened carefully as Kevin ran over the various dials and buttons. It was a tiny vehicle, two seats in a bubble, two short wings and a propeller a foot and a half from their noses. It felt horribly like learning to drive all over again but with the added level of difficulty of an extra axis thrown in.

Kevin's general briefing poured out a long string of information and detail at him. Soon most of this stream began to merge into an incomprehensible babble that washed over him. His mind went blank; what did all this rubbish mean?

'Let's start her up,' said Kevin finally.

Peter snapped out of his daze, nodded and followed his instructions. The engine shuddered violently and, shaking the cockpit, the propeller spun into action. As ordered, Peter steered gingerly towards the runway area with the rudder pedals.

'Okay, we are going for take-off. When the column feels light just pull back on it and up we'll go.'

Sweat appeared spontaneously all over Peter's body. 'When it feels light, pull back?'

'You've got it.' Kevin leant slightly forward and pushed the red throttle handle in fully.

The engine roared and the pointer on the RPM dial went into the yellow and wavered unpredictably as if to indicate an imminent explosion. The airplane accelerated along the grass, bouncing and bobbing at an ever increasing rate. Kevin's prophesy was fulfilled; the column went light and Peter pulled on it. The yoke eased towards him and in an instant they were airborne.

'Okay, hold it about there.'

Peter held the grip and saw through the corner of his eye the ground shrinking below and the grey clouds become his horizon.

'That's all there is to taking off,' said Kevin, maintaining his off-hand air. 'Landing is a bit trickier.'

———

He had not been bothered for long by the phobia. Everything had happened so quickly. The amazement of being suspended in the air with only the slightest of material between him and the elements had overwhelmed all other feelings, except for a progressive disease in his stomach. The plane flew over East London and he tried in vain to pick out landmarks. On the ground he had a perfect sense of direction and would navigate himself around purely by following his nose. Wherever he wanted to go he would just set off and follow his bonnet. In the air, he was lost; he searched for motorways and buildings, but from four thousand feet up, he could not pick out a single detail that fitted with his mental map. Only the Thames declared itself and he was glad that it was not down to him to find the way back.

Kevin showed him how to fly straight and level, trying without success to explain to him how different 'trims' affected the way the plane flew.

They were soon coming back into land, but though he looked carefully, he could not see the airfield. Then suddenly he saw a green mark down below, an emerald postage stamp, an impossibly small bullseye. It was a relief that he wasn't in control. From his point of view, the task of getting onto the ground looked not dissimilar to jumping off a table onto a box of matches.

Kevin brought her in smoothly, describing fluently the procedure as he did so. He pulled the nose up and they touched down.

They taxied to the flying school, Peter driving in as directed. Kevin talked through the power down procedure and then booked Peter in for another lesson.

Peter was happier now that they had stopped and happier still when both of his feet were on the ground. Flying was fun, but he hated being taught, he hated being lost, it made him feel sick and worst of all it had cost a hundred pounds.

———

As he padlocked the shutter on the shop front, the door of a Granada parked by the curb opened. A tall man in a raincoat stepped out. Normally, someone leaving a car would go unnoticed, but the individual's attention was solidly fixed on Peter.

Peter sensed intent and turned his attention away from the fiddly job of locking up. As he straightened up, their eyes met and the link was confirmed. The man was caught off balance by the recognition. His arm went out, too far away to have any hope of touching him; it signalled imminent attack. Peter resisted the urge to recoil and stood back onto his heels, off balance and prone.

'Get into the car,' said the man as the driver's door opened and another figure began to appear.

Peter was transfixed, his mind wrestling with the unknown. The hand made solid contact with his left shoulder, grasping him. The force sparked his reaction.

He knocked the arm away with the back of his right wrist and drove his stronger left into the side of the man's head. His right sunk into the solar plexus and his left repeated a similar blow to its last, back to the temple. The man fell to the floor like a felled tree, a dramatic unrestrained collapse. Peter sprinted forward and in front of the Granada. The traffic baulked him so he turned to the other man, out of his vehicle and backing away from him. His new opponent was middle aged, a cheap ill-fitting suit covering a flabby body. He had fear in his eyes, a look of someone unprepared for violence. Peter dived through a tiny gap in the traffic into the no-man's buffer of the middle of the road. A fraction later again he bolted onto the far pavement, horns blaring around him. He snatched a glimpse behind as he ran for his car. He saw no one coming after him.

His Mercedes leapt out of its space, clearing the bumper of the car in front by more inches than his judgment deserved. The dusk was turning into night. He drove around the streets randomly, looking to see if he was being followed.

He rang George on the car phone.

'8 5 9 7.'

The line hissed and buzzed. 'George?'

'Boss?'

'I've just had some hassle George, someone just tried to jump me.'

'Jump you, where?'

'Outside the office, just now.'

'Who were they?'

'I don't know.'

'The Old Bill?'

'I hope not, I laid one out.'

'Better the Old Bill than some.'

'They weren't in uniform, they didn't show ID.'

'Blimey . . . They still after you?'

'I don't think so.'

'So you're away clean.'

'Yes, I think so.'

'That's okay then.'

'Okay?'

'Peachy.'

'Peachy?' his voice rose involuntarily. 'What do I do now?'

'Go home.'

'Go home?'

'If it's the Old Bill they'll call on you. If it ain't they'll leave it for a bit.'

'That sounds all well and good in theory.'

'Trust me, I'm a Doctor.'

'I'm not sick.'

'Look boss, if you are overly troubled, pack some things and book into a hotel. Come round my place if you like but you'd do better to go home. You've got locks, haven't you?'

'Well I don't live in a castle.'

'Nor did Ronnie and Reggie. You'll be okay.'

'You're not convincing.'

'Look, don't worry.'

'I am worried. I don't get jumped on every day of the week.'

'Don't get scared,' said George. 'Someone's most probably feeling us out.'

'What do you mean?'

'Putting the frighteners on us.'

'Why?'

'Why, 'cause you're making stacks of illicit wonga.'

'And?'

'I mean, they might want some of it.'

'And?'

'And if we go showing we're soft, they'll terrorise us for all the money they can.'

Peter pulled into the curb. 'You think that's what it is?'

'Could be, I dunno, like I said, if it's the Old Bill they'll look us up and you can tell 'em it's all a big mistake. Just remember old George is senile, got it?'

'Fine and dandy!' Peter said sarcastically.

'I'll get you bailed out, don't you worry. It's better than going into hiding.'

'Oh great, thanks.'

'You can't expect to keep your nose clean forever,' said George jauntily through the hiss. 'People are going to make waves sooner or later. If you do it right you'll make enough to get out ahead or make a couple of years on the Isle of White a bit of a holiday.'

'Well I'm not planning on getting arrested just yet. We're not actually doing anything wrong.'

George laughed. 'Leave it out, I'm no legal brain, but if they say what you do is illegal, it'll be illegal, whether it is or it ain't. Whatever we are doing, we ain't working for the Salvation Army.'

'So . . . You reckon I should go home?'

'Yer, it'll sort itself out.'

'Shit, who the hell were they?'

'Don't worry, you'll see, nothing to get het up about. You've got to let it transpire. Save your energy. Anyway, we've got enough money to ease the way, whatever's up.'

'I'll take your word for it.'

'Relax.'

'Alright, I'll relax. Let's hope you're right.'

'You watch, George knows.'

'Well I hope so.'

'You laid one out, huh. We must be wanted by the Boy Scouts.'

———

There was no police car waiting outside his flat when he drove into his parking space. He wasn't sure whether he was relieved or worried by this.

Even though only a short period had elapsed between the confrontation and his arrival home, it already seemed a long time ago. This made him feel depressed. It was as if, somewhere inside of him, there was a true desperado trying to take over. Since New York, there was no way to ignore the fact that what he was doing, however accidentally it had come about or even technically legal, was on the wrong side of the tracks. He had to find a way out, but a way needed to be found that wouldn't place him in further difficulties. The trouble was, he was rising to the wrong kind of challenge and worse still, he seemed to have a natural talent for it.

He never usually put the chain on his door, but tonight was an exception. There wasn't anything of value in his flat, so it was scarcely protected, save by the obligatory Yale.

Although he only rented it, the flat was home. It was a scruffy, comfortable place where he could switch off and relax. He watched television, toying with the idea of taking off to a hotel with his still half-filled suitcase. He thought about what George had said and decided to stay.

At midnight he went up to his bedroom and put his pillows on the floor at the far side of the bed. He lay down on the carpet and pulled the duvet over himself. He hoped that he would sleep lighter there and if anything began to happen in the night he would not only wake up quickly, but be where they didn't expected him.

———

His alarm clock buzzed. Peter felt groggy and faintly stiff. The night had apparently passed without event. He showered and dressed, then drove to the office.

'Any more trouble?' said George by way of greeting.

'No.'

'Told ya.'

Peter dropped into his chair and rocked back on it.

'What next then?'

'Dunno, something will turn up.'

'As long as it's not me in a flyover.'

The door buzzer sounded and George went down to answer it. He reappeared holding a brown envelope.

'A geezer in a raincoat with a farking great black eye just delivered this.'

Peter shot forward on his chair and craned his neck to see out of the window to the street below. A Granada pulled into the traffic.

'It's them!' He lunged forward and grabbed for the letter. 'Give me that.'

George handed it over. 'Looks official.'

'Maybe it's the tax man,' said Peter sarcastically.

Peter ripped the flap open and pulled out the contents. 'It's an invitation to lunch at the Ludgate Cellars on Thursday, with a Rodney Mojo-Smith.' He examined the paper. 'You're right, it does look official. It doesn't say it's official, but it looks like it.'

'I told you something would turn up.'

'Yes, but what?'

George shrugged. 'So long as we're not headed for the clink just yet, I'll leave you to worry about that. Tea?'

———

Later that evening, Peter and George visited the Ludgate Cellars to check it out.

It was an extensive City wine bar, a massive underground vault beneath a railway bridge that crossed the Thames. It consisted of a labyrinth of nooks and crannies where tables lurked in the gloomy shadows. Peter imagined that at lunch it would be packed with bankers and brokers drinking their tension away over platters of high cholesterol, up market junk food.

George downed his pint before Peter had paid for the round. 'Same again,' he told the barman, 'and two whiskey chasers.' He pulled out some money. 'This one's mine.'

Peter almost cancelled his part of the premature round, but noting George's pleasure in buying, held himself in check. 'Cheers.'

'It's been a long time since I've been able to really stand a shout,' said George with glee. 'You know, get one in and not have to worry about the gas bill.' He watched the barman serve them up, then passed him the tenner. 'And one for yourself.' The barman acknowledged and brought back his change. 'So what do you reckon? Who is it and what does he want?'

'I think I'll find out tomorrow.'

'I was thinking,' said George, pulling himself up onto a stool. 'That fellow you did in, was, well, quite 'uge. How come you did that to him and you didn't get touched?'

Peter slipped onto one of the circular perches. 'Is this twenty questions?'

'No, but go on, I'm interested, I mean, he looked a bit like a gorilla to me.'

'It's a long story, but I used to box when I was a kid. You know, amateur stuff, ended up at light-middleweight.

Just to keep fit and for a bit of sport. It's good fun, if you get into it.'

'Did you fight much?'

'Not really. A bit. Enough.'

'What made you pack it in?'

Peter laughed. 'Not wanting to be a cabbage.'

'And what else?'

'Nothing.'

'You chucked it in 'cause you got beat?'

'No, not beat,' said Peter indignantly.

'Right, well why then?'

'It's not something you do forever, like golf.'

'Go on, you can tell me. Were you any good?'

'Well, I was good, as a junior anyway.'

'How good?'

'Sufficiently good to be able to fight and not really get hurt. You know what I mean.'

'Ever thought of going pro?'

Peter laughed. 'No, I'm not cut out for that. When I got into the seniors I had a few fights and they were okay, no problem. Then I came up against this guy called Briggs and he was as good as me, maybe he was even better on a good day. He kept catching me. I won, but it hurt. I mean really hurt. The sort of pain, no not pain; hurt, distress, sort of agony, it's indescribable really. It's like a head on collision. You want to win at all costs and the other side is someone who's capable of taking all your punishment and giving it back, there's no escape, no pleasure, no sport, just pain. I guess I got a taste of how I used to hurt other kids, only I wasn't expecting it. So I thought, sod this, this can only get worse, and I packed it in right there. Get out while you're ahead.' Peter paused and reflected. 'I was eighteen. So what's that, five years ago now.'

'You miss it?'

'Not really, a little I guess. It's got a lot going for it, so long as you're not on the wrong end of it. Anyway, I like my nose straight and pointy and I've still got all my brain cells. I was never hungry, like you need to be. I was just good enough for it to be a kind of pleasure. Then I reached a level when I wasn't and it wasn't. Up against your own class, it's just a matter of who can take the most pain and who gets lucky. The higher up you go the harder you get punched.'

'You don't look like the type.'

'I wasn't, that's why I didn't keep it up. Just not hard enough for it. Yesterday, it was strange having to use it, you know, outside of a ring. It's like walking down the street in cricket pads. Punching someone on the pavement isn't really in my physical vocabulary.'

'Well it's always handy to be handy, I say.'

'What? Even if the guy just wanted to invite me to lunch?'

George sunk his whisky. 'Ahhh, luverly-jubberley.'

———

A good night's sleep in bed only partially compensated for his hangover. By mid-morning it had lifted. George, who had drunk more much than Peter could remember, seemed completely unaffected.

'I don't know,' said George, smirking at Peter's fragile condition. 'You youngsters, don't seem to have any oomph these days.'

'Ha,' replied Peter, reaching for the ringing phone.

A smile came over Peter's face as he pressed the handset to his ear. 'I'd given up on you.'

'I'm sorry,' said Laura, 'but I've been totally rushed off my feet. I've just about had it.'

'I didn't know Britain had that much sculpture.'

'You're talking about the country of Henry Moore. Turn over a rock and there's a piece of work under it. Anyway, I've been, gone and come back.'

'How long before you're off again?'

'Three days.'

'Where are you going next?'

'Home.'

'Fancy dinner, tomorrow night?'

'That would be exciting.'

'Where are you staying?'

'Brown's. Do you know it?'

'No, but I can find it. Does it serve Waldorf salad?'

'I'm sad to say.'

'Look, I'll pick you up at seven and we'll go somewhere. Somewhere real. Sound good?'

'Not too real I hope.'

'Real nice, I mean, real London.'

'Cockneys and warm beer?'

'It can be arranged, but I thought of something a bit more sophisticated.'

'Oh, okay, sounds fine.'

'Do you like music?'

'Yes, mostly.'

'Anything you don't like?'

'Not really. Heavy metal I suppose. You know, kid's stuff can get a little difficult.'

'Alright, leave it to me, you're in good hands.'

———

Peter spent the afternoon putting together a new machine. If anything happened to the operational computer, it might take a number of days to get the system running again. To be assured against this eventuality, a second machine could be brought into immediate use and the last day's backup installed on it, and as far as the users would be concerned there would be no break in service.

The next step would be to link the two up to run in tandem so that if one broke down the other would take up its tasks immediately. He didn't however have the experience to implement that in one go, so one waiting in the wings as a backup would have to be good enough.

The 'client accounts', where a user put in money to purchase other users' data, had started as a trickle of money. Compared to the steady flow of joining fees its early income was hardly noticeable. That had steadily grown and now Peter was the custodian of a sizable chunk of deposits. There were regular shifts in account balances as notional amounts were transferred between users and their 'services'.

On his return, he printed out a transaction report which showed that while a large amount of money had changed hands, only a small number of trades had taken place. It surprised him that although business had gone on with money debited from one account, being credited to another, no one had yet asked for a withdrawal. Before his success had been placed within the real framework of his users, he would have wondered about this, but not too much. It was all on deposit, earning a good rate of interest at the bank. Now, however, he understood what was happening. When business is good but illicit, cash can be embarrassing. His business was legitimate, so who better to keep it? He had made the perfect conduit and now he was their banker as well as their messenger.

'To whom much is given much is expected,' thought Peter. He seemed to recall something nasty had happened to the guy who said that.

———

Peter sat by the bar, a copy of Personnel Computer World spread in front of him. He sipped a Coca-Cola.

A very short man dressed in a pin-striped suit walked up to him. He smiled, exposing a compressed bite of incisor teeth.

'Peter Talbot?' He offered his hand.

Peter looked down on him. 'Yes.' He dropped off his stool.

As far as Peter could tell Mojo-Smith was in his fifties. A large head with a squashed mottled face leading to a pointy chin, perched on a withered doll-like body, gave Smith more than a passing resemblance to an impish gargoyle.

'Nice to meet you,' he said in a sharp high staccato. The barman passed unoccupied and Mojo-Smith caught his eye with the merest of glances. He ordered a gin and tonic.

'I must admit to finding this place most delightfully troglodytic.'

'Eh . . . Well it's certainly dark in here.'

'It reminds me of a stay I had in some caves in Borneo. Frightfully dank, but after a few months it was just like home.' He paid for his drink and pointed to a table in an alcove. 'Shall we?'

Mojo-Smith sat himself down, his back to the far wall of a short tunnel, while Peter sat facing him, his back to the rest of the wine bar.

'It's a fascinating business you're in, Peter.'

'Not really, I suspect it's pretty much like any other, except a bit more high tech.'

'Ah, but there you have it. Technology, the science of opportunity, don't you agree?'

'The science of bugs and errors mostly. I tend to think what you gain in absolute efficiency you can lose in reliability. If you know what you are doing, you are onto a winner, but the learning curve can be more costly than staying with old ideas.'

'But when you know what you are doing, surely the scope for achievement is broad.' Mojo-Smith's neck sunk into his body, his head nesting on his shoulders. He sipped his drink then smiled inscrutably. 'How do you see the future of all this change?'

'Do you mind me asking your interest? I don't wish to be rude but, how can I say this, who are you and what is your business?'

'I am an observer and that is my business. When something is interesting, I am interested.'

'I see, and?'

'And you and your business are of interest.'

'I see, so?'

'So, I thought we should meet.'

'I'm sorry, but I don't feel enlightened.'

'Ah, a difficult state ever to attain. Whereas change, on the other hand, is constantly enforced on us.'

'You don't strike me as a journalist.'

'I am sure that might be taken as a compliment.' He stopped to drink and then stared into Peter's eyes. 'Are you a patriot?'

'A patriot? Well I'm not really sure what you mean.'

'Simply, are you a patriot?'

'I guess so. As I understand it. Why?'

'It is important to me.'

'I see, or rather I don't see, but go on.'

'I have to make a decision about you and I need to establish a few reference points. What made you start Online Data?'

'I've always been into computers and I thought there was an opportunity to get into business with a souped up BB.'

'What is your net margin?'

'Net margin, of what?'

'Your net margin on sales?'

Peter shrugged, 'If I knew, it sounds like the sort of thing I wouldn't tell you.'

'What's your protection against an Anton Piller order?'

'Depends on what that is?'

'It's no matter. What speed are your modems running at?'

'300, 1200/75, 1200, 2400 and 9600.'

Mojo-Smith's head rose up momentarily and his eyes flashed. He took a silver case from his pocket, offered a filter-less oval cigarette to Peter, then lit up.

'It seems that perhaps we may help each other. Let me try to explain. My business is information. Not gross information with explicit content, but a patchwork of small pieces that build into pictures. A jigsaw puzzle with no edges. My best endeavours build this tapestry up from as many sources as possible, to give an insight into what is happening in the recesses of our society. Take for example, a small incident. All the milk bottles disappear from the doorsteps of a neighbourhood. A mystery of no importance, perhaps. Two days later a major riot erupts of considerable ferocity, many petrol bombs are thrown. The milk bottles have reappeared.'

'So who counts the milk bottles?'

'Who indeed? No one, no system can watch everything. It would be neither practical nor beneficial. Quality has to be all important as there is only so much, as you would probably say, data, one can access.'

'Process.'

'Process, quite. Now this is where you may help us.' He stubbed out his barely smoked cigarette with dainty taps. 'You are the custodian and recorder of information of the highest order and you have become the associate of a good proportion of the kind of people that raise my interest.'

'All client information is confidential.'

'Quite so. Secrecy is the first tenet of a successful operation in both our businesses. Likewise it is the only way to remain in business. It is essential.'

'Secret and confidential are different.'

'As are covert and illicit, but their modus operandi are remarkably similar.'

'So what are you asking me for?'

'Insight.'

'And what would you do with this insight, if someone gave it to you?'

'Assemble it. You see, although information may be directly relevant, it is often more important because of the light it throws on other matters.'

'What does that mean?'

'Let us imagine we, or rather a person, discovered that a man was forging twenty pound notes, to the value of, say, five million pounds. Should it be enabled that the man be arrested or should it perhaps be facilitated that the man who buys the money be detained? Might it be better to step in at the point when the currency purchaser is importing heroin he has used the phoney money to buy? Unpleasant elements in the Far East end up with amounts of useless money, drugs are impounded, a very serious felon is incarcerated and the bait remains in place, but compromised. Additionally the font of the original information remains obscured.'

'That sounds all very tidy.'

Mojo-Smith pulled out a calling card with just a number printed on it. 'You may at some point wish to phone me to establish my credentials.'

Peter took the card. 'So basically you want me to spy for you.'

Mojo-Smith winced. 'Such an ambiguous word.'

'But nonetheless.'

'Nonetheless, a very positive solution to what would otherwise be an awkward problem.'

'Problem?'

'Unfair advantage.'

'How do you mean?'

'Consider the idea of teams. We have, by far,' he accentuated the phrase and repeated it, 'by far, the biggest team. But sadly it is not as driven or dynamic as the opposition. At present, you are on the side of the other team, even if perhaps you may consider yourself as merely neutral. You provide them with an advantage they have never before enjoyed. One way or another they must not retain an advantage. To remove such an advantage at this stage would be a simple matter but not I believe to the best result.'

'So, you want me to join your team.'

'Indeed.'

'It occurs to me the opposing team's strength is that it is spread out and hard to trace. Whereas you are concentrated and potentially obvious.'

'We have that latency.'

'This might be unfortunate for someone helping you. If he was ever found out he would be in deep shit.'

'A risk.'

Peter drank some Coke. 'Okay, so you want me to spy for you. Why shouldn't I just take this as a warning and shut up shop?'

Mojo-Smith grinned, 'We would be grateful if you didn't.'

'Grateful?'

'We are not ungrateful people. We would like to value you. We know that you have made a relatively considerable amount of money. Undoubtedly enough to remove yourself to a safe distance and continue selling your skills on a different basis.'

'Or the same basis.'

'Potentially.'

'Alternatively I could co-operate with you.'

Mojo-Smith nodded. 'For which you would not only elicit our gratitude but also gain the ability to continue on with your affairs unmolested.'

'Unless you blew it.'

'A risk, always a risk.'

'Which might land me buried in a motorway somewhere.'

'Unlikely in this country, but not impossible.'

'Grateful, I take it, doesn't just mean that I get to continue helping you indefinitely.'

'Open briefcases, Peter.'

'Open briefcases?'

'Need is an empty briefcase. Gratitude is a full one.'

'Full with what?'

'It depends on the need and the worthiness.'

'Look Rodney, you're being too obscure for me. You want me to spy for you. If I spy for you, you'll be grateful, whatever that is, and I get to keep going unmolested.'

'In essence.'

Peter sat himself up in the chair. 'Well, it's been very interesting talking to you and if I have any more questions I know where to reach you.' He fished out the calling card and looked at it again.

'Quite prudently said.'

———

His phone rang just as he was going to bed. It was George.

'Well, who was he?'

'A potential investor.'

'With heavies? Leave it out!'

'Bodyguards.'

'Alright, so?'

'So nothing. I told him I wasn't interested.'

'You sure?'

'I'm sure.'

'Mare's bollocks!'

'Those too.'

George grunted. 'I don't want you going round getting into trouble without me.'

Peter smiled. 'George, if there is going to be any trouble I'll make sure you are invited.'

———

The next morning Peter rang the number.

'Department of Trade and Industry.'

'Rodney Mojo-Smith, please.'

'Putting you through.'

The phone rang.

'Department 87,' said a woman's voice.

Peter hung up and turned to the computer. He sat at the keyboard and typed in some commands. The laser printer started to work, a faint buzz signalling the first page was about to be printed. He got up and walked to the stairs.

'I'm off flying,' he called down. 'Don't be up to anything when I get back!'

'Me?' called George. 'Up to what?'

———

The lesson was an hour long slog. His fear of flying was now totally replaced by a nauseous feeling in the pit of his stomach. Taking off and flying straight and level was easy, knowing where he was going was another matter.

Coming into land the instructor talked him through it all again, but it meant nothing. He was too busy searching the quilt of the ground for the landing strip. Then, they were coming down and only at the last moment could he see the runway.

'The trouble is I just get totally lost up there.'

Kevin turned the engine off and they stopped amongst the parked planes in front of the club house.

'It's to be expected to begin with. If God had meant us to navigate, He'd have put compasses in our shoes.'

——

'How did it go?' said George as Peter climbed the stairs. 'Shoot down any jerries?'

'Only one.'

He collected up the output of the printer and pushed it into a large brown envelope from his desk drawer. He rang the number again.

'Trade and Industry,' said the voice of the switchboard after a long delay.

'Department 87 please.'

'One moment.'

'Department 87.'

'Hello,' said Peter, 'I have a package for Mr Mojo-Smith from Peter Talbot. Can I have it sent around?'

'Certainly sir.'

'What address?'

'29 Monmouth Street. WC2.'

'Thanks.'

'Thank you.'

'Bye.' Peter hung up. 'George!' he called.

'Tea?' George enquired.

'Nope.' He wrote on the envelope.

'Can you take this round straight away?' He held out the package.

George took it and looked at the address. 'Okey dokey.'

'And make sure it's the Ministry of Trade and Industry.'

'Okay.'
'If it isn't, come back with it.'
'Message received.'

———

Brown's was a formidable structure, a large Edwardian building with an unmodern airiness about it. Laura met him in the
reception wearing a stripy French-style t-shirt covered by an
open jacket, topped, like an onion seller, with a small red scarf.

'Hi, how are you?' She looked nervous.

'Fine and you?'

They kissed gingerly as friends.

'I'm ready to see the sights.'

'What would you like to eat?'

She pulled a face. 'If I see any more haute cuisine, I'm
going to fake death and get shipped home in a body bag.'

'Do you like jazz?'

She raised her hands. 'Don't ask me, just take me!'

'Okay, let's go then.'

Outside they flagged a cab.

'Ronnie Scott's, please,' said Peter as they climbed in.

'Right you are mate.'

For a minute or so they settled down, Laura taking in
the atmosphere.

'You know, London cabbies are so knowledgeable. In
New York a cab driver is lucky to know his way home.'

'They have to do a lot of training here. You see them
out on mopeds learning every street, turn and landmark.
If they don't know them, they don't get a licence.'

'In New York some of them can't even speak English.' Laura became more relaxed and with that she seemed to grow younger. 'God there are only so many artists and experts I can handle. Meeting new ones every now and then is okay, but after a while they drive me insane. Here she comes, the big cheque from America. Roll out the red carpet.'

'Must be terrible.'

'You are so right.'

'So I won't talk about statues then.'

'If you do I'll jump onto the road.'

They entered Piccadilly Circus. 'Cover your eyes, there's a statue right in front.'

She covered her eyes and laughed. 'Is there no escape? How much is it?'

'It's not for sale.'

She put her hands down and they passed Eros. 'Not for sale? I must have it then, name your price.'

'Twenty quid.'

'Quid?'

'Twenty pounds.'

'Twenty quids, I don't like it anymore, it's too cheap. It's gotta be junk.'

The cab turned into Soho.

'Damn, caught out by a professional.'

'So they keep telling me.'

'How did you get to be a curator?'

She shrugged. 'First I got to be an assistant curator, then I got promoted.'

'So, were you a junior assistant curator before that?'

'No, but I should have been. I'm actually a potter by training and for that matter, I'm a potter by nature. It was one of those things, the post came up, out of state, during my divorce, I applied for it and I got the job. Potters don't get to have much to leave behind, except maybe a wheel and a kiln, so I suppose it was inevitable that I would gravitate away.'

'Do you miss it?'

'Oh yes, one hell of a lot. I keep sneaking terracotta pieces into the collection out of pure angst.'

The cab pulled up outside Ronnie Scott's and Peter paid. As he turned towards the door, Peter glanced at Laura. She did something to him that he couldn't quantify. Something in his blood quickened, something animal stirred. Women always raised his tempo, but there was a profoundly exciting allure about her that was apart from that, entirely separate. She was pretty and chic, but that wasn't it. She was intelligent and successful but that had no great resonance. Whatever it was, it was the difference between a wine and a spirit. She was a definite kick to his system.

They sat in the dimly lit club at a table near the back of a low dark room. The place was busy, filled with the relish of people eating, drinking and listening in a venue they had actively chosen to visit rather than merely drifted into.

They talked between the sets and ate the snacky food on offer. Peter didn't like the music much but he appreciated the musicians who obviously knew their trade.

A thin, half-starved singer came onto the floor. She looked like a waif from some Victorian print and sang a squeaky doleful song. He could not make out the lyrics and the melody was far too extrapolated for his untrained ear.

Laura smiled at him over their barbeque chicken wings. The singer ended on an impossibly high note that sounded horribly out of tune. The crowd applauded rapturously.

'What do you think?' shouted Peter over the crowd noise.

'It's real,' Laura shouted back.

Peter nodded.

The evening drew on and as the hours passed it seemed to Peter as if Laura changed. Her manner lightened, became less serious and cynical. Her face became more full, her movements more open. He was mesmerized; he watched her, almost detached from his surroundings. Laura was a masterpiece, a complete, whole woman. Not a girl, not a young thing finding her way and unsure of her place in life, but a fully qualified, bona fide, class A female.

Then the club part of the evening had run its natural course and they left. It was 11.30.

'Do you fancy a walk?' asked Peter. 'We can't be more than half a mile from your hotel, as the crow flies.'

'That sounds like a nice idea. I've got my Mace.'

'You don't need Mace in London.'

'Damn, does that mean I have to take it back to the Tower of London?'

He laughed and they set off slowly, joking and chatting, meandering out onto Charing Cross Road. They headed towards Oxford Street. She stopped by a wall plastered with gig posters and began to study them under the dim yellow street light.

She straightened up and looked at him seriously. 'I love British music.'

Peter floated forwards a foot and they kissed. They embraced tightly, her tongue touching his. Her breasts pressed into his chest as he felt her taut back muscles through the thin fabric of her t-shirt. They moved back into the itinerant shadow of the wall, lost in their private passion. Her crotch pressed against his. His left hand moved down her body, sensing her form through the cloth. She moaned quietly, pressing her right hand against the base of his neck.

They stood locked together in the gloom, prisoners of their clothes. He tore himself from her lips.

'Let's get back.'

She grasped his hand. 'Quickly.'

He threw his arm up as a black shape rattled towards them. 'Taxi!'

———

As the lift door closed they kissed, alone for a few moments. The lift slowed and they entered the hushed corridor. Holding hands they walked along the plush calm hallways to her room. She opened her purse and took out her room key. The door clicked open and they entered. The light switch was not to hand and the door swung closed behind them leaving them in darkness. He felt her close. They touched and kissed again. Her hands began to roam his body, unfettered now. He cupped her breasts then eased her jacket from her shoulders. She pulled off his tie and as they moved further into the room, he pulled his own jacket off. She began to unbutton his shirt. He held her again, then found the fastenings on her skirt and flicked them open.

His shirt was undone and her hands began moving over his chest.

They said nothing, only the sound of whispering kisses breaking the silence. With the zip of her skirt half down, it fell to the ground. She stepped slowly out of it as his fingers slipped under the elastic of her panties. His hands moved around, touching the cool globes of her buttocks and then the crisp warmth of her pubic hair. He eased them off, until they too fell away. He moved away for a moment and yanked his shirt inside out and off. His flies were open and now his buckle was undone. He slid his right hand under her t-shirt to her bra clasp, and pinched it open. He kissed her again and with both hands lifted her bra away, caressing her breasts. She tugged his shorts over his erect penis and then held him in her hand. He lifted her t-shirt up. She let go of him and ducked down to let him lift it over her head.

They stood apart for a moment. He pulled off his shoes clumsily, then pushed off his trousers and pants with his feet. She slid out of her bra. His eyes had become accustomed to the blackness and he could pick up the outline of the bed. He took her hand and led her there. They lay down and he slowly pulled off her ankle socks and then tugged off his own. He began to kiss her body. She took his hand and pulled it down. Her body vibrated to his fingertips. Her hand moved down for his manhood but he was out of reach. He lifted to move up and her other arm urged him on top of her. She held him for a moment and he pushed forward and entered her. She turned her head away from him and he kissed her neck. He raised himself up onto his hands and increased the strength of his thrusts. She pushed up on his chest and supported some of his weight on her forearms.

She made no sound. Her head began turning from side to side, her neck arching with his thrusts. With her hands she began to grip his back, kneading his skin, her undulating movements turning into counter thrusts. Gasping, she looked up, held his buttocks and stopped his motion. Arms aching, he lowered himself down. They kissed again, turning onto their sides like a human X. Peter watched Laura watching him, moving slowly, exploring. Her body was full, soft and comfortable, without the edged hardness of a younger women.

She pushed him away and onto his back. She kneeled over his waist and joined him in a single fluid manoeuvre, then began to move back and forth. Peter sat up and began to kiss her breasts, caressing them with both hands. He leant back and urged her down on top of him. Laura pushed her right leg back straight and they rolled over.

Her eyes were closed again and his, too, were heavy, losing their will to see. He concentrated on the feel of her, her shape, her warmth, her rhythm. He could hear her gasping, again and again, in time with his thrusts. He was filled with an urgent impulse, a demanding rush of energy. His groans replaced hers; his movements took on a new purpose. His pleasure rose like boiling milk, instantly out of control. The moment passed like a bursting bubble.

He opened his eyes; she was looking at him with a shadowy smile. She lifted a sheet to his forehead and mopped his brow.

'Can I take you home?' she said.

'If you like.'

'I like, I like very much.'

'Okay.' He rose up onto his elbow and began to move inside her again.

'You're meant to take a breather now,' she laughed, wriggling slightly.

He pushed provocatively. 'I'm still a kid, make the most of it.'

'Oh my God, you're insatiable.'

He held her arms. 'Only on the full moon.'

———

The digital clocked showed 6:43. He looked at Laura, sleeping on her stomach under the thin white sheet. He gently touched her back. She was hot like bread from an oven. He ran his hand down over her bottom to her thighs. Her legs widened to his touch. He moved his hand over her legs, feeling them on his fingertips. He touched her; she was damp and yielding, her thighs parting. He moved towards her, exploring her with his fingers, feeling her move to their probing. He lay between her legs and entered her. She began to breathe heavily, lifting herself up to him, pushing backwards. She rose up on all fours and he knelt behind her. Clasping her hips he rode her slowly.

Humming rhythmically, she craned back her head, dipping her waist forwards. She sucked a finger, her hair covering her eyes. Peter drifted away; the morning sun sparkled through the curtains onto her back, sprinkling her body with golden fingers. Laura grasped her pillow and began to puff. Peter felt her orgasm around him. The urgency was long since out of him now, minutes of easy pleasure passed. She came again, this time in a single long silent shiver. Then the tide of pleasure rose in him once more, slowly at first, then surging fast. He fell forward onto her and they parted as she lay forward. He hugged her back and they fell into sleep.

———

He listened to the shower in the bathroom as he called the office.

George answered, 'Online Data, good morning.'

'George, it's Peter. I won't be in till this afternoon, I've got to see someone off at the airport.'

'Right you are boss. Whenever.'

'Cheers.' He hung up.

He walked over to the bathroom door and opened it. The small room was full of steam, the large mirror covered in condensation.

'Room for one more?'

———

They held hands in the cab to Heathrow and didn't speak, except when the silences seemed to have gone on too long. He wondered if things would feel less poignant if Laura lived only a few miles away. Was he excited by a desperate romance or was he just excited?

Heathrow was compulsive by design, something inexorable about its configuration forced everything towards the departure gate. He carried her suitcases to the check in and they queued.

'We could wait for an hour, but I'd prefer to go on through customs,' she said as she put her boarding card into her purse. 'Otherwise it will just be such a drawn out thing.'

'I don't mind waiting on,' he said.

'I hate goodbyes.'

Peter nodded. 'I do too.'

'Especially long goodbyes.'

He stopped and she turned to him. 'Okay,' he said, 'if you want.'

She looked bitterly at him. 'It's impossible, you know that?'

'Impossible, what's impossible?'

'It's, you know, it's.'

He kissed her, holding her tightly. She began to struggle, but then hugged him. For a moment the darkness of the night returned.

'Nothing's impossible.' He looked her in the eyes. 'Difficult, improbable, even stupid maybe, but not impossible.' He turned and walked away.

——

The light was bright above the clouds. The glare dazzled him. It was a turbulent day and the bobbing motion of the plane was taking its toll on him again. Peter looked across the cockpit at the instructor. 'I'm feeling really airsick, I think it would be a good idea to call it a day.'

'Okay, we'd better get down.'

Within a couple of minutes the plane was descending through the cumulus and making its approach. The instructor set the plane down with the usual bump and they taxied to their normal parking spot.

'I hope you won't take this personally, Kevin, but I don't think I'll be having anymore flying lessons. I don't think it's for me.'

'I'm sorry to hear that.'

'It's just that I've succeeded, in so much as I wanted to get over a fear of flying. I'm cured but now flying just makes me want to vomit. That's no fun.'

Kevin shrugged, 'It's a shame but there's no point if it makes you feel ill.'

Peter walked dizzily to the car. He was driving through London before he began to feel better.

——

'We've a visitor waiting downstairs,' said George, as he walked into the office. 'A young lad.'

'Who?'

'Colin Fordham.'

Peter thought for a second. 'Oh, the hacker, right, well tell him I'll be down in a few minutes.'

He set the printer running and wrote out an envelope. The printer whizzed quietly.

George returned. 'You know,' he began, looking sheepishly at Peter, 'I've been doing a little thought. You know on the quiet like. And it comes to me and don't take this the wrong way, but, it seemed like, if you don't mind me saying, you should be thinking of ways of doing something with all this money. Alright we've stashed a lot and there is more we haven't stashed but it's all sitting there collecting dust. Why don't you get yourself an accountant?'

'An accountant,' Peter leant against the desk. 'Sounds like we'd have a lot of explaining to do.'

'I thought that too, but I could make enquiries.'

'Enquiries?'

'Yeah, enquiries. I mean, villains have accountants you know.'

Peter scowled.

'Well you know what I mean,' said George, holding up his hands. 'Not that we are or anything of course.'

'Well yes, but how will you make enquiries?'

George pointed at the computer. 'We move in the right circles, we are the right circles. I'll consult the Oracle.'

Peter looked at George and smiled wryly. 'Of course.'

'I've helped a few people on the system. I'll email a few connections and see who they recommend.'

Peter laughed. 'You'll make a dodgy geezer out of me yet.'

George grinned. 'The trouble with you is you'll never be a dodgy geezer. If you had an ounce of wide-boy in you, you'd not be in this mess, you'd be long gone.'

Peter scooped up the output of the laser printer and pushed it into the envelope.

'If you don't mind me asking, are we giving that to the Old Bill?'

'Did you see any blue helmets?'

'No, that's what I thought.'

'Well then.'

'Well then, it must be the heavy mob.'

'Heavier than the heavy mob.' He handed George the envelope.

George took it and checked the address. 'That's good then, I think that should mean we don't end up in the slammer.'

'It could mean we're working for the good guys.'

'Oh, them. The ones that send you over the top then bugger off back to HQ for dinner. That's happy news. All we've got to worry about now is not finding ourselves up to our ears in a car park.'

'Don't worry, I'll tell them you're senile.'

———

Colin was a thick set, over-weight individual with short light hair. His diet of junk food kept his complexion pale and blemished with red outbreaks of acne.

He had a deep voice that naturally broke into a high nervous laugh.

George had redecorated downstairs into an intimate lounge with potted plants, sofas and low smoke glass coffee tables. Peter introduced himself and sat down.

'So, did you bring me a report on our security?'

'Yep.' Colin pulled out a folder from a battered portfolio.

Peter read the three page document and handed it back. 'Yes, I agree with your general points on security, but I don't see how they impact on us.'

'There's plenty of other things that I haven't covered in my report. I like to build up a relationship with my clients before I get into some of the more worrying security loopholes. It would be reckless to reveal them to everyone.'

'I see.'

'I thought at the early stages we might keep things general.'

'You mean vague.'

'No I don't mean that.'

Peter tried not to look too unimpressed. 'To be honest, talking about the theoretical side of computer security is not what I had in mind. Excuse me if I say so, but it's been some time since we spoke and it doesn't seem you have managed to come up with anything substantial.'

'How do you know?' retorted Colin.

'Are you saying you have?'

'Not necessarily, but that's the problem with security. Just because you think you are safe, doesn't mean you are.'

Peter sat forward. 'Come on, don't give me all this cyberpunk shit. Either you have got something or you haven't. If you have something I need to know, I'm interested. If you haven't, I'm not. You hacked it once and I closed you out and now you don't seem to have come up with anything else.'

Colin looked unsettled. 'It's not my security skills that might interest you, but my development skills.'

Peter frowned, 'Skills for developing what?'

'Your system for example, I could develop some new features for your service.'

Peter shook his head. 'No, I've already thought about that. You're a hacker, you admit that. I don't think I can afford to let a hacker near my machine. I'll take my chances on getting attacked from the outside, but I won't risk getting attacked from within.'

Fordham reddened. 'My interest in security is purely academic.'

Peter stood up. 'That's as maybe, but I'm afraid I'm not interested in new services. Look, you hack in again and I'll pay you to close the loophole, okay?'

'Well, I'm not sure that I want to work on that basis.'

'That's fine.'

Colin stood up and put the pages back in his briefcase.

'I'll be off then.'

'If you change your mind then you know the system's number.'

'Yes, but I can't promise I'm interested.'

'I understand.'

'I could give you a lot of good feedback if I could get a proper look at your setup from the system console.'

'You get in from the outside and I might show you.'

'I'll think about it.'

Peter pointed him at the door. 'Yeah, do that and this time don't wait for years to call me.'

———

During his lunch break, George had bought himself a suit and swaggered into the office with a larger than usual grin on his face.

Peter didn't notice.

'Tuesday,' he pronounced.

Peter looked up from his printout. 'Tuesday?'

'Tuesday it is!'

'Tuesday.' He looked back at the listing, wondering whether he was missing something. His mind jumped out of computer mode. He looked at George. 'Tuesday, bloody what?'

'Tuesday, is our man.'

'What are you going on about?'

George pointed at his maroon waistcoat. 'It's hard to find quality like this nowadays.'

Peter grimaced in frustration. 'Yeah, yeah, very nice.' He looked at the suit and realized it was new. He smiled; George could pass for a retired major or a country squire in such finery. 'That's very smart.'

'Not bad, I must say. I got it off my mate Moshe on Bethnal Green Road. Better than Saville Row and half the dosh.' He waved his index finger. 'Tuesday, William, for it is he; our man with the golden numbers. I asked around and this is his number. Bookkeeper to the illicit and wide. Satisfaction or your money back.' He pulled out a slip of paper from his trouser pocket.

————

'Yes, I've heard a lot about you recently,' said Tuesday, just comprehensible through the noise of a portable phone. 'Computers and things, yes, interesting.'

Tuesday's tone was the very essence of upper middle class propriety. It was a high, smooth, modulated voice, straight from the yacht club. 'I can pop by this afternoon if you are free. Client dropped dead yesterday, left a hole in my diary, not to mention his.'

'Oh, sorry to hear that, but yes I've nothing fixed.'

'Jolly good, see you in an hour or so.'

————

George ushered Tuesday in. He was a small man in his late forties with fine, mousy hair, an angular face and a raffish moustache. In one hand, he carried a small black briefcase with gold fittings that looked suspiciously like they actually were solid gold. In the other he held a gleaming red and white full face motorcycle helmet.

He put them down and introduced himself.

'So this is mission control,' he said, looking around. 'Reassuringly low-key.'

'Exactly.'

William smiled. 'How may I be of assistance?'

'Advice, I think we need some financial advice.'

————

Peter stood on his tiptoes and peered at an angle to watch Tuesday mount his 750cc racing bike in the street. He set it off its stand, glanced out into the traffic then shot out and away with a ballistic surge of acceleration.

'If he was any wider he wouldn't fit through doors,' remarked George. 'Did any of that mumbo-jumbo mean anything to you, Boss?'

Peter raised an eyebrow. 'I think he said tax was optional, or words to that effect.'

'So are kneecaps.'

Peter sat down and glanced at his screen. 'Yes, I think I know what you mean.'

George pulled up a chair and sat in front of the desk. 'I've been meaning to ask, but I thought it might get clear in my head, all on its own. It hasn't, so I'm gonna ask flat out. Whose side are we on? Not that I give a monkey's but I'd like to have an idea just so I know. I don't want to get into trouble and not deserve it, you know, it's pride.'

'We're on our side and then we're on the goodies' side. In that order.'

'That sounds 'biguous to me, draw me a picture and colour it in a bit.'

Peter pointed at George with his biro. 'You and me come first. Then come the good guys. I'm not sticking our heads in any nooses for anyone. We're helping the good guys because we are the good guys. We've just got to find a way of getting out from under all this shit. Then we can sod off and do something legitimate.'

'So how are we gonna do that?'

Peter leant back on his chair. 'We've got the right friends, we've got a lot of money.' He stared up at the ceiling. 'All we need now is the opportunity to reverse out gracefully.'

'What kind of opportunity?'

Peter tipped forward, 'Fuck knows!'

'So you'll need my services for a time yet.'

Peter smiled; he could sense a concern. 'George, don't worry, I'll always need a safe pair of hands whatever happens.'

'What, like a chauffeur?'

'Yes, and bodyguard of course.'

'I better brush up on the karate.' He waved his tubby hands in the air. 'Lethal weapons these.'

———

It amazed Peter, just how much junk mail he received in the post. He found it hard to imagine how he had got onto so many mailing lists, though he guessed it was due to his regular visits to computer shows. Often he would be invited to the launch of one sort of equipment or another but he never went. He felt guilty about throwing some of the mail away, as it was obviously the result of a vast amount of money and effort. Sadly, there seemed little alternative but tipping it straight into the bin. 'Thank god email would never go the same way,' he thought.

He was thinking about the junk mail as he stood in the middle of a wood dressed from head to toe in camouflage.

A distant sound signalled approaching enemy. He checked his gun and waited in the strange roaring silence of expectation. All that he could hear was the rushing of blood and the pounding of his heart. Suddenly he heard the sound of heavy steps. They came closer; uneven, clumsy steps, probably the product of a single person. He swung from behind the tree and caught her at almost point blank range, aiming between the eyes. She shrieked, crouched and shielded her face with one hand. She fired wildly and missed. She toppled over backwards onto her back, her legs in the air. He jumped forwards, grabbed her by her baggy fatigues and fired the paintball into the flap he pulled away from her body.

'You're dead.'

'Shit,' she said, looking up at him through her protective glasses.

'See you later.' He turned, running out of sight into cover.

He hunkered down in some friendly ferns and wondered what had possessed him to sign up for this stupid game. It made him feel like a kid, admittedly, a refreshingly warm nostalgic sensation, but some of the players seemed to take it all much too seriously. They stormed up and down the copses, trying to capture the opposing team's flag. They shouted and screamed as if it was for real.

The moment he had kitted up, the dynamics of the game became totally clear to him. As both teams were rabbles, the numbers the same and the fire rate made pretty constant by the reload procedure, it was just a free for all. He decided to lurk and pick off strays.

Why a computer manufacturer had invited him for a day out to shoot at reps eluded him. He had bought their machine because it did the job at the right price. The computer hadn't come with a paint gun day out ticket and he was certainly not going to buy the next machine on the basis of a battle in the bushes. Such were his thoughts as he waited to ambush the next lost salesman.

There was another trudging sound coming his way. Once fired, the gun took about five seconds to reload, so it was important to make sure he got a hit first time. If you fired first and missed, you were in trouble. Apparently combat was all down to Pythagoras' right-angled triangle theorem and this had all become clear on the analysis of dog-fights after the First World War. This illumination came too late to help the pilots. They were under the impression that chasing a plane at all costs was the best strategy; instead they should have taken pot shots at the enemy then left with as much haste as possible.

Peter jumped out of the bush, his adversary ten yards away. 'Go ahead punk, make my day,' he announced in the worst Clint Eastwood accent imaginable. The man started, aimed roughly and fired. The paintball arced its way towards him and Peter stood smartly aside. He ran after his quarry and shot him in the backside. His opponent cursed. Three figures appeared at the top of a rise ahead of him and, yelping, dashed forwards.

Peter turned on his heels and ran. 'What the hell am I doing here?' he thought, charging blindly through the undergrowth.

———

A broad smile came over Peter's face as he looked at the message stuck on his screen.

'Malcolm Collins from Uridium called, 01 879 6239.'

Peter rang the number immediately and was greeted by an answer phone. 'This is Peter Talbot calling you back, I'm in all day. Bye.'

He set the laser printer running. Maybe he could get out via Uridium. Getting out clean would be the difficult thing. Even now he could just drop everything and disappear, but to be safe he thought he would have to go so far and lay so low, what would be the point. The world was too small.

He wondered what Mojo-Smith was doing with his print-outs. Was there a room of analysts pouring over the pages or were they stacking up in an in tray somewhere? After the first package, he had spoken to Mojo-Smith's secretary and enquired whether they would like the information to be sent on disk but no reply had been forthcoming. Perhaps there was some impenetrable security reason that precluded non-paper media; perhaps they just didn't use the technology.

George answered the phone then buzzed him on the intercom. 'It's Malcolm Collins from Uridium.'

Peter took the line. 'Hi, Malcolm, how are you?'

'Well, quite well, thank you. And you?'

'Great, great. You called yesterday while I was out playing soldiers.'

'Yes I did, thanks for getting back to me.'

'What can I do for you?'

'I'd like to set up a meeting, if I can; I think I've come up with a formula which might put a deal together between you and Howard.'

'Howard?'

'Howard Kendal, you met, my client.'

'Oh yes, sorry, I've a bad head for names.'

'Right, fine.'

'Why don't you just tell me on the phone? I don't have to look you in the eyes.'

'No, quite so. If we can all meet however, then if there are any little points that need straightening out, we can do it there and then.'

'Hum.' Peter played cool. 'Well okay, where had you in mind?'

'How's Friday at the Park Lane Hilton at eleven o'clock sound to you?'

'Sounds inconvenient to me, but possible.'

'Ah well if that's a problem . . . '

'No, just a bloody slog through traffic. Don't worry, I'll manage.'

'Okay then, that's good of you.'

'Malcolm, can I ask you something?'

'Yes, please, go ahead.'

'Are you in a position to put together really big deals, I mean multi-million pound deals?'

'Well yes, for the right business or the right project.'

'And what is the right business?'

'That's a tricky one, but generally a business with a strong positive cash flow or easy liquidable assets. Cash cows or assets strips. The sort of gilt edged opportunity that you don't need a degree in business studies to see the profit in. Why?'

'Just wondered.'

'Why, do you think you might qualify?'

'You never know. Your client, I'd guess he hadn't got much of a ceiling for his deals.'

There was a silent pause, 'I can't answer that one without prejudicing our talks one way or another.'

'No, I appreciate that, but I don't want to waste everyone's time.'

'I'm sure you won't.'

———

Peter had given MonoLog a special call up number for the system to ring Online. Since its installation it had lain idle. He had faxed Andretti with his bank details but no bill. Every Wednesday the bank called him to confirm that five thousand dollars had been deposited into the Online Data account. Sometime soon, something worth five thousand dollars a week would start to pour up and down that line. He waited with a fascinated dread for the connection to go live.

He had worked methodically on upgrading his equipment and the link of his backup machine had gone well; now if the main machine crashed, the other would immediately take over. It was all now installed in a nineteen inch rack with uninterruptible power supplies to protect them from power-cuts and 'dirty mains.' Even without a mains supply the system would run for hours. With the new burglar alarm, the service was protected from all but a nuclear strike. The area in front of his desk hummed with cooling fans and bristled with cables linking one grey slot to another. It all looked like a stereo system gone mutant. The monitor and keyboard on his desk were now merely connected to it as a remote terminal. George could do what he liked on his desk, his hard disks were elsewhere.

———

George returned from his drop with a letter.'

'It's a note from Q,' he said wryly.

Peter opened it. 'He wants me to meet him tonight for a rendezvous.'

'Have you got to wear a pansy in your buttonhole?'

'Apparently not.'

———

Peter sat at a table near the bar and waited. The cellar seemed very fitting for a clandestine meeting. It had two entrances, each onto a different road; it would be easy to enter and meet and leave again without being noticed. Inside there was much scope for hiding away from watching eyes, in a remote quiet cubicle.

Mojo-Smith materialized from the gloom, smiling at Peter with a toothy grin. He bought them a round of drinks.

'Pleasing, very pleasing,' he said after of moment of pleasantries. He interlaced his bony fingers and flexed them gleefully. 'Very gratifying indeed.' His joints retorted like a string of fire-crackers.

Peter winced at the sounds. 'What is?' he asked, fishing for the concrete in his statement.

'The work, the work. Most useful.'

'My material, you mean?'

'Inextricably.'

'I'm glad.'

Mojo-Smith sipped at a gin and tonic. 'More to come, I hope?'

'Yes, I don't see why not.'

'Good, excellent.'

'As long as I don't get any backwash, I don't see why I can't help you further.'

Mojo-smith smiled. 'Your help is much appreciated.'

'Does that mean you are becoming grateful?'

'Definitely.' Mojo-Smith lit a cigarette and Peter joined him. 'I see you are becoming part of the band of brothers.'

'Which band?'

'The great fraternity of smokers.'

Peter winced again. 'I have one now and again.'

A cloud of grey smoke floated around Mojo-Smith's head. 'Expertise is a precious commodity,' he expounded like a Buddhist sage.

'Yes, I guess. As long as you can find a buyer for it.'

'To my mind, it is the only value. From iron ore to a prestige car, the only unnatural ingredient is expertise.'

'I never followed economics at school.'

'Many of our best results are performed with experts. A small piece of specialized knowledge can often open up great horizons of understanding.'

'Well I'm glad I'm being of some help.'

'Oh yes, help, very good. It came to my mind that it would be most interesting to gain access to more computers, perhaps around the world, and be able to monitor them quietly.'

'You mean hack into them.'

'Hack, yes, splendid word, full of vitality.' He smiled a crooked grin. 'Yes. "Be able to hack into computers", he said, sampling the phrase. 'Quite so.'

'I would have thought you would have done that long ago.'

'Sadly no, at least not us; friends, perhaps. It's not the sort of breed we have, freelancers are so hard to find. At least, types one can rely on.'

'Oh? I'm surprised.'

'Perhaps you might help us.'

'Hack other people's systems?' Peter restated.

'It would be of great use.'

'I'm sure it would. What sort of systems had you in mind?'

'I gather then, you could be interested?'

'Interested is not the way I'd put it. I might give it a go though, on a no promises basis.'

Mojo-Smith pulled out a sheet of paper with phone numbers typed on them. 'You may notice that we have many interests abroad.'

'It's just a list of phone numbers.'

'Yes.'

'And you want me to get into as many of the hosts at the other end as I can.'

'Then pass the codes on to us.'

'I'll need a funny line from the exchange, so I won't get any funny traces or big bills winging their way home.'

'We have good relations with Telecom security.'

'You realize I'll be breaking the laws of the countries these computers are in.'

'I imagine that to be a possibility.'

'I'll need to.'

'Very well then.'

Peter looked closely at the list then folded it up. 'Alright, I'll see what I can do.'

'Pleasing, most pleasing, thank you.'

———

Peter lay on his bed and looked at the street light filtering onto his bed through the ill-fitting curtains. A scenario was opening around him. Ideas formed and floated about in his head like themes and melodies in a yet to be constructed concerto. He strained for something to pull everything together.

Hacking, spying, running messages for the mob, everything was now utterly out of control. The problem in his mind was grasping how all the pieces fitted together. He had got himself into some kind of lobster pot. He had to find the way out before someone yanked him out of his element and served him up on a plate.

———

Colin hadn't expected to go back to Excalibur again, but the word was out on him and the advances had dried up. Now he needed the thousand pounds for the demo he'd promised them all those months back. He was hopeful that they would still want the product and the money would be enough to tide him over for a while.

'Graham Spilsby please?'

'Who's calling?'

'Colin Fordham.'

'Hold on, I'll try and put you through.'

Tinny music played for a few bars, then stopped. 'Colin? I thought you'd died.'

'Not quite.'

'How goes it?'

'Not so bad, been working hard on Anthrax.'

'Anthrax? We canned that.'

'Oh.'

'We took a new guy on to finish it. He couldn't cut it, so we cancelled the title.'

'Oh I see.'

'We tried to contact you, but you seemed to have fallen off the face of the planet.'

'I sent you my change of address.'

'Did you? Really?'

'Yeah, I had cards printed up and everything.'

'Didn't get one.'

'Bloody Post Office.'

'Something like that. Anyway, what can I do you for?'

'You still interested in Anthrax then?'

'Depends.'

'On what?'

'On what you've got. Your name's been doing the rounds, you know. Bad karma!'

'What do you mean?'

'I mean how many projects are you working on?'

'Just a couple, serious mainframe stuff, you know?'

'Yeah, I know.'

'You interested in Anthrax?'

'Look, bring me something I can play and sell and we'll see. We've done all the advertising, but I know Mike would throw a fit if I part with any money to you without something concrete in my hand. Really, I should be asking you for our equipment back.'

'I'll bring you a playable demo and you can make your mind up.'

'Okay, when are you coming in?'

'Tomorrow afternoon?' suggested Colin.

'Okay, when?'

'Two-ish.'

'That's fine, I'll see you then. Bye.'

Graham hung up and buzzed through to the office secretary.

'Judy, can you put me down for a two o'clock tomorrow with Colin Fordham and remind me not to take a long lunch.'

'Um yeah, right you are.' She jotted it down in the appointments diary. She grabbed her handbag, took out her pocket book and dialled a number. The phone answered.

'Dragin's Balliffs.'

'Is Pete there? It's Judy Aps.'

There was a pause.

'Hello, darling, how are you?'

'Fine thanks. You know that guy you were asking about a while back, a programmer? Well he's coming in tomorrow. Do you still want his address?'

'I'm not sure love, when's he coming in?'

'After lunch.'

'I'll check but I think it's all blown over now. If my memory serves me, he paid up. Either way, I'll send you something for thinking of me. Thanks darling.'

'Tarra then.'

———

Peter dusted off his briefcase and went to the tube via the bank. He caught the Metropolitan line to Liverpool Street station, changed onto the Central line and got off at Marble Arch tube. He walked down Park Lane towards the Hilton and examined the fine houses as he strolled by. What untold wealth must the people who owned these properties control? He looked over at the park on the other side of the road. Cars chased along, expensive bubbles encasing stressed people. At moments like these, a peasant life of simple labour seemed an attractive option.

He entered the Hilton and walked through the foyer into the lounge area. He was beginning to hate expensive hotels. The velvet glove too thinly covered a cold grasping hand. In a corner Malcolm Collins sat crouched over a low table, reading some papers.

'Hello, fancy some coffee?'

'Yes, great,' said Peter, sitting.

'Howard will be right along, he just called me on the portable; he's caught on the Edgware Road and will be about fifteen.'

'No problem.'

'How's biz?'

'Booming as usual.'

'That's good to hear. I am sorry our last meeting didn't get off on the right footing, but these things happen. Howard can be a bit fierce, but he is an alright guy.'

'I'm sure he is.'

'He only just sold out his company, Maserati Expansions. It was a double glazing business, very successful too. Now he is looking to investing some of his cash into new ventures.'

'Everything has its price,' said Peter accommodatingly, 'but it has to be the right price.'

'Obviously.'

'Good, I'm glad you agree.'

Something warbled in Collins' briefcase. He opened it hurriedly, unclipped the phone's cover and answered it. A distant voice reported inaudibly. 'Yes, okay, see you in a minute.' He pressed a button which bleeped. 'He's in parking now, so he'll be right with us.'

Peter crunched through a pink wafer biscuit and they waited in silence.

Kendal strode over to them. 'Morning fellows, sorry to keep you hanging around but the North Circular's fucked.'

They all shook hands.

He dumped himself down. 'Right, let's get to it. I want to buy, you want to sell, what could be simpler?'

'Sorry,' interjected Peter. 'You want to buy, I'm interested.'

'Alright. Same difference. I want to buy, you want to sell, probably. Probably, right? Like the beer ad.'

'Okay, probably.'

Collins smiled and turned to Kendal. 'I mentioned that we would have a proposal that might suit both parties.'

'Yeah, I'm coming to that. I was thinking, you want a good whack for Online Data, and I can pay a good price for it, but I can't agree to any formulas until I know about the quality of the variables. You know what I mean?'

'What Howard means is that he doesn't want to pay for questionable profits, inflated stock, work in progress, intangibles, those kind of soft assets.'

'We haven't got any of those. I mean, you can exclude them from your calculations, if you like.'

Kendal sneered at Collins. 'Alright then, that's good. How about this for an offer? I'll pay you six times profits for the company, spread over three years. Twice this year's, at the end of year one, twice second year's at the end of year two and twice third year at the end of year three.'

'I don't like the sound of that. It's too long and too low. I like the sound of buy and goodbye.'

Kendal poured himself a cup of coffee. 'It could be arranged. How much are you gonna make this year?' He took a mouthful.

'Half a million.'

Kendal nearly spat his coffee out onto Collins, but sat a moment, his jowls bulging. He swallowed. 'Half a million, pigs might fly. You've only been registered for a year.'

'That may well be the case, but there it is.'

'Let's get serious. I'll pay you fifty thousand up front then twice profits for three years.'

Peter smiled. 'Look Howard, I'm making at least half a meg a year, that's 300K after tax minimum. Fifty grand is not an object to me. If you want to buy me out it's five meg.'

Kendal didn't quite laugh but still pulled all of the facial expressions. 'Look son, don't get me wrong, but you can't expect me to believe that you're making half a million a year in a few months from nothing. Life just isn't like that and I don't appreciate being treated like I'm a carrot cruncher from Noddyland.'

'Do you bet, Howard?'

'Sometimes.'

'How much is that Rolex worth on your wrist?'

He shrugged, 'A bit.'

Peter took his cheque book out of his pocket. 'I'll bet you 5K against your watch that I've got a hundred grand in my briefcase.'

Kendall grinned widely. 'Is your cheque good for that?'

'Yes.'

Kendal chuckled evilly. 'You're fucking winding me up.'

'Well, it's put up or shut up time.'

Kendal looked at Collins. 'Where did you get this guy from?'

Collins blushed and laughed weakly. 'It's all quite out of the ordinary, this, you know,' he whined at Peter.

'Well I'll be off then. I think you know my price point. If you are in that league, you know where I am.' He stood but Kendal caught his arm.

'Sit down a moment.' He looked into Peter's eyes. 'Write that cheque out to me.'

Peter took his cheque book out again and filled one in. Collins read it and Kendal took his watch off and placed it on top of the blue piece of paper.

Peter held his face as impassive as possible and put the case onto the table. He unfastened it and lifted the lid.

'Fuck me,' exclaimed Kendal. 'Fuck me.'

Collins looked around nervously.

Kendal reached forward for one of the bundles. 'I want to check one.'

Peter held his hand. 'Malcolm can.'

Collins gingerly pulled out a bundle and stripped a note from the centre. He handed it to Kendal who held it up to the light. 'You must be fucking crazy carrying all that cash around.'

Peter took the note back and closed the case. He took the watch and cheque from in front of Collins. The watch was too light to be gold. 'It's a fake.'

'Yeah, Taiwanese.'

Peter stood up and looked at Collins. 'When I said half a meg, I was being conservative. 700k plus by the year end.'

He threw the watch back to Kendall. 'Sayonara.'

———

As Colin walked down the road towards Excalibur Games, he ran over the pitch in his mind. He had spent the last few days hacking other games to pieces, changing graphics, pulling routines from one and putting them into another. The results were unrecognizable, although likely to flicker and crash unexpectedly.

He was pleased with the demo, and he was sure they would be too. He had written none of the code, just stolen it and kludged it together from a number of existing products. This was hidden by new visuals, modified and remixed sounds and some joystick control tweaks. After all, wasn't one game very much the same as another? He hated other people's code, it was ugly, but hacking it was quick.

A car pulled up alongside him and a figure leapt out. Without thinking he bolted away and found himself being pursued by a man in a suit. The Jaguar started off up the street after him. He jumped the crash barrier at the side of the road and ran blindly into the street. The car drove at him, but he was in the oncoming lane before it could reach him. A learner car swerved out of his path and ploughed into the saloon but he barely noticed the accident, running away, his vision blurring.

Colin's mind switched in. Online Data was about two hundred yards ahead, while Excalibur was another quarter mile on towards the city. He turned his head to see if he was still being chased. Running flat out, he couldn't tell. Had he known his pursuer had stayed by the accident, his get-away car compromised, he might have slowed up and had that split second to discover that the chase was over. Without that clarity, he hadn't the time to do anything but dash headlong for safety.

Chapter Six
HOTTER

There was a violent banging on the door.

'Who the fark's there?' said George, picking up the intercom.

'It's C-C-Colin Fordham, let me in,' he cried.

'You got an appointment?'

'Let me in, let me in, now, it's an emergency.'

George pressed the buzzer and went to the stairs. 'What's all this about?'

Colin was red and covered in sweat. A life in front of a terminal hadn't trained him for the eight hundred metre dash. 'Eh nothing, is there a back way out?'

'Nope. What's up, you in trouble?'

———

Peter walked along the Whitechapel Road from the bank towards the office. Someone had had a nasty crash with a learner vehicle and he tried not to gape. It looked like some kind of hit and run, but nobody seemed hurt.

Colin looked out of the window onto the street. All seemed clear, but he could see only half of the picture.

George came into the room. 'He's got nothing in his book saying he's expecting you.' The door clunked close. 'That's him now.' George went onto the landing. 'It's Colin Fordham; he says you are expecting him.'

Peter shook his head and shrugged. 'Don't think so.'

'If you ask me,' whispered George, 'he's in some kind of bother.'

Peter walked into the meeting room. Colin stood by the corner of the window peering out into the road. 'What's up?'

Colin turned round. 'I'm being followed.'

'By who?'

'I don't know?'

'I'll call the police.'

'But I can't see them, they're not in sight.'

'Oh I see. You can leave then.'

Colin burst into tears. 'No, don't make me leave. See this . . .' he opened his mouth and slipped down a plate accounting for half his top teeth, 'they did that to me.' He pointed to a scar on his forehead. 'And that.' Tears began to roll down his face. 'Let me stay, please.'

Peter was taken aback by the sudden outburst. 'Who are they?'

'Some people I did some work for. They're going to do me over again.'

'What did you do to them?'

'Nothing, nothing.'

'Don't give me that.'

'Nothing I swear.'

'You're lying; no one does that for nothing.'

'I swear,' he cried desperately.

Peter glared at him. 'Go on then, get out of here.'

'No, no, don't, I'll do anything,' he pleaded.

Peter sat down; he felt he was missing a trick. He thought for a second and the idea that was clearly forming jumped into his head. 'I'll do you a deal.'

Colin blew his nose. 'Anything,' he said after a muffled sniff.

'You tell me the truth and if I can get you sorted out, you'll teach me to hack.'

'Sorted out?' Colin looked at him as if Peter didn't understand the trouble he was in. 'These people are seriously bad.'

'Let me worry about that. Is it a deal?'

'Only if I can stay here.'

'Only if you are up front with me.'

'Okay, it's a deal.' Colin smiled suddenly. 'I'll owe you forever if you save my arse.'

————

'Get me a cab for Box Office Video will you, George?' He picked up a letter from America that lay in the centre of his desk.

'One cab coming up.'

He opened it, it was from Laura.

'Dear Peter,

Thank you for a lovely time. Sorry it's taken a while to write you, but I've been feeling hectic about life and work, you know how it is?

I've been asked to write a book about the catalogue and I'm wondering if they are nuts. I guess it's a kind of job security though.

I think I'm missing you, I don't know why, if you know what I mean. I should be over all that sort of puppy-goo. Perhaps ten thousand miles and ten years has had a positive effect on me. Perhaps distance makes romance safe.

I feel like FedExing me over to you.

Love,

Laura

P.S. You were right, it's just impractical.'

He folded the letter and put it into his top drawer.

———

Roberts' phone intercom buzzed. He picked it up. 'Yes?' he said absent-mindedly.

'I have a Peter Talbot in reception for you.'

'What?' He looked up from the papers on his desk. 'I haven't got anyone in to see me this afternoon.'

'He says he's come about Colin Fordham.'

'Who the fuck's that?' The name registered and he frowned. 'Tell him I can't see him and show him the door.'

The receptionist looked up from her console to Peter who stood gazing at a picture on the wall. 'I'm afraid he's tied up this afternoon and can't see you.'

'All afternoon?'

'I'm afraid so. If you'd like to call in the morning, we might be able to set something up for you then.'

'Tell him it's very important and that I just need five minutes of his time.'

'I'm afraid that's not possible. He was just going into a meeting and can't be disturbed.'

'Okay, tell his secretary now, that I have a very important and highly confidential message for Mr Roberts, which she will have cause to regret if he does not receive.' He smiled at her. 'Can you do that?'

She jabbed some buttons. 'Ravi, I have a Mr Talbot down here for Mr Roberts. He says he has an urgent message concerning a Colin Fordham for him. Mr Roberts is in a meeting, do you think you can come down?'

'I said it was confidential.'

'Mr Singh is the Finance Director, I'm sure he will be able to help you.'

———

Box Office Video had a small meeting room. It was little more than a cubicle of thick glazing.

'What may I do for you?' said the small wiry Asian, dressed in a dark, over-tailored suit.

Peter smiled. 'Your boss is trying to kill one of my employees and I've come to straighten things out. Take me to him.'

Singh looked nervously at him. 'I don't think I am understanding you and what is more I am not sure I can do this thing you are asking.'

'Let's just say, you tell him I'm a serious man wanting to sort out a serious matter.'

'I can try to interrupt him, but I am not promising an advantageous response.'

———

'So who the fuck is this Talbot, what does he look like?'

Singh shrugged, 'He is young, he is well dressed, also he sounds like he has a need to speak to you.'

'And he says it's about Fordham?' He screwed up a piece of paper and began squeezing it down into a tight ball with rhythmical gripping motions. 'Alright, send him up. Meanwhile do a check on him.'

———

Singh ushered Peter into the room and disappeared immediately. Roberts pointed to a chair in front of his desk. 'Sit down, tell me all about it.'

'Thanks.'

'Now who is this Colin Fordham that you're so worried about?' He tried to smile pleasantly.

'Colin is a hacker that cracked your system and trashed your disks. You've had him beaten up and now he thinks you are trying to kill him.'

Roberts curled his lip. 'What a load of bollocks, where do you think this is, America?'

Peter rubbed his eye. 'Come on, let's not play footsie. Fordham is mine and I want him left alone.'

'He's yours. I see, but I don't see how I can help you.'

'You can help me by calling off whoever you have that's after him.'

'You've got me all wrong, I'm a business man, I'm in videos, not drugs. I don't know what you're talking about.'

'Okay, let me put it another way. How much compensation do you need?'

'Compensation, what compensation?' Roberts looked puzzled, a broad smile on his face. 'I don't understand you.'

Peter sighed. 'I can see you are a busy man. I've got one more thing to say and then I'll leave.' He looked Roberts in the eye. 'Don't fuck with me.'

Roberts leapt up. 'Fuck with you? Fuck with you? Who the fuck do you think you are that you can come in here and threaten me?'

Peter stood. 'I'm leaving now.' He turned, glimpsing as he did an approaching blow. He ducked and then came up with a right hook that landed. Roberts fell back heavily into his chair, banging its back heavily against the wall. Peter turned fully and faced him, ready to knock him back down again. Roberts held his mouth and looked up at him. He wasn't coming back for more. Peter dropped his guard, reached into his jacket pocket and pulled out his cheque book.

'How much do you want for him?'

The phone buzzed and Roberts snatched it up. 'Yeah,' he mumbled.

'He's heavy, bloody heavy, heavy,' said Singh. 'Really heavy indeed.'

'Out of ten.'

Peter and Roberts stared at each other.

'Sixteen. Class one.' His boss sounded funny. 'You alright?'

'Fine, what videos are we talking about?'

Singh reeled off a list of hits. 'Dirty Dancing, Aliens, Batman.'

He hung up. Fuck, this guy was as heavy as Batman!

He smiled. A punch in the mouth suddenly turned into an honour. Someone that heavy and that young would be an asset to know. 'You've got a fucking good right hand,' he said, touching the bleeding split in his lip.

Peter took out a biro and clicked it. 'How much?'

Roberts waved his hand dismissively and straightened himself in the chair. 'No, I don't want your money. Don't get me wrong, I fly off the handle like that sometimes.'

'So can I take it that my guy doesn't need to lose anymore sleep?'

'As I said, I'm a business man; I don't go in for that sort of thing. I'll tell you what, I'll look into it. If there are any outstanding problems they'll be closed. Okay?' Roberts stood up.

Peter couldn't raise a smile. 'I'm glad we have an understanding.'

'You know, it's good to meet you,' he said chummily. 'It's always good to get acquainted with new faces.'

———

George wasn't a happy man. 'That little toerag is wrecking the place. I hope he's not staying. Practically had to thump him to keep him away from the system. When are you going to throw him out?'

Peter sat down and went through his messages. 'Don't worry, he's going.' He waved a post-it note. 'When did Collins call?'

'Soon after you left.'

Peter smiled a smug cat grin. 'Vunderbar! Vunder-bloody-bar. Call our friend up.'

George stuck his head out of the door. 'Colin, get your 'orrible person up here.' He pulled a face. 'I don't like him boss, does it show?'

Colin appeared clutching a comic. 'Hi, eh, hi.'

Peter stood up. 'I've got some good news for you. I've got you sorted out with Box Office Video.'

Colin jumped into the air. 'Yesssssss,' he screamed. He fell to his knees, 'Beautiful, beautiful.'

'I thought you'd like that.'

Colin stood, 'Thanks, you don't know what that means to me. That's amazing.' He clenched the comic and pointed it at Peter. 'Thanks, I really appreciate it. I'll pay you back someday.' He went to turn.

'Good, you see as long as you keep coming, I make the payments and you'll stay out of trouble.'

Colin turned back, his smile gone. 'Oh right, I see. Yeah, fine.'

'Tomorrow at twelve?' suggested Peter.

'Yeah right, twelve.' He frowned. 'How many payments?'

'Six monthly payments. Don't worry, if you stick to your agreement, I'll stick to mine.'

Colin smiled weakly. 'Yeah, fine.'

———

As soon as Fordham left, Peter rang Collins and spoke to his answerphone. Twenty minutes later, just before six, his call was returned.

'Hi Malcolm.'

'Peter, I hope you got that money banked safely. I've been making a few calls since I got back. I think I can arrange something more fitting for you. I've put some feelers out and I'm getting interest. I broached the lie of the land to a few of my more moneyed contacts and the signs are positive.'

'Good. Two per cent on success.'

'Sorry, come again, I didn't quite get that one?'

'Two per cent for you on success.'

'Oh I see. There's a problem there; strictly speaking I earn my percentage from the purchasers I represent. You see there would be a conflict of interest.'

'Does that mean you would object to it turning up at your door after the event?'

'It depends on if it was from anyone.'

'I wouldn't expect so.'

'Well then it would be hard to return.'

'Ah I suppose it would.'

'I think we may be able to arrange a nice package. I understand a clean break for you is worth a discount, but I think I might make a nice match, to make it easier for you to stay on for a time.'

'It depends on how long is long.'

'No, I understand that, after all we all have better things to do then spend our best years behind a desk.'

Peter wondered if he knew his secret. 'Exactly. I'm really not interested now that things are running smoothly. The challenge is over and it's time for something new.'

'I'm sure a period for a changeover wouldn't be too invidious.'

'So long as I won't be chained to it for long. A couple of months maximum perhaps.'

'Hopefully I can put you in touch with someone who will want to step into your shoes immediately.'

'That would be good. All the numbers are available, but I'm not interested in teaching someone else how to set up in competition. They can see the figures but they don't get a disassembly of the business. That's proprietary.'

'I understand. I will get back to you in the next ten days or possibly sooner.'

'Fine.'

'By the way, if you want any free advice on what to do with that cash, just give me a call.'

'I'm looked after on that front, but thanks anyway. Speak with you shortly.'

———

Colin stayed up all night and added some more effects to his demo. He felt less confident than usual. His call to Excalibur had met with an icy reply. When he arrived no one was pleased to see him; even his old work-mates ignored him. The look on Spilsby's face reminded him of the day he had managed to infect them with a deadly computer virus.

'I seem to remember having an appointment to see you, yesterday at two, but I suppose a day late is a pretty minor delay considering your normal form.'

Colin laughed. 'Sorry about that, got caught up in an accident up the road. A Jag and a learner driver had a smash, I nearly got run over. I was so shaken I had to go home.'

'Tough break, so close but so far.'

'Eh . . . yeah.'

'I've got ten minutes, then I've got another meeting.'

'That's all I need Graham, let's do it.'

Somehow the old magic wasn't working. Graham watched the screen stony-faced as Colin ran him through the levels. At every glitch and crash Graham's manner darkened, until finally he flipped the disk out of the machine and handed it back.

'I can't do anything with this, Colin. Normally I could advance up to a couple of K on this sort of demo, but not to you.'

'Ah come on Graham, that was then, this is now!'

Spilsby shook his head. 'Exactly. You've burnt too many people. In fact you've burnt me so many times I've lost count.'

Colin put the disk away. 'I'm sorry you feel like that.'

'Me too. If you can bring me something we can sell. Finished. Testable. Complete. Then we can do business.'

'Okay, but the price will go up.'

Graham yawned and rubbed his eyes. 'So be it.'

———

Walking down the road he ran down the list of companies likely to sign his demo. Graham was right, he had run out of fingers to burn. He might have to finish a game after all, but then again maybe Online Data would part with some money.

———

The Telecom engineer was a happy, young builder type, who had the new line installed by Peter's desk in a couple of well-focused minutes. He hoovered up a little pile of sawdust with a handheld vacuum, plugged his phone into the jack and made his checks.

'I don't usually get this sort of work,' he said, looking at Peter with a sardonic grin. 'Business lines aren't my department. My area head put this job on my desk and here I am. First time I've ever seen him. Weird.'

Sitting at George's table, Peter looked up from his magazine and nodded. 'Ah, right.'

'And this line request code is very unusual, no sales department reference or nothing. You know, we've had to bring a new line in from the exchange for you.'

Peter shrugged. 'It's all gibberish to me.'

———

After the engineer had left, Peter began to call the list of numbers given to him by Mojo-Smith. All but two of the forty answered with the high-pitched whistle of a modem. He wondered what kind of operations were on the end and determined to try the UK numbers first so he could at least read the language if he got through.

Colin turned up half an hour late so he kept him waiting for a further thirty minutes.

'Right Colin,' he said, coming into the meeting room with a pad. 'Let's start then.'

'I'm going to need a computer.'

Peter smiled. 'First I'd like the basics, then once I have got that straight in my head, we can take it from there.'

Colin grimaced. 'It would be much easier if we had a computer in front of us.'

'I want you to tell me all you know first. Okay?'

Colin scowled then his face brightened. 'Is there any money in this for me?'

'It depends if I am happy with what I learn. You're already overdrawn at the bank of Online Data, remember?'

'How about expenses?'

'Good point, it cost me a few quid to get to Box Office but I'll let you off.'

Colin looked down at his feet, a broad smile spreading over his chubby face. 'You wouldn't have to try hard to be a bastard you know.'

Peter sneered at him. 'I wouldn't have to try at all, so let's get started.' He sat down and took the top off his biro. 'Let's say I have a number and when I call it, it goes bleeeeep. What next?'

Colin pursed his lips, 'You could have called a fax machine.'

'Okay, it's not a fax.'

'It depends what you are after and what you have rung.'

'Let's worry about what we've called.'

'There are lots of types of connections but two main types, a network or a dial up.'

'What's the difference?'

'A network is just a collections of lines into which any number of computers are plugged. The number you call might be in London, but once you have given it the codes it can then connect you anywhere in the world on that network without adding anything extra to the phone cost. If you get access to a network, that's only really like being able to ring a number of machines up, but it doesn't get you onto the machines themselves.'

'Okay, I know about dial-ups, we are on a dial-up. So what next?'

'It depends if you want backend access or user access.'

'Let's say user access.'

'Well if it's a public system, like yours for example. You join it for the minimum amount. Nose around and take down people's IDs from their posting or wherever else they are shown. That's half of the puzzle. Then try and guess their passwords. It helps if you can work out who are the novice users or stupid individuals as that will help you guess. You would be surprised how often the same words get used as codes or how frequently the same ID and password are the same.'

'Give me some examples.'

'FUCK for example, that's really common. SECRET too and even PASSWORD. Some people put their ID or name in backwards or if they are JBLOGGS they have their password BLOGGSJ. Some systems have guest accounts and will let you on as such.'

Peter finished his notes, 'Let's say I can't join. What then?'

Colin looked really happy and from his enthusiasm, Peter could tell that this was a subject he loved.

'You've got to work out what machine and which operating system software they are running.'

'For instance?'

'Well, the system could be a Unix box like yours, or a VAX running VMS or a Prime.'

'Go on.'

'Or say an IBM running OS370 or DEC 10 or 20 running Ten X or Tween X.'

'How will that help?'

'Each system has its own kind of user ID. Unix is going to have a user ID like jsmith, whereas PrimeOS will have abc123 or VMS [12,1234]. That then gives you something to play with.'

'That sounds like a hard way.'

Colin grinned. 'If they've got their security at all right, it's pretty near impossible. Happily a lot of systems still don't. You just have to slog through it.'

'Okay, what about backends?'

Colin paused and bit at one of his fingernails. 'Now that's where things get interesting. If you can get in the back, then that can be very nice. With a bit of luck you get your hands on the password file and then have free reign with the accounts as well as the machine.'

'What about the password encryption?'

Colin grinned. 'They can scramble the codes so you can't unscramble them, but I've got the scrambler and I've scrambled all the words in the dictionary. I just give it the scrambled password and as long as they are in the dictionary, my program matches them up and gives me the password. Voila!'

'Okay, but how do I get in the backend? If I can close you out, won't most systems be locked tight?'

Colin stuck his bottom lip out. 'Okay, you locked me out and I didn't get back, but I got in, didn't I? If I wanted to, I could get back.'

'How?'

'It depends how far you are willing to go.'

'Alright then.'

'I could burgle you. I could sleep with George.'

Peter laughed. 'You're not his sort.'

'I could get into your confidence.'

'You've tried that.'

Colin scowled. 'I could sit on the roof of the building across the road with a pair of binoculars and wait till you type in your password. Remember, I already have your ID,' he smirked, 'and your password isn't your car number plate.'

'Okay, apart from haunting me, how else can you get in?'

'System accounts. All machines come with backend system accounts which sometimes don't get changed. Like SYSTEST, ID and password on VMS.'

'And the hole you went through on our system.'

'You're not wrong.'

'Can you get me a list of them for as many systems as you know?'

'What's it worth?'

'Let me rephrase that. Get me a list of them for as many systems as you can. I may even give you a bonus. Okay?'

Colin tried to look as sour faced as he could. 'Okay.'

'So I'm in a backend. What now?'

'A system is like an onion and the closer to the centre you get, the more power you get on the machine. What you need to get is operator privileges and the password file. That's complete power and access. Then the world is yours.'

'How do I do that?'

'Find a trap-door.'

'For instance?'

'Well, every system will have its own; but basically an operating system will have features.'

'You mean bugs.'

'Yeah, features. Which will enable you to mutate the privileges you have into higher ones.'

'I'll need a list of them too.'

'Oh, that's not so easy,' Colin groaned.

'Why?'

'Well some of these things aren't easy. It would take forever to write that all down. I mean, I'm not a technical writer.'

'How long is forever?'

'Forever, forever. It depends on how you get in, where you get in, and then loads of other stuff.'

'Okay, let's concentrate on getting in and then I'll be able to be more specific. How does that grab you?'

'I like that better. Anyway, what are you going to do with all this stuff?'

'I'm interested. What was it you said? It's academic.'

'Going to break into a university computer then are you?'

Peter snorted. 'No, I don't think so. I'm trying to build up an understanding, maybe even an expertise.'

'You can't get expert without doing it.'

'Perhaps.'

'I can help, if there's somewhere specific you want to get into.'

'No, it's okay. I just want to get the theory straight.'

'I'm not squeamish.'

'I remember.'

'It wouldn't cost you much.'

'I know.'

'I could do it from home and come in with the results.'

Peter put his pad to one side. 'Get me that list of pre-set system accounts and passwords. Then if there's more I need to know, and I suspect there might be, we can take it from there.'

'Shame. I'm sure I could make things really easy.'

'Get me that list for Friday and some identifying behaviour to tell machines apart.'

'Have it your way.'

'That's Friday, not Monday or some other time next week.'

'Friday, that's as in the day before next Saturday.'

'Yes, that's the one.'

'If I can have an account on Online I could email it to you,' said Colin keenly.

'No chance.'

Colin sighed. 'Please.'

'No.'

'Please, please, grovel, grovel.'

'No.'

'Humph. I'll see you Friday then.'

Peter pulled twenty pounds from his pocket. 'I wouldn't want you to have to walk.'

Colin stood up, took the money and jammed it into his back pocket. 'Can't buy many drugs with that,' he said gravely. He laughed. 'That's a joke.'

'I'm glad you told me.' Peter rose. 'A nice complete list for Friday.'

'Yeah, yeah, my middle name is complete.'

'Complete what?'

Colin laughed, 'That's a good one.'

'Goodbye Colin, see you Friday.'

Colin went to the door. 'See you then.'

'On Friday.'

'Yeah, and thanks for the twenty quid.'

'No problem.'

Peter stood at the landing until the bottom door slammed close.

———

There was a cup of tea waiting for him on his desk.

George looked at Peter disapprovingly.

'I'm not mad on him either, George.'

'So why are we entertaining the dodgy sloper?'

'Because he's got something we need.'

'And what may I ask is that?'

Peter took a sip. 'A little expertise.'

'As my brother used to say, before he got killed, a little expertise is a dangerous thing.'

'I think you mean knowledge.'

George turned his nose up. 'That as well.'

Peter looked at the message stuck to his monitor: 'Malcolm Collins called. Will call again.'

He plucked it off his screen and waved it at George. 'This could be one of our tickets out of here.'

'Whats the SP?'

Peter screwed up the message and threw it in the bin. 'Even money, in a field of one.'

The phone rang and George picked it up. 'Online, can I 'elp you.' There was a pause. 'Hold on please sir.' He put the call on hold. 'It's the man.' He hung up.

Peter took over. 'Talbot.'

'Peter, just a call to say I'm onto a couple of leads but no real news yet. People are going away making interested noises but seem to want to do a bit of homework on this type of business before taking the next step. I thought you would like to have a brief update though.'

'Thanks.'

'These things are either immediate or they're not.'

'I see.'

'But I'm confident, very confident, that some of my contacts are going to get back to us with firm interest. Cash cows are always in demand.'

'I'm happy to hear it.'

'I expect to get something a bit more concrete in the next couple of weeks, if not it might take longer.'

'Right. Okay, well I look forward to it.'

'Speak to you soon.'

'Cheers.' He hung up and looked at George. 'Make that six to one.'

George yawned. 'Talk's cheap, money buys houses.'

'The trouble is,' said Peter, 'if anyone realises who we cater for, they wouldn't take the business if we gave it to them.'

'What a sad situation indeed,' muttered George. 'People keep giving us thousands of pounds and we can't make it stop.'

———

Every time Peter looked at his watch another hour had passed. He had been following Colin's list of default user accounts and user ID and password combinations since seven in the evening. Nothing had worked. FUCK no longer seemed to be a favoured password and none of the backend trapdoors seemed to have been left lying around. He kept telling himself that these machines were probably military or governmental and therefore used rigorous security precautions.

It was four in the morning. His little macro program, which did the donkey work of hacking, was running the permutations into the last system on the list somewhere in Silicon Valley. The line dropped for the last time. He had failed to crack into a single computer. Times had moved on.

———

'None of your bright ideas worked.'

Colin looked forlorn. 'I didn't say they would necessary work. Anyway, I thought you just wanted to master the subject.'

Peter snorted indignantly. 'How can this stuff help me master anything? It doesn't work.'

'If you're hacking, let me do it with you. Then we will get in.'

Peter shook his head. 'If I were hacking, I certainly wouldn't do it with you.'

'Oh come on, be a sport. It's what I really dig.'

'You're not exactly Mr Discrete, if I remember.'

Colin looked disgruntled. 'There's always a way in. Always. And I'd find it. Just give me the number and I'll sit here and hack in. You'll see. Might take a few hours, maybe a day or two, but I'll get in. That would be worth a few quid to you.'

'No and no. I just want information that works. I want state of the art techniques, not yesterday's ideas.'

Colin scratched his head and then rubbed his hands on his black t-shirt. 'How state of the art?'

'How state of the art can you get?

'In theory?'

'Yes in theory.'

'You could blue box.'

'Which is?'

'Well, there's black box and blue box. A black box gives you a free phone call, a blue box gives you something else.'

'What?'

'Well, if you know what you're doing, it gives you free access and control of the telephone exchange you are calling to and then on to any other in the phone network, then so on anywhere in the world. So long as you know the codes, you're in business.'

'What codes?'

Colin did his phone impression, 'Bleep, bleep, bleep, bleep, bleep, bleep, bleep,' he sang, 'the tone codes. You know, except the blue box has got two extra.'

'So how does that help me?'

'Well, if you had your box and you knew your codes, you can do pretty much anything.'

'I get that, but how does that help me?'

'How would a conference call help you out?'

Peter caught on. 'Oh, you mean hold a conference call with a modem on the system you wanted to hack. Better still redirect the calls to that number, from there to here and read the users' attempts to log into that system. As they were trying to get into it you'd get their passwords.'

Colin grinned. 'Even cooler would be to redirect the calls from the system you want to hack with your blue box, read the traffic with a modem and log it on a printer. Then redirect it back down another line to the system you've diverted them from. That way they'd never ever know.'

Peter felt excited. 'Yes, that would do it. That way you'd get a lot of user access passwords and maybe a few back-ends too. Have you got a blue box?'

'No.'

'Do you know how to use one?' Peter threw his hands up. 'To know how to use it, you would have to have one.'

'Well theoretically I know how to use one. But I haven't got any codes.'

'So how would I get a blue box and the codes?'

'You'd speak to this guy I know.'

'Okay.'

'But it would cost.'

'In what way?'

'The blue box would cost. So would the codes and how to use them.'

'How much of this cost would you be getting?'

'Is that an offer?'

'No, it's a question.'

'Something I suppose, I've got to live. Pickings are thin. I'm nearly down to my last Big Mac.' He grinned amiably.

Peter thought for a moment. 'Get me a price on a blue box and the knowledge and I'll pay you something. If I choose to take delivery, I'll pay you double. If it works I'll double it again. If it does everything I want it to do I double it again.'

Colin worked it out in his head. 'Fifteen quid,' he squealed. 'Wow, I'm rich.'

'The quicker you work the more you'll get.'

'Incentivise me a bit.'

'I just did.'

'Alright then, incentivise me a bit more by telling me about the first payment.'

Peter grimaced. 'If you get me the price by tomorrow, call it two hundred quid. If it's Tuesday call it one hundred, if it's Wednesday call it fifty. Then ten pounds less every day.'

'Can I renegotiate next Monday?'

Peter shook his head in exasperation. 'Look, just do it. Okay?'

Colin grinned triumphantly. 'Don't worry Uncle Peter, I won't let you down. The three grand is mine. Consider it a done deal, done.'

Peter sighed. 'I make that sixteen hundred.'

———

He picked up the phone. It echoed. It was Andretti from MonoLog.

'Hello Peter. I'll come straight to the point.' There was a pause. 'I'm disappointed.'

Peter felt a sinking feeling in the pit of his stomach. 'Disappointed?' He voice thickened. There was no response. 'Why?'

'I'm disappointed because I thought we might build a relationship.' This time Peter kept the silence. 'So I'm now perturbed.'

'I'm sorry to hear that. If you can be specific perhaps I might understand your problem?'

'Long term relationships are very important to us. You cannot build a business like ours on deals. The stakes are too high.'

'Okay, I understand that.'

'It has come to our attention that you wish to sell your operation . . . '

Peter's mind began to race. If he had a good answer ready, he might be able to get away with calming Andretti down.

' . . . I would have expected you to have come to us first if you were looking to move on from the industry.'

'I've been approached by a broker who wants to know if I want to sell. I told him what I would tell anyone. Online is always for sale at the right price.'

Andretti snarled, 'Peter, you can't go selling yourself like that. The business is too deep.'

'I'm not selling my business. It is for sale, it always was and it always will be. It only ever needs the right purchaser and the right price. If someone shows interest, I will respond.'

There was another long silence. 'I'll tell you what I'll do. Consider us the potential customer. Pay attention to THE, in that phrase. I'll send someone over to see you and we will crank up some action.'

'Alright, that sounds like a good idea.'

'So what makes you want to quit? You're smart enough to have anything you want.'

'I don't want to quit, but I'm not going to work if someone's going to pay me enough that I can stop. This is a business to me not a religion.'

'Okay,' said Andretti. 'We can work with that.'

———

'That Colin ain't going to come back, by the look of things,' said George. Peter sat staring at his desk. George put a brown bag filled with hot bacon sandwiches in front of him. He hesitated. 'You okay boss?'

'Humm,' grunted Peter.

'Woz up?'

Peter turned to him, his face screwed up in thought. 'Fuck, fuck, fuck.'

'Ah . . . ' he looked puzzled, 'fuck what?'

'Our New York friends want to buy and they are a little bit pissed off that A, we want to sell and B, we didn't offer them first bite.'

'Fuck 'em.'

Peter grimaced. 'I suspect they've had rather more practice at fucking people than we have.'

George sat down and extracted a sandwich from his bag. 'Don't let yours get cold.'

Peter picked up his packet, which left a shiny halo on the wooden surface. 'I'll think of something.'

The phone rang once and George snapped it up. 'Online Data, good afternoon.' He held the handset over to Peter. 'Sandy from America.'

Peter dropped his sandwich onto the paper bag, and swallowed quickly. 'Sandy. Hi.'

'I'm to come and see you. When are you free?'

He raised an eyebrow at George. 'Whenever.'

'How's Monday sound to you?'

'Okay. You bringing anyone else along?'

'No, just me.'

'Do you need me to make any arrangements for you?'

'No, I've got it covered.'

'Pick you up at the airport?'

'No, that's fine, I'll come in Sunday and get an early night.'

'Dinner Sunday at your hotel?'

'That would be nice. I'll fax you details to confirm.'

'See you Sunday.'

'Ciao.'

'Ciao.' He hung up and looked at George. 'They're sending her over Sunday.'

'Well I hope she ain't a hit man.'

Peter picked up his now cool bacon sandwich and took an oily mouthful. 'No, that she isn't.'

'A gangster's moll then?'

Peter nodded. 'Kind of, well no, ish. Let's just say, she's a hot potato. But, I don't get it. Why would they send her over?'

'Maybe they want to test drive you.'

Peter hesitated, 'Do you think so? What will they be looking for?'

George shrugged, 'Don't ask me.'

———

When Peter arrived, Colin was waiting for him.

He was grinning widely. 'I've got the information and price.'

'How much?'

'A grand.'

'A grand?'

'Yep, a grand.'

'Including VAT?'

Colin laughed. 'Yeah, including VAT.'

'And the codes and instructions?'

'All included.'

'Hold on a minute. I've got some dummy numbers I'm going to need put into documented examples.'

'Okay, don't forget my two hundred.'

'You're late!'

'Where am I? Jeeeez amnesia. My mind is fading, memories slipping away. Who are you?'

'Alright, alright. You can remember again. I'll let you off.'

Peter returned with the £1,200 cash and a sheet of paper.

'When do I get the box?'

'Dunno, soon.'

'Soon?'

'ASAP.'

'Soon! Soon!'

Colin smiled, finishing his counting. 'Sooooooon. As soon as poss.' He laughed at Peter's annoyed glances. 'Hey, be happy, I sweated blood for you.'

'Good,' Peter grunted. 'Now sweat some more.'

———

Peter lay awake. Sunday would be important. What information did they want Sandy to gather? What would she be after?

He didn't imagine that she could go through the company's finances and get a picture of the business, so why was she coming instead of some dull bookkeeper? Maybe he had underestimated her.

A character reference seemed likely, but what did they want him to be? He felt he was neither a villain nor a techno geek. Where did he fit in their picture? What was he? Perhaps he was a hardened villain; after all, he headed something that was so deeply buried in nefarious operations that from the outside there might seem nothing to distinguish him from the criminals he served.

Nevertheless, he did not feel he was part of the underworld fraternity and although firmly snagged, he held onto the fact that he was struggling to set himself free. However, she mustn't realize it.

His mind focused on his predicament. Perhaps a slower, studied approach to the snare might extricate him. Trying to force things could merely tighten the trap.

———

At the office the modem lights flickered and the traffic of information moved invisibly around the system. Messages, data and money transferred across the ether, important events, held as faint electrical charges, stored as an infinitesimal magnetic imprint. The whole nexus was travelling a world of intangible surfaces, existing on the borderline of reality.

———

That evening he had delivered another parcel to Mojo-Smith. The shrivelled spy smiled gleefully at his bundle.

'Very productive, very!' Mojo-Smith studied Peter carefully. 'It would be regretful indeed to lose such a valuable source.'

Peter's left eye began to twitch. 'I can imagine, however, the time will arrive.'

Mojo-Smith's head began to bob slowly from side to side. 'Will, is a strong word, don't you think?'

Peter picked Mojo-Smith's cigarette case up and went to open it for a cigarette.

Mojo-Smith cried out, lunged and snatched it away from him. His composure returned, but flushing even redder than normal. He opened it gingerly. 'Cigarette?'

Peter took one nervously, pausing to frame his words in 'Mojo-speak'. 'If that time comes sooner than later, I will be pleased. Though I will be sad not to be able to continue the work with you.'

Smith leant towards him, his lighter ablaze. Peter bent forward to meet it and lit up. Smith put his Dunhill away. 'You could still help us.'

Peter nodded. 'If you had work you felt I could do.'

'We always have work for the right people. In the meantime, you will do what you can?'

'Yes, of course.'

———

On Saturday he went into the office at about midday and made the weekend backup. The tape, about half the size of a video, went into the boot of his car. There was no point in putting it by the machine, if for example there was a fire or a flood. Why make a security copy if it too might be destroyed by the same accident? The cartridge held a complete record of all the software on the machine, its layout and all its data records. It was his only insurance against disaster. With it the system could be restored in minutes on a new machine, even if his office burnt down.

He drove into the West End and spent a couple of hours playing pinball in an arcade. He hated the weekends. Nothing ever happened.

———

Peter waited in the foyer for Sandy. He had called her room on the house phone and he waited in suspense. Standing under a huge chandelier that hung in the centre of the room, he watched the lifts' floor indicators for her approach. The doors opened and he appreciated a beautiful platinum blonde who stepped out and walked towards him. She wore a white low cut dress and short jacket. Something about her walk was familiar. He realized with a jolt that it was Sandy.

'Peter,' she said smiling, 'how wonderful to see you.'
She kissed his cheek and he, hers.

'Sandy, you look marvellous. You've changed your hair.'

'Thank you, I like to keep fluid.' She touched the arm of his new jacket. 'That's beautiful leather.'

He reached his arm around her waist. 'That's beautiful lipstick.' Pulling Sandy slowly forward he kissed her.

She pressed forward against him and tilted her head back, looking at him with eagerness.

'I'm not hungry, it's still the afternoon for me.'

'Not a bit tired?'

'Not a bit.'

Sandy took his hand and led him to the elevator.

————

She lay across his chest and ran the nail of her left index finger up and down his throat.

'What's the itinerary then?' he said, pinning her finger with his neck.

She wriggled her digit free. 'Oh, a few days of shadowing, I guess.'

'Is there anything particular you need?'

She lifted herself up and sat on his waist. 'Now or later?'

'Later.'

'Nothing comes to mind right now. I just need a picture to take home with me.'

He touched the reflex at the bottom of her stomach and ran his hand lightly over it. Her navel twitched left then right.

She giggled.

'I hope you don't mean a Polaroid?' he said.

'No, I don't think so.'

He sat up, cradling her in his arms. 'Are you hungry yet?'

'I guess so. What's on the menu?'

'Room service?'

Sandy looked at the clock. 'Jeez is that the time?'

Peter turned his head. It was four o'clock. 'Breakfast?'

———

Peter woke up, blurred but aware that it was an abnormal time to be in bed. Sandy was sound asleep. He ordered breakfast to be brought up, even though lunch would have been more appropriate. Twenty minutes later it arrived. Dressed in a hotel towelling robe, he took the tray, tipped the waiter and took it back with him to the bed. Sandy was still asleep. He shook her, but she didn't react. He shook her again and she moaned distantly.

'Time to get up.'

She rolled over. 'What time is that?' she murmured distantly.

'Eleven thirty.'

She forced her eyes open. 'Ahh sheesh.'

He poured a coffee and handed it to her as she sat up slightly.

'Jetlag?'

She paid him no attention and sipped. 'This better shock me.'

Peter moved the tray of two continental breakfasts into the middle of the bed. He dropped out of his robe and slipped under the sheets.

'Ah, luxury,' he said, plumping up some pillows behind him. 'So what do you want to do today?'

'Acclimatization.' She looked over at him. 'Some more R and R.'

'In which order?'

She blew onto her coffee. 'Rest I guess.'

———

Sandy leant over the dressing table, her head back, watching him in the mirror. He looked into her reflected eyes. Her head moved to his thrusts, tilting up, her mouth opening, lips a natural fiery red. She arched her body sensuously, responding to his lateral penetrations. Peter held her just above the thighs, gripping her torso by the hard muscle that seemed to flow from her legs, into her waist. She felt stronger to him on her feet, even more exciting. Seeing her walk across the room naked, bathed in daylight, had pulled him out of the bed as if wrenched by a lustful magnetism. Sandy laughed, but his caresses soon turned her silent and then husky. She was nimble, animate and reciprocating. She danced to his tune.

The previous night's glut of sex had drained him, but his desire for her remained.

They sat in the corner bath of her suite, slowly soaking in hot perfumed water. Their legs entwined, they sat in silence, wallowing. Sandy seemed absorbed in her own thoughts, preening herself like a royal bird. Her face was wet, moisture running down her smooth hot pink skin. He watched her like a voyeur as she bathed.

She looked up from her thoughts with a splash. 'What got you into this business, Peter?'

'Money.'

'Anything else?'

'I like computers.'

'Anybody help you?'

'Family and friends. You know, they helped by putting up some of the money.'

'Do they hold stock?'

'No, they just lent me some cash, which I paid them back as soon as I could.'

'So how do you feel about working with people like MonoLog?' she said, lying back.

'In what sense?'

'Any,' she said languidly.

'For instance?'

'I think you know what I mean.' She looked at him knowingly.

'Okay. I'm a mute carrier. If a Mafia boss wants to send a letter instructing someone to break the law, they don't arrest the Postmaster for sending it.'

A finger ran across his toes. 'Okay, but how do you feel about it?'

Peter flicked some water at her. 'Is this the Spanish Inquisition?'

'Monty Python, right?'

'Eh yes.' He stood up and stepped out of the bath, then turned to her. 'Let's just say we are in the same business. So why should it bother me?'

————

The hotel charged him twenty pounds to get his Mercedes out of the underground garage. The attendant seemed extremely pleased at taking the money from him. Perhaps, Peter thought, it was his revenge on all those who lived such high a life.

The traffic was terrible, their progress reduced to a snail-like crawl down Park Lane, along Green Park to Piccadilly Circus.

Peter tried to maintain a running guide of the route, but the traffic had been reduced to such a pace that the sights were not going by fast enough for him to keep the commentary up.

'So what's the schedule?'

'Have a look at your facility. Examine your site, evaluate the situation, quantify the functionality.'

Peter turned to her, an amused smile on his face. 'Oh I see, and then?'

'Go shopping, see London.' She shrugged. 'Screw.'

He laughed. 'I'll go for that.'

————

Sandy sat on the other side of his desk, typing furiously on her laptop computer. George had made himself very scarce, passing them in the hallway, every time they went up or down stairs.

'Pardon me, miss,' he said each time.

'This is all very clean,' she said, looking up. 'Low profile, low maintenance, low overhead, low headcount. It's really impressive.' She typed a sentence without breaking his gaze. 'Do you realize how much we spend making sure we don't have any loose jaws at MonoLog? You add one staff to the roster, you practically double the chances of someone blabbing. We get around it by compartmentalization, but your minimalism is class. We could learn a lot from you.'

'It makes sense to let the technology work for me,' said Peter.

'That's the theory we try to implement, but we don't get as close as this.'

She took a phone wire from her briefcase and clipped it into her computer. She held the end up. 'Have you got somewhere I can jack in?'

Peter took it and plugged her into the telephone socket. 'Contact!'

She tapped at the keyboard and the modem dialled into MonoLog, singing the tones that represented the number.

Peter got up and walked into the kitchen. He picked up a teaspoon and wrote invisibly with its blunt end onto the wall calendar, '515 273 9196'. Why was there never a pen when he needed one?

'Fancy a coffee?' he called through.

Sandy looked up from her screen. 'I'd love one.'

———

Peter laser printed out some statistics for the system, to show her how much of it was used at any one time. As he knew and she expected, the throughput compared with the system's capacity was negligible but it was enough to keep the money kept rolling in.

'Quality traffic,' she said, taking down the figure on her machine.

It had been a better than average day. Every time a messenger arrived, he put the package in front of her and told her to open it. George brought up the ultraviolet torch for Sandy to shine at the money.

'You can't be too careful,' said Peter. 'We don't want cash with a history.'

At four o'clock, he excused himself. 'I'm going off home to change. At five George will get you a cab for your hotel. I'll meet you there about eight for dinner. I've told George, you can have anything you like except user info or backend access.'

'Sure thing.'

As soon as he left, Sandy got up from Peter's desk and went downstairs to where George was reading the papers.

'Hi there.'

George looked up. 'Hello, can I get you anything?'

'Oh no, I just wondered if I could join you for a chat, as you Brits would say.'

George smiled. 'Fine and dandy.'

She sat on the couch end nearest to the armchair George had made his own.

'This is some operation you have here. How long have you been working for Peter?'

'About a year.'

'What did you do before?'

'I was a man of leisure.'

'That sounds like fun.'

'It can be. What does a lovely lady like you do?'

'I'm an analyst at MonoLog.'

'And is MonoLog in the same kind of thing as us?'

'Pretty much.' Sandy crossed her long legs at him. 'Pretty much,' she winked. 'Now Peter, he's a real dynamic kind of guy. What's it like working with him?'

'He's a big man. The heart of a bear and the balls of a rhino.' George blushed a bit. 'If you pardon the vernacular.'

Sandy laughed. 'So how do you feel working in this business?'

'I think I could be doing worse, don't you?'

Sandy smiled. 'Go on.'

'I could be chopping down the ozone layer, or something similar.'

Sandy smiled. 'I think that might be a serious mistake. We are certainly in an environmentally friendly business. A little power is about the only thing we consume.'

'Yeah, I'll take your word for it.'

'Do you have much to do with the customers?'

'I don't talk about punters, 'cause we don't know nothing about them. They could all be vicars as far as I know.'

Sandy laughed charmingly. 'George, do you think they might all be vicars?'

George smiled. 'When I was jumping outta planes in the war, there was this poster. There was all these officers, stood around this pretty girl. She looked just like you. Prettier than eight score draws on a Saturday afternoon. Now they obviously fancied her, because they looked like they were going to tell her about how important they were and what was going to happen. Loose lips cost ships, that was the poster's motto.' He tapped his nose with his index finger. 'Loose lips cost ships. Now if you were the Queen, and I've been a guest of hers, I still wouldn't be forthcoming. My old mum once said to me, 'George, remember the Monkeys.' He put his hands over his ears, 'Monkey see, monkey do!'

Sandy smiled. 'I respect that, but don't you mean see no evil, hear no evil, speak no evil'

'That as well. Can I get you a cuppa?'

———

Peter stood in front of his bathroom mirror and combed his wet hair back out of his eyes. Things were going well; with luck she was ticking the right boxes. He wondered how George was getting on.

———

She knelt, straddling him, resting on her elbows, raised on her knees.

'Will you tell me something, Peter?' Sandy nuzzled him.

'What?'

'Why do you want to sell out?'

Peter pushed her buttocks forward and up, forcing her head up to his face. 'I don't want to sell out.' He squeezed them in a firm grip. 'I've got enquiries to buy me out and I've followed them up.'

She pushed back with her right arm, holding him with her left hand. As she moved down onto him he entered her. She moaned a sharp shivering gasp, sitting back on his waist.

'The right people, the right money,' his voice clipped as if he were in pain. 'I'm not going to say no.'

————

Sandy spent her last morning at the office then took a cab to Heathrow.

'You look shagged out,' said George to Peter, moments after she left.

'All in the cause of duty.'

George dropped a sheet of paper on his desk. 'Done some nosin' around for you.'

Peter looked at the list of words with percentages next to them, 'What's this?'

'Our passwords and how many we've got of each. I thought it might help you out. I've taken the liberty to express 'em as a percentage.'

Peter raised an eyebrow, 'What made you do this?'

George frowned. 'If young wazzocks can hack, so can I. Colin told me all about it yesterday, while you were gallivanting about with Miss Hot to Trot.'

Peter glanced through the list. 'You got these on your own?'

George frowned again. 'What do you think, I let Colin get it for me?' He pointed at his head. 'It might be old but it still works.'

'Well George, I'm impressed!' Peter looked at the top of the list. 'N C C 1 7 0 1. 3.5%. What's the significance of ncc1701?'

George held his hands out. 'Search me, but its Top of the Pops.'

'When's Colin coming back?'

George pulled out a piece of paper and handed it to Peter. 'Here's his number, give him a tinkle.'

Peter stared at him in amazement. 'How did you get this out of him?'

'I persuaded him we needed it.'

Peter dialled the number. A modem answered. He rang it again and the machine answered again. He dialled a third time and Colin answered. 'Eh, sorry, but I left my HST in. What's up?'

'What does ncc1701 mean to you?'

Colin laughed. 'Live long and prosper man! It's the serial number of the Starship Enterprise. Got tribble trouble?'

'Okay, you win the holiday to Lerwick. Got my blue box?'

'Yeah.'Hhe blew a kiss down the phone. 'It's wonderful. Where's Lerwick?'

'The Shetlands. I take it from that, it works.'

'The Shetlands, gross. Yeah, the blue box, mega, no problem.'

'Repeat after me! I'm on my way over right now.'

Colin laughed. 'Yeah Pete, but one question though.'

'Nope.'

'Okay, one question anyway.'

'One question then.'

'Why are you the only set up it doesn't work with?'

'No idea.'

'Wierd!' muttered Colin.

'See you in a bit then?'

'I will get in, you know, somehow.'

'Through the front door in about an hour.'

'Alright, I'm coming.'

Peter hung up. 'Wazzie's on his way.' He got up and went to the wall calendar. He took it back to his desk and shaved the carbon of a pencil into a small pile. He rubbed it onto the impression he had made two days earlier, then wrote the number down on a notepad.

———

Peter called up to George. 'Okay, we're going for a test.'

Colin typed the codes into the blue box then rang his home number. The phone was picked up; it was George upstairs.

'Online Data, can I help you?'

'Okay Pete, that's redirect working.'

Colin reset the line with the box and dailled again. His answer phone replied.

'There, it's back to normal.'

Peter picked up an envelope and handed it to Colin. 'There's an extra thousand in there.'

Colin opened the envelope, and checked to see if Peter had just made a joke. He hadn't. 'Muchas gracias! Arriba, arriba!'

'When we need you again, I'll call.'

Colin stuck the envelope in his kit bag. 'Thanks.' He shook Peter's hand. 'Thanks a bunch.'

'Bye.'

———

George watched Peter check and double check the set up.

'Follow me through this, George. If something sounds wrong . . . '

'I'll holler.'

'Blue box redirects the call made to any phone number we wish to intercept, to our incoming line. The incoming line has modem number 1 connected to it. Modem 1 answers and sends the call to the PC. The PC connects the call to modem 2 which connects to the outgoing line. Modem 2 redirects the call to the original destination. PC is connected to laser printer. A call to the target system gets redirected to us, we answer and connect back to the target system so the user notices nothing. The PC logs the logon ID and password to the printer.'

George looked confused, 'Sounds like magic to me.'

Peter redirected his home number with the blue box to modem 1's line and set modem 2 to call the office number and route it through. He ran upstairs then connected another modem to a different PC and dialled home. A few seconds passed and the office phone rang. He picked it up and there was the hollow clicking of modem 2 trying to make a connection. He dropped the line on the modem and the dialling tone on the office phone returned.

'It works!'

He went downstairs again with George and reset the numbers.

'Now let's find out a bit about MonoLog.'

He double checked the set up then dialled the codes into the blue box. Immediately the lights of the modem flashed alive, then with a whistle the printer began to feed through its first sheet of paper.

'Bingo!' said Peter.

'House,' said George.

Chapter Seven
OPEN DOORS

For the next two days, Peter babysat the blue box, watching with a fading fascination the call logging.

MonoLog's traffic was in a loosely veiled code. It seemed to represent what he expected, a mixed bag of gaming transactions, money transfers, vice and drug-related messaging. He extracted the login IDs and the passwords, browsed the rest of the sessions and passed them through a shredding machine that George had bought.

He turned his attention to Mojo-Smith's list and while he ran the blue box on them, he wrote a simple program to ignore the bulk of the transmissions that came after the password and ID had been entered. This saved the reams of paper that the printer has started to churn out.

Just as he was about to test it, Sandy called.

'I've discussed my report with Mr Andretti and he would like you to come over to finalize the arrangements.'

'We haven't discussed the price yet.'

'Don't worry about that, Peter, I'm sure we can make you a suitable offer. Can you come over Wednesday? I hope that's convenient.'

'You want me over on Wednesday?' Peter looked up at George and pulled a face. 'I'm washing my hair that night.'

Sandy laughed. 'Hey, don't give me a hard time over this. Is Wednesday a problem?'

'No, Wednesday's fine.'

'I'll fax you.'

———

'I'm coming with you,' said George as Peter hung up.

Peter shook his head. 'I'll be okay.'

'I hope you know what you're doing?'

Peter smiled. 'No, but I'll be okay.'

'You sure it's not a stitch up?'

Peter shook his head. 'No.' He picked the phone up again and dialled. 'I've got to take that risk.'

The phone rang. 'Department 87.'

'Mojo-Smith please, it's Peter Talbot.'

'Putting you through, Mr Talbot.' The phone went on hold.

'Thanks Moneypenny.' He grinned at George.

There was a click on the line. 'Mojo-Smith.'

'Rodney, I've got a bundle for you tomorrow. Are you free?'

'Eight o'clock?'

'No problem. Same place?'

'Excellent.'

'See you then.'

'Good day.'

———

Peter took the disk from his drive and went downstairs with it. George followed him. As Peter was installing the program George flopped down into his chair.

'I've been thinking. You've got 750 thou in the box. Why not do a runner? I could look after the shop for as long as I could. Should be a mill by then.'

'No, it wouldn't work.'

'You could keep your head down for a few years with that sort of dosh.'

'This isn't the kind of business you can just wind up. You've got to look after the customers.' He laughed. 'Look at how quickly MonoLog got to hear of our sell out attempt. We are important, a lot of business is dependent on us, that's why we are getting so much money. You've heard of Dr Faust, well I'm him; the trouble is I didn't choose the deal, it chose me.'

George looked like he was struggling for inspiration. 'You could hide away?'

'Are you saying, don't go to the States?'

George slapped the table. 'Yeah, I am, I don't like it. I think those yanks are too fucking iffy.'

'Why?'

''Cause I think they could try and bump you off.'

Peter sat cross legged on the floor. 'It might be cheaper. In fact it would be a lot cheaper. However I've got to take that as a risk; there is a real opportunity to get out in one piece with the MonoLog deal.'

'I don't want to make a big song and dance, but if I were them, it would make much more sense to bump someone off on your own manor.'

Peter rolled his eyes. 'Not exactly an uncommon thing in New York either.'

'If I were you, I'd bail out.'

Peter smiled. 'Anyway, it's we. I've got to look after you as well.'

George smirked. 'Okay, I don't think I passed myself off as the janitor to Miss Hoochiecoochie, so that's a nice thought, but I'm at the end of my glorious career, so you've got to look after yourself first. This is all extra time for me.'

'Extra time or not, where would we go?' He picked up a few sheets of paper from the printout. 'Spain, Australia, Brazil. They are all here. The world's too small. You can run, but you can't hide. I would have sold to Kendal, if he had wanted to pay enough that he couldn't have just dropped it as soon as he realised the game.'

'So what's the answer?'

'I've got to sell to someone who can't afford to drop it or who won't want to. Either that or just keep on doing it.'

'New York or bust then.'

Peter nodded.

———

Peter handed Mojo-Smith an envelope. 'I've got about the first third of the numbers cracked at user level and two of them at backend level.'

Mojo-Smith opened it and took the pages out. 'Any footprints in the snow?'

'None. The accounts haven't been used by me so at the moment this information is unused.'

'I don't follow.'

'What you've got there is a list of passwords for systems and their IDs. None of them have yet been used by an unauthorized user and therefore there is no obvious way they can know they've been penetrated.'

Mojo-smith smiled inquisitively, pushing his head forwards on its stalk. 'How, may I ask, did you achieve that?'

'If you don't mind I shall leave that a trade secret.'

'By all means. It's undoubtedly beyond my grasp in any event.'

'Now I have a favour to ask.'

'Indeed?'

'Indeed.' Peter explained the situation with MonoLog.

Mojo-Smith looked earnestly at him. 'Unfortunate. I suggest a visit to my office tomorrow may be in order.'

'I should have the rest of the information after I get back from the trip.'

Mojo-Smith raised his glass. 'Here is to a successful visit.'

———

He had learnt his lesson from the first time he flew. He bought an economy ticket and a window seat in smoking. The plane was relatively full, but the passengers obviously didn't like the idea of sitting amongst the fumes and the back of the plane was practically empty. The last five mid-section rows had no one in them and armed with the knowledge that his window seat was assured, he moved to the rearmost seat, just before take-off. His flying lessons had done the trick. During the rush of acceleration he felt no emotions at all. He was cured.

After take-off he put up the arms of the other seats, pushed the belts between the cushions and lay down across all four. Soon, he was asleep under his new heavy jacket on the only transatlantic flying bed. Eight hours later the stewardess woke him; he felt groggy but for him it had been a very short flight.

'We are coming into land. Please fasten your seatbelt.'

Sleeping on a plane was like sleeping in a waiting room. While not particularly restful, it was far better than staying conscious.

At JFK, he queued for an hour behind the passengers of an Air India Jumbo. Immigration did not like the look of them at all. The officers poured over their passports, scowling importantly as petty clerks are trained to.

Peter suspected that the tendency of the patient visitors to pull large quantities of photocopied documents from various pockets when asked any questions didn't help his slow progress. However, the seething impatience of his thoughts didn't move the line along any faster. He watched mournfully as US citizens came and went through their own gate.

Outside the customs hall a limousine driver waited with a board:

PETER TALBOT
Online Data

He walked straight past him and got a cab. The cab driver's face was not the one on the permit and he seemed unable to communicate intelligibly. At least, in the yellow cab, he could only get overcharged.

He checked in at his hotel and was pleased to find it booked. If the trip had been off the plane and straight into the river, then they might not have gone to the trouble of actually booking the room. He thought again; what if they were just being careful? MonoLog was, after all, a professional outfit.

'Your room is Suite 1650.'

Peter grimaced. '1650, that's my unlucky number. Have you got a different one?'

The clerk looked troubled. 'I'll see what I have. I have a 1742, but it's not a non-smoking suite.'

'That's fine, I'll have it.'

He went up to his room, threw his case onto the bed and went down in the elevator again. He walked out onto the street, across the road and into the Sheraton.

'I'd like a room for three nights.'

'Certainly sir, is that smoking or non-smoking?'

'Eh . . . non-smoking.'

He handed over his credit card, showed his passport and filled in the paperwork.

He felt pleased with himself. Cat and mouse had started to become a way of life.

He threw his jacket onto the spare double bed of his new suite and then lay down on the other. It was a heavy handsome leather jacket, lined expertly with bullet-proof Kevlar. So were his trousers. They made him feel a lot safer, as did the room.

———

He called MonoLog and got put through to Sandy.

'Hi, I made it.'

'Thank God,' she said, 'we were getting so worried. You must have missed our driver.'

'Oh bloody hell, that would have saved me a cab fare.'

'Is everything okay now?' asked Sandy.

'Yeah, fine.'

'See you tonight?'

'I'd love to but I'm really tired,' he said mournfully. 'Tomorrow after the meeting?'

'Ah, and here I am actually missing someone.'

'I'm sorry, but it will give me time to acclimatize. You wouldn't want me off form, would you? Anyway, I wouldn't be able to keep up with you.'

'Oh well, if you put it that way.'

'I'll see you tomorrow at ten?'

'Sure thing. Get refreshed now!' She blew a kiss.

Still quite fresh from his sleep on the plane he decided to walk up and down Broadway and see some sights. New York was definitely alive. A few hundred yards along a single street and the atmosphere changed like the odours from a busy kitchen. The night fell, but unlike London where the pace of living dropped away with the light, the city still jangled with life. He went into a bar and bought the most American-sounding beer he could see. O'Reilly's bar wasn't Irish, for all its pictures of four leaf clovers. It was as American as hamburger and as foreign to Peter as the Gobi Desert would be if he were ever to visit it. He drank the Budweiser, a distant stronger relative of the light fizzy drink introduced into Britain, and pondered the permutations of the next day.

———

Sandy met Peter at MonoLog's reception. He was wearing a black suit and looked like he was on his way to a funeral. He had swept his hair back and oiled it lightly. He appeared quietly menacing.

'Peter, you look great. All the guys are dying to meet you.' Sandy led him through the offices to a boardroom of shiny ebony. He wondered how much rainforest had been felled for it and at what cost.

Waiting for him across the well-appointed room, in front of windows that opened onto a cityscape, were four middle-aged men. All fat and slightly balding, they looked like a group of tailors meeting for reminiscence about old times.

Sandy took him to a seat on the other side of the black oval table and excused herself.

Peter shook their hands and Andretti asked him to be seated. The nameless three eyed him, like buyers in an auction.

'These are my friends, they are non-executive members of the board and represent our syndicate of investors. They want to ask you a few questions.'

'Please,' said Peter, 'feel free to ask what you like.'

'Coming somewhat quickly to the point,' said the smallest of the four, perching forward on his chair, sharp flinty eyes glinting. 'Why do you want to sell your business to us?'

'Mr Andretti thought that rather than consider other offers that have been made to me, I might consider one from you first. I agreed that I would give you first option. I'm very happy to do that. I'm a businessman; a sizable offer for my business is not an opportunity I wish to pass without investigation.'

'How would you see your future if we were to take control of your company?' asked Andretti.

'That would depend on the details of any arrangement we might come to. Obviously I would like to consider that I was selling the business as opposed to myself.'

Peter felt Mojo-Smith's influence hovering in his mind. 'Speak oblique,' it said.

The small man to the left of Andretti sat back, 'So would you want to work for us after we took over?'

'Would I be prepared to work for you afterwards? In principle yes, but again that would be subject to any arrangement we might make. What did you have in mind?'

Andretti answered. 'We have thought this whole thing out. It makes sense for us to do this deal with you in England. Our reports are that you have a tight operation and a low key position. We think it would cause too much interest if we were to buy you out and replace you with an American. It would attract too much heat.'

'I see.'

'I'm sure you understand that we aren't exactly unknown, but we are left alone, because we have friends and strictly speaking, we do not offend any regulation. However, I don't see that it would be good to make an investment and risk publishing the fact, even with our buffered posture.'

'So how would you see a deal panning out?' asked Peter.

'We buy you out. You run Online for a few years and we pay you over that time.'

'Do you want to know my price?'

'Well, the way we see it, it's worth nothing without you. A little if you stay around for a short period and a whole lot if you stay, say, five years. It's where your price crosses our need curve, that is the important issue for us.'

'Five years is longer than I planned,' said Peter.

The right wing of the panel croaked and then snapped gruffly, 'Be happy, five years is a short period. It is a greater percentage of your life when you're my age but for you it's of no matter.' He looked at his fellows, flexing his grey eyebrows and then looked back at Peter. 'You don't have to look to your old age yet.'

Peter smiled. 'Even so.'

Andretti continued, 'We thought a million bucks for the company. Then a million a year for years two to four and a million at the end of the fifth.'

The short man rocked forwards. 'What do you think about that?'

'I think I'm making the yearly figure already.'

The short man grinned. 'But for how long? We can make sure you don't have any competition. Someone might go up against you, but up against us, that's a different matter.'

Andretti shrugged. 'He's got a point; this kind of money attracts all the wrong types. Bad people are capable of anything for this kind of money. They're not practical people like us, just animals who want a fast buck.'

Peter thought for a moment. 'I'll tell you what I'll do. I've got about 700K, I guess about 1.3 million dollars, spare at the moment. I'll take that and the deal. You pay me into a Swiss bank account and I'll promise to work a three year minimum. Maybe five, maybe four, but I won't guarantee more than three.'

Andretti glanced around. 'If you work three years, you get three million from us.'

Peter nodded. 'Agreed.'

Andretti looked around at his confederates, who remained impassive. 'I think we can handle that.'

'It's a deal then,' said Peter.

Andretti grinned. 'Welcome to the club.'

The four stood and he shook with each one in turn.

As he took his hand, the fourth member of the syndicate, who had remained silent, looked Peter in the eyes and smiled a thin grin. 'Remember, we will be relying on you.' He held Peter's gaze.

Peter laughed calmly. 'I understand.'

To Peter, the snare had tightened another notch, but perhaps it could now start to loosen and eventually come free. He knew his urge to bolt would simply throttle him.

'Gentlemen, it's a pleasure to be aboard.'

———

It was a dark moonless night lit by the lemon sodium of street lamps. It had been raining and the road shone in patches with a silver grey glitter. A Ford Sierra stopped outside the tailors shop below Online Data. It was three o'clock. A man of average height and average build got out of the driver's seat and made his way to the rear passenger door. Whitechapel was empty, except for the occasional car that dashed past with a swish of wet tyres. The man produced a long pair of bolt cutters, four feet in length and shaped like a large lawn-edger. He carried them quickly to the iron shutters and efficiently chopped the hasps from them with four fierce wrenches. The locks fell with a clatter.

He returned to the car and placed the cutter back on the rear seat. A youth got out of the car from the front nearside and joined him at the grill, which they both lifted.

The man produced a gun-shaped object from within his jacket. Placing a wire protrusion at its barrel end into the lock, he squeezed a trigger and unlocked the door.

'Go,' he said, opening the door and letting the youth past. The teenager had a torch in his hand and moved quickly up the stairs. His ears followed the sound of the pre-alarm warning, tracing it with his beam of light. The flash-light located the alarm box. He moved his face alongside the panel with its key buttons and shone the torch across the plane of its fascia. The angled light picked out the round patches of impression made by the daily routine of repeated finger presses. The code was a four digit number of the permutations 1, 4, 6 and 0.

He had approximately forty-five seconds to crack the code.

0146
0164
0614
0641
1046
1064
1406
1460
1640
1604
4016
4061

The pre-alarm bleep stopped. It had taken him twenty-five seconds from the door to silence it. He trotted back down the stairs.

'See you in an hour,' he said, catching a set of car keys thrown to him.

'Nice work, lad,' said the older man, going in. He closed the door behind him, turned a dim torch on and made his way up. He had been a 'creep' all of his adult life, working his way up the ladder of larceny, from petty crime and random house breaking to stealing to order. There was more money in pre-planned robbery, with no nasty surprises and a prearranged sale at the end of a night's work. Nowadays, he was more likely to be paid to steal paperwork than commissioned to acquire a painting or some jewels.

He went into the first floor meeting room and unlocked the window. He always unlocked every possible exit in case he needed to use one in a hurry. The older he got, the greater his fear of prison. As a younger man it hadn't entered into his thinking; now it dominated his attitude.

Eyes now accustomed to the faint light, he switched off his torch. He went out into the pitch black passageway again and went up the stairs. The door looked interesting. It was bolted and with a little effort the bolt came undone. He hesitated for a moment and listened. Something bothered him; his professional antenna sensed a problem. He twitched his moustache and expelled a dismissive grunt. He was getting too old for the job, he thought, opening the door and darting across the threshold. A thrashing moment of confusion passed and he gave a sharp cry. There was a heavy thud in the courtyard below. The door swung back with a slam.

An hour passed. The Sierra returned and parked outside the office. It waited for a minute then drove away. Five minutes passed and the car reappeared. No one came out from beneath the shutters and after a minute the car vanished. Ten minutes passed and it returned once more, then again half an hour later.

At five o'clock, a teenager walked around the corner of the road, stopping outside the tailors shop. He looked around nervously and lifted the shutter. In thirty minutes the sun would be coming up. The door was still unlocked.

'Joe?' he called in a whisper, his heart pounding, 'you there?'

He went into the meeting room and noted the window slightly ajar. The next landing door was ajar.

'Joe?' He held the handle and pushed. As he started to lean forward, he felt a faint draft round his feet. The door swung open. He grappled the doorframe with his forearm, his hand filled with a torch. He swung half out into the void, grasping the frame with his other hand. He yanked himself in, dropping his torch in the process.

'Oh shit, fucking shit,' he gasped. Looking into the black pool of the bricked-in space below, a shiver of horror ran through him. He picked up the torch and pointed it down, pushing the switch forward. Below lay an outline of a broken body, a pool of blood reflecting with a dark fiery red.

'Jesus, oh Jesus Christ.' He turned and fled.

———

George felt the colour drain from his face as he drove past the tailors to his normal parking place.

'More police than a Mason's ball,' he muttered. He parked up and made his way slowly toward the office. Across the road he could see an ambulance. It gave him some hope; they had never taken him away in an ambulance before. A postman stood watching from his side of the road.

'What's up over there?' asked George.

'Someone's topped themselves, by the look of things,' said the postman, wrinkling his nose.

A shade of pink came back into George's complexion. 'Blimey, not a nice thing.'

George crossed over the junction and walked between two police Rovers. He noticed the shutter and its broken hasps.

A stout policeman, who was talking into his radio, signed off and stepped over to intercept him.

'Can I help you sir?'

'Yes officer, what's happening?'

'I'm afraid there's been an accident sir and this area has been closed off for the time being.'

'I work here,' he pointed upstairs. 'Can I get through?'

The policeman smiled politely. 'Ah, if you'd like to come this way sir? You see, someone fell out of your building last night and died. Perhaps you can help us with a few questions?'

'It's not a young bloke is it?' asked George anxiously.

'No sir, not young. Why do you ask?'

'Thought it could be my boss. Thank gawd.'

'You've been broken into and it seems one of the miscreants came unstuck.'

'Bloody hell. What happened?'

'He left by the wrong door.' There was a hint of satisfaction in his voice, but nothing that could have been proved in court. 'Most unfortunate. We had a call early this morning.'

'Blimey.'

'Theft of computer equipment. It's getting to be quite a common crime. Lucky for you he didn't get away with it.'

'Not so lucky for him.'

'No sir, not lucky at all. Would you care to follow me?'

'Lead on, officer.'

———

The night had drawn in and even through the thick glass of the hotel room's window, he could hear the sound of the city. It rumbled like a distant river, a rushing, coursing roar that set his nerves on edge. Sometimes he felt excitement and then, at other moments, dread. He had done the deal, but it wasn't over for him until he walked away. Even now they might double-cross him. The presence of the other board members gave him a degree of faith in the arrangement. He imagined they would not have brought them into a meeting, if all they had wanted to do was lower his guard. If he could escape in one piece, he had made himself four million dollars, but getting out would be a task worthy of such a high fee.

The success and excitement cast a spell all its own. Soon perhaps he might not wish to escape. Perhaps he would become a criminal in spirit rather than a prisoner of circumstance. Now at least there was a defined route out of trouble, so that avoiding further complications could now be top priority.

Peter rang the other hotel to check for any messages. Sandy had called several times, so he rang her on what appeared to be her home number. An answerphone replied.

'Hi,' said the message, 'I'm not in right now to answer your call. At the tone please leave your message and I'll reach you as soon as possible.'

'Hello, it's Peter, I'm just calling . . . '

The handset was picked up. It was Sandy. 'Peter, where are you? You're not supposed to disappear like that. I was worried for you.'

'I took in some sights.'

'I was planning to celebrate with you.'

'Oh I'm sorry, I didn't think. I'm still in a bit of a fug. I took a walk after the meeting and got distracted. There didn't seem like any more business to do.'

'I was thinking about coming over. I have something for you, are you free?'

'Yes, but I was just planning to get some sleep. My brain thinks it's two o'clock in the morning. Anyway, what had you in mind?'

'Just to drop by,' she sounded sad, 'and, you know, see how you are? I've got these papers I need to get to you before you go.'

'Okay, but I am knackered.'

'Oh gee, that's bad news. Anyways, I'd like to drop them off now if I can. Maybe I can stay for a quick nightcap.'

He closed his eyes. 'How could I say no?'

'I'll come over right away. I'll be thirty.'

———

Peter sat in the foyer bar behind a pillar. He looked into a mirror as he sucked on a coke. The mirror reflected onto the main lifts leading up to his official room. The leather jacket was heavy and hot, but he could cope with that better than the idea of an unwelcome visitor coming to see him instead of Sandy.

Then, exactly half an hour after he had spoken to her, Sandy appeared as a reflection. She was alone and as she entered a car, he got up and went to the lifts. In moments, he too was on his way to the nineteenth floor.

Sandy was standing outside of his door waiting. She knocked again, looking down at the floor with a sour expression.

'He's probably asleep, can I help?' said Peter.

She looked up with a start. 'Peter! You made me jump.'

'I had a walk to wake me up a bit.' He unlocked the hotel room door, kissed her cheek and ushered her in.

'So what have you got for me?' he said, closing the door behind them and turning the dead bolt.

She reached to her purse and opened it. For a second he imagined a Derringer was about to be pulled, but an envelope appeared instead.

He took it, letting out a barely muted sigh of relief. He flipped up the unsealed flap. It was a cheque for a million dollars. In that first glance at the blue slip of paper he felt surprised and happy then regretful and sad.

He looked grimly at Sandy, 'I guess this cheque is the contract.'

She nodded. 'It sure is.'

He raised his eyebrows. 'To whom much is given, much is expected.'

'Right, but you don't have to take it. It's the only get out you'll get.'

Peter shook his head. 'A deal is a deal. I don't need a piece of paper, either. What would I do, sue?' He laughed.

She stepped forward to him.

'You're a lucky man,' she whispered in his ear. 'You can have anything you want.'

'Anything?'

'Anything.'

He kissed her, holding her tightly.

She gripped him passionately, sighing to the motions of his embrace.

Their lips parted.

'But not sleep,' he said.

She smiled at him. 'Not yet.' She grabbed him by the arm, pulled him to the bed and pushed him onto it.

'This subtle approach will never work on me,' he protested.

———

He woke early in the morning. The bedside clock showed 5.30. He looked at Sandy, asleep at the far side of the bed. Having sex with her, he thought, was like starring in a porn movie. The only difference was that the camera was concealed. He wondered if she thought he trusted her and whether she was ever off-duty with him. He tried not to flatter himself; he was business.

The phone by his bedside rang. He awoke from a uneasy doze and reached over Sandy to answer it. It was seven.

'Boss?'

'Yeah.'

'We've had a bit of hassle.'

'What? Is the system okay?'

'Yes, it's okay, don't worry.'

'What then?'

'We had a break-in and the thief fell out the landing door into the courtyard.'

'Shit.'

'He's brown bread.'

'Dead?'

'As a dodo.'

'Bloody hell.'

'I've sorted the Old Bill out, but I reckon they'll be back to check and double check.'

'Have you got it covered?'

'No problem, they weren't asking any awkward questions.'

'Hum. Did anything get taken?'

'Nothing, he must have gone straight out of the door.'

'Lucky for us.'

'Looked like a very professional job.'

'How do you mean?'

'They got past the alarm. All the locks were picked or cut.'

'Get some locksmiths in and get some extra security.'

'I'm already onto it.'

'I'll be flying back tomorrow and I'll be in the next morning. Change the password on the alarm.'

'Trying to do it. Bloody terrible manual.'

'Okay, I'll call you later.'

———

Sandy sat wrapped in a towel, her head to the phone.

'I've just checked my voice mail, Peter, can you stay another day?'

Peter grimaced. 'If I absolutely need to. Why?'

'There a meeting that Mr Andretti wants you to attend.'

'Uh huh.' Peter tried not to appear distrustful. 'What kind of meeting?'

'With some Japanese associates who want a gateway.'

'Yes, and?'

'Frank wants you along as our European representative.'

'That's nice.'

'I'll book a flight for you on Saturday.'

'Thanks.'

'Want to see some sights?'

'Sounds good to me.'

———

In Peter's mind, Central Park was a jungle of muggers. It was an easy cliché that had been planted then nurtured in him by the media ever since he was a small child.

Sandy took him along 5th Avenue to the park. They sat by a lake, inside a wooden covered jetty, and watched the waterfowl paddle around. The park was obviously not the battleground he automatically expected. Even so, there was an atmosphere that made him wonder what changes took place once the daylight had gone.

Peter had run out of things to tell Sandy. Her gentle probing was now striking a hard inner core behind which the truth lay. A burbling tone from within her purse announced that she was carrying a portable phone, which she answered.

'Yeah.' She smiled at Peter. 'Sure.' Her face went solemn. 'Sure.' Her gaze became distant. 'It's covered.' She nodded to herself. 'No problem. Right, I don't see any reason why not.' There was a still silence. 'It's cooked. Yes, confidence is high.' She straightened up and pressed the handset off. She turned to Peter. 'The meeting with the Japs is all in place.'

'When?'

'Mr Andretti, Meyer and Mark Skink are saddling up for the meeting in about an hour, so we better go.'

'Okay.' Peter grimaced. 'So long as I don't have to speak any Japanese.'

'Just say Hi and bow a little. You are way above them in the rankings. You're practically the European data shogun.' She smiled. 'They are the ones that have to bang their heads on the floor.'

Skink was a short, bald, disagreeable-looking man. He scowled pugnaciously as he shook Peter's hand. 'So you are the Brit everyone's talking about. Good to meet ya.'

Meyer looked more intently reptilian than on their previous meeting, his skin's opalescent pallor glinting like scales. He seemed to have something on his mind.

'I like your jacket. A heavy jacket suits you.'

'I would have worn a suit, but Sandy sprung this on me.'

'That's okay, Peter,' interjected Andretti. 'It'll rap the Japs around the axle and we are in for a hot one.'

Sandy came into the board room with a large leather holdall and a heavy case.

'Hardware, guys,' she said, clipping the case open. She unzipped the bag. 'Holsters.'

Andretti watched Peter's face which remained unchanged except for an uncontrollable rise of his right eyebrow.

He laughed. 'You've got balls, kid; you've got steel balls.'

Meyer interjected coldly. 'These are just a precaution, relations are a bit under-load. Don't worry, the weapons ARE purged.'

'Police think they still own them,' commented Skink for Peter's benefit.

'You better pick one for me and show me the right end.' Peter smiled. 'They don't have these where I come from.'

Skink threw him a revolver. 'Have the Commissioner's piece.'

The 35 under his arm was a comforting companion. The weight transmitted a feeling of security in a different way to the layers of Kevlar. The implied forceful brutality of the weapon felt like a best defence, even though he had no real idea how to use it.

———

The flight out was for Zurich and it was full. There was a weary tense atmosphere made by an airplane packed with people all hoping that time would pass faster than they knew it could. His flying bed ploy was baulked by the number of passengers, but he managed to twist and curl in his seat till he gained a position where his head was sufficiently rested that he could fall asleep.

———

Smitt, the banker, received him with detached politeness in a small marble lined room. The stone table reflected the gold painted mouldings around the room.

'Once I have opened an account, how do I transfer money?'

The banker nodded. 'Just send us the details of the transaction and it will executed. The number is the key to the account and it is that which is the authority under which we operate.'

Peter smiled. 'A kind of password.'

'So.'

'What happens, say, if the British authorities enquire about the account of a holder? What do you do?'

'We do not receive letters from foreign authorities.'

'Ah, but what if you did?'

'We do not receive such enquiries.'

'Right, I see. But if you did?'

Smitt tore a piece of notepaper from the embossed pad in front of him, screwed it up and dropped it in the bin. 'We do not receive communications concerning the business of our clients. We never have and never will receive such things.'

Peter took the envelope with the first payment from his jacket and passed it to Smitt. He had shown it to an attractive clerk on the reception desk, in a blunt attempt to meet the right man. It had done the trick but he now felt gauche in such an atmosphere of restrained splendour and wealth. What was a mere million dollars to these people? He had felt more at home with a handgun by his heart.

Smitt rose and a minute later returned with royal blue folder. He sat down and drew out a letter and handed it to Peter. 'This is your account number,' he said, pointing to a long serial number at the top of the page, 'and your balance.' He replaced the letter and handed Peter the stiff card enclosure. 'If you require any further information on our many services I would be pleased to help you at any time.'

———

George looked overjoyed to see him.

'Thought something happened to you, boss.'

'Had a detour, George.'

'Right you are. How did it go?'

'We are out.'

'Out?'

'Out. We have just got to hang about for three years.'

'Three years. I'll be dead by then.' He grinned.

'I doubt it.'

'So what's the deal?'

'The mob's bought us. Over three years.'

'HP?'

'Kind of.'

'How much did you get? Mucho denarii?'

'Mucho.'

'Lovely.'

'Anyway, what about the burglary?'

'Sorted. Coroner's report in a couple of weeks. The Old Bill says it's a formality. We don't even have to show up.'

'Good.'

'We were bloody lucky.'

Peter grimaced. 'That had occurred to me.'

'I've had four different alarms put in, so there is no way those bastards can get in now. I've also taken the liberty of bunging the Police Benevolent fund a couple of gorillas, so if the bell goes ding-a-ling, expect the cavalry.'

Peter laughed. 'You better remember all the passcodes or they'll be around here sooner than you think.'

'286, 386, 486, 586.'

'George, you'll be a programmer yet.'

'I am. I'm learning C.'

'You're a head case. You know that?'

George grinned and pointed a thick digit at Peter. 'Someone's got to back you up. I'm just watching your arse.'

Peter looked at the old man. George was packed with the energy of a youth but filled with all the experience of the years.

'We're a team, George. I know it. I know you know it. Wherever it is this is going, it's good to have you along.'

George smiled. 'And with a bit of luck we're going to be scot free and happy as Larry.'

'Just thirty-six months to go.'

'Thirty-six months, it's a cakewalk.'

———

Peter couldn't sleep. He had adjusted to American time and now he was wide awake in the middle of the night. His mind wandered aimlessly, jumping from thought to thought. He had fallen far in a short time and become rich, but none of the upside meant much. Nothing was of interest to him while he was trapped.

———

'Jolly good,' said Mojo-Smith, his face inflating into a rare beaming smile. 'Three years. Excellent.'

'I expected that would please you.'

'Pleased, yes, an apt word. Very pleased indeed. So you must have been well remunerated.'

'Okay. I suppose. I just need to get to enjoy it.'

'I should expect you will not have many problems on that score. Even retired, you will be very valuable to all parties.'

'To you perhaps, but to them I might become a significant liability at some point, regardless of whether they found out about our little relationship.'

Mojo-Smith's head bobbed for a moment in thought. 'I would expect, afterwards, that a retainer would give them a security that would reassure them. Perhaps you should cultivate a lifestyle that would suggest a quiet neutral attitude to the future. It might also be a good idea to fade out in a planned manner. No rude changes of state.'

'Maybe I should join the priesthood?'

'That's exactly what you shouldn't do.'

'Okay. I'll buy a castle and never come out.'

'That is certainly an alternative. Perhaps a move to a foreign location for a few years of sabbatical. New Zealand comes highly recommended.'

'Bloody Hell, New Zealand. There's only grass and sheep in New Zealand.'

'Nonetheless, a reassuringly distant location.'

'Not much better than the Falklands.'

'You might consider continuing to work for your new partners.'

Peter grimaced. 'Forever and ever? I wouldn't fancy my long term chances of survival, somehow. I expect they would love it, but it's very low on my wish list. The people give me the creeps.'

'You seem to have become important very quickly and I can't imagine that you will be able to make yourself unimportant as fast.'

'Irrelevant would be better,' he mused. 'Unimportant could be dangerous.'

'Quite so,' agreed Mojo-Smith characteristically. 'The trouble is, one man's asset is another's liability. While the debtor thinks he's a creditor, everything will operate smoothly.'

'Yes, if I follow that correctly. As long as they don't find out about us, it should pan out.'

'It may be a good job that you have friends in high places.' Mojo-Smith smiled.

'Is that you or someone else I don't know about?'

'Possibly.'

'Well, either way, I hope if it ever comes to it, that will be the case. I may need some heavyweight help.' Peter studied Rodney's face intently for reassurance.

'It has to be said,' Mojo-Smith looked reflective, 'that I can only act within my powers. With those that I am granted, it must be understood that they apply only to the world within which we operate. Outside that arena, we do not exist and cannot and will not try to influence anything. Our actions cannot be seen to intrude into the normal world, as what we do and how we operate are unacceptable, against the basic principles of the very powers we serve. In certain instances this means that we may be powerless to help no matter our feelings or obligations.'

'Run that by me again.'

'It is difficult for me to be more specific.'

Peter smiled sarcastically. 'I know that, but try.'

'If you were to be caught robbing a bank, we would be unable to help you. If on the other hand you were caught inside someone else's house in the course of our investigations then it would be most unlikely that anything would come of it.'

'I take it all this works on the basis of common sense and which way the wind is blowing at the time.'

Mojo-Smith looked blankly at him. 'Life and eventualities are always more complicated than we can possibly make allowances for. Therefore common sense is always the ultimate recourse. The American services would put it all in an employment contract, classify it and then go back on it when they needed to.' He grinned evilly for a moment, then his face became stern. 'Never forget, always be prudent and always be precious. That is the key.'

'Precious.'

Smith smiled again and nodded. 'Precious.'

'I see.'

'Precious,' he repeated, biting the word sharply.

Peter smiled. 'I'll try.'

Mojo-Smith nodded. 'Indeed.'

Chapter Eight
LAST EXIT TO DOCKLANDS

There was a knock at George's door. He opened it to two bible-holding men dressed in black.

'What can I do for you boys?'

The foremost barged forwards, bowling George over onto his back. They dashed in and slammed the door behind them. The first pulled a pistol and as George rose, bent down over him.

'Just do as we say and you won't get hurt,' he said, pointing the gun at his chest.

George froze. 'Alright, alright, all my money's upstairs under the mattress.'

The thug prodded George with the barrel. 'We don't want your money. We want the backup tapes of your work's computer.'

'I ain't got them.' The man pressed the end of the pistol hard into George's chest bone. He groaned in pain.

'Where are they then?'

'I don't know.'

'Get up,' said the second one.

George struggled to his feet shakily. They pushed him into the parlour and shoved him down into an armchair.

'Look,' said the first, passing the gun to his fellow, 'my friend here is a bit trigger happy, but I'm a reasonable sort of fellow.' He fixed George with his black beady eyes. 'Just answer a few questions and we won't hurt you . . . ' He smacked him round the head with the bible. 'Any more . . . Get it? Where are the backup tapes?'

'I don't know.'

He hit George across the face with the book again. 'Wrong answer,' he sang. 'What are the passwords to the office alarms and where are the door keys?'

'I've got keys but not the alarm numbers. Only the boss has got the numbers.' He was hit again and his nose began to bleed.

'Look,' said the man with the pistol, 'go upstairs and search it. I'll show the old man my game.'

George's tormenter threw the book down and walked out.

'My name's Fred,' said the gunman, dropping five bullets out of the handgun, 'and this is a real weapon, not a toy. It wants to know where the tapes are and you are going to tell it.' He spun the chamber. 'Click,' he said, 'and maybe boom.' He sat down in the other armchair. 'Well?'

'I don't know, I really don't know. If I knew I'd tell, I'm not stupid.'

Fred spun the cylinder again. 'You better be lucky old man,' he said slowly, pulling the trigger.

Georges face widened with fear as the hammer pulled back. Fred's smile grew. There was a sharp metallic snap. 'Lucky fellow.'

George clutched his chest and stumbled to his feet with a gasp. 'Heart, me heart' he croaked. He tottered heavily onto the fireplace bracing himself with his left arm.

Fred jumped up, ready to push the sick man back into the chair.

As he reached the balls of his feet, a golden flash sped across his field of view.

The end of the poker struck the side of his temple. The pistol went off with a loud bang as he fell like a sack of coal.

George grabbed the pistol, found the three bullets and loaded them. Fred lay quivering on the carpet, blood streaming from a deep gash on the side of his head. George heard the other man coming down the stairs.

'Shit, you idiot, you . . . ' The door swung open. There was an instant of recognition as he saw the old man aiming at him. He started.

George fired into his torso and then, pausing an instant, fired the other two rounds into the transfixed and collapsing figure.

George walked unevenly to the phone and dialled.

There was no reply from Peter's home phone. He checked the bodies; neither was breathing. He tried Peter's car phone, but it was not switched on. He tried again ten minutes later but to no avail. Perhaps they had paid a visit to him too.

He pulled out his little book and dialled another number.

'I'm sorry but the department is closed for the weekend. If however you have an urgent message please call the voice mail box on 0482 343212.'

George rang the new number and left a message. 'This is George from Online Data; I've got two dead geezers laid out in my house. The address is 42a Wordsworth Rd, E11. I'm not sure, but my boss Peter Talbot may be in trouble too, so look out for him first.'

———

Peter was dreaming about Mojo-Smith. They were meeting at the Ludgate Cellars. Peter knew that every word that Smith uttered meant something and that however convoluted and hidden, there would be a message attached.

'Where is the point in talking plainly when it is a deeper understanding that is needed? If I had the desire to be bold how could it possibly be compatible with my role?'

Peter began to realize from within the dream that something was wrong with his slumber. There was a roar and a shaking around him. He felt wet around the face. A throbbing pain soon joined his increasing consciousness and then he began to feel he was somewhere strange, dark and claustrophobic.

He was immobilized and his mouth was closed with something. Waking, it seemed that he must be in the boot of a car, but how did he get there?

He head ached, pulsing beneath a heavy pall of congealing blood on his face. From a faint tingling sensation and a warmth he associated with falling down as a little child, it felt like he might still be bleeding.

He could hear nothing except the road noise and from the smooth undeviating path of the vehicle he guessed they must be on some sort of motorway.

The last thing he could remember was Mojo-Smith. What had happened in between then and now? How long was it? From the pull of his clothes on his body, it seemed he was wearing a suit jacket. He moved in the restricted space, confirming its edges. When he had seen Mojo-Smith, he had been wearing a jumper, a gesture to try and be less formal. At the very least, now must be the next day, but perhaps it was some other time altogether. Whatever had happened, he was obviously in deep trouble.

Peter tried to work his hands and legs free, but they seemed to be trussed together with some sort of tape. If it had been rope he could have slipped his arms out with ease. It was crudely wrapped but it stuck unremittingly to his skin. If he could just work one of his hands out, he could get it off. Then he could start having a go at releasing the boot catch, but there was no give to the bonds.

Without warning he woke again. He had not noticed any faintness coming on, he had merely passed out for a moment. This time he felt stronger but still his bindings had no play. The direction of the car shifted and he was tilted left, then right and rolled forward further into the boot. He pressed uncomfortably against the forward bulkhead and then tumbled back as the car sped up again. The road began to twist and turn, throwing him helplessly around. He struggled with the fastenings, feeling limp and useless. Time was clearly running out. As he struggled his mind sped through anything that might help him and when the possible was exhausted, the impossible was considered for fleeting desperate moments. The car moved onto rougher ground and travelled at a slower, bumpier pace. His efforts became more frantic but it was to no avail.

His old trainer pointed to the ring where two young fighters danced.

'Look,' he said, pointing at the taller, 'he's lost, he's gone blind. He's thrashing out in the hope of catching a lucky one. He's given up on his mind and he's hoping his heart will find the spot. You can't expect luck to give you the punch.' He pointed at his head. 'It all comes from here.' As if by magic, the smaller fighter sprung forward and hit his opponent square on the nose. A moment and a splash of blood later and the referee jumped forward and stopped the bout. The trainer shoved Peter with glee. 'See. Remember that! Don't go blind. Rage doesn't get you any-where, except out of it.'

Peter lay back and took a long drawn deep breath through his nose. He had to wait for an opening and then act. If he didn't get the opening, then that was that. If it came, he had to be fit for it.

The car stopped and for a time there was silence. He thought he could hear the sound of metal doors opening and a moment later the car started up again and pulled slowly ahead. The sound of large roller doors was louder and from the echo he guessed he was now within a large empty warehouse building.

The boot opened and the light blinded him. His legs were freed and he was dragged out of the car and bundled across a clicking concrete floor. He struggled to see but his eyes screwed up with searing pain. Then just as they started to become accustomed, his manhandlers flung him through a doorway into the darkness of a small windowless room. The door was slammed shut and he could hear the sound of bolts being closed. He moved toward the door which let a small stream of light in at the bottom and touched its cold steel surface with his face.

He groaned. 'What now?'

Through the faint glimmer he could see the edges of his small confines, a tiny storage space with wooden floors. The walls seemed bare, but he begin carefully moving along them, hoping to find something useful. Halfway along the back wall his prayers were answered. A nail, a small jutting edge sticking from the surface, rubbed against his arm. He fell to his knees and twisted his head, trying to see it in the gloom. It was too dark, but with his face he searched it out. He stood up and pressed his taped wrists against it and ran them up until the edge reach the tape wrapped around them. He worried and worked at the interface of flesh and adhesive, trying to catch the head of the nail and then tear into the bonding.

How long would it be before they returned? Any moment they might come back and kill him where he stood. He snagged his flesh but in doing so ripped a tiny piece of the tape. He lined it up again, running the rusty metal painful across the now bleeding cut, riding up a small notch of the tape.

The head gripped and he pulled and twisted it under the glued layers. His body was sweating profusely and he began to soak. His arms were wracked with pain from the straining unnatural contortions. They demanded that he drop his stance, but that would only lose the nail's cutting position. He tried to breathe slowly but the tension began to make him suck heavily through his nose, which felt congested and inadequate.

He tried not to pull too hard, as he feared he could rip the nail from its hole or crumple the tape and harden it with corrugations. His jacket restricted his movement, the cuffs further complicating the operation. He began to ease the tape out further in small tugs, cutting it little by little, slowly prizing the glued surface away from his skin. A small pocket of cut and warped tape formed and by running the protrusion back and forth he opened it up along a further length. The nail-head snagged then snapped out of the cutting channel.

He cursed. He lined his wrists up again and ran the nail head along the edge. It slipped out of the end and he realized it was cut. He exploited the tear, millimetre by millimetre opening a flap that ran along the line of his right arm.

The temptation to try and wrench himself free became too great and he began to twist his arms. His jerks became more desperate as he felt a change in its grip on his wrists. The tape gave and came away, tearing at his skin, ripping his hairs from their roots. It glued to itself, becoming a cable attached only to the back of his left hand and the side of his right.

He continued to wrench his hands in a scissor movement until with a sudden yank, his right arm pulled out. Putting his hands to his face, his right hand pulled his mouth to one side as he scratched with his left to lift a corner of his gag. His face was slippery and hot, covered in sweat, grime and blood. At last he picked out an edge and with a yank ripped it off his face. He felt an inrush of air into his mouth as he gasped in with pain and relief. Now at least he could respond. He took his jacket off and slid down the wall to the floor, trying to clear his mind.

'Calm and objective, calm and objective,' he repeated. He pulled the tape from his left hand, still clinging tenaciously to the back of his left wrist and threw it to the floor. 'Bastard,' he cursed under his breath. Ripping from his skin hurt more now it was no longer a mortal enemy.

The floor, unlike the outside area, was made up of old splintery wooden boards, saturated with engine oil that had dried into them. He went to the door and listened. He couldn't hear anything, but it felt as if someone was out there. He put some weight on the door with his shoulder and there was no give or sign that it might yield to some greater force.

He remembered the hollow rattle from the right corner of the room as he had moved around in search of something sharp. He returned and found the spot again with his feet. He bent down.

A board was loose, the nails that once held it down no longer sunk into the batons below. Peter levered it up with trembling fingers and pushed it quietly to one side. He probed the hole. There seemed enough room for him to squeeze down into it. Reaching in, he could feel no end to the gap. He lowered his feet in and then his body. Lying like a corpse in a coffin, he pulled the board in on top. There was a chance that if they found the room empty they might not find his hiding place. However slim the chance, it was a ruse worth playing. He imagined they would be back soon. With difficulty, he began to roll over onto his stomach. There was only an inch or two of clearance on any side.

Rubble in the run under the floor boards stuck into him as he eased forward. It was such a restricted space he gained only an inch or so of ground with each effort. There was dry warmth in the tight passageway and an airless heavy scent of grime. He twisted carefully around the sharp spike of a jutting nail. Getting back, if he needed, would be very difficult; he had travelled his own length at about a foot a minute and reversing would be much slower.

He pushed his right arm out but felt nothing in his way. Surely the course had lead under the wall. At least he was going to be able to get far enough away to make it hellish for them to come after him without tearing up the floor. He pulled himself further along on his elbows. It felt as if the run was becoming tighter, or perhaps he was tiring.

The tunnels lead on and every small movement was taking him away from his captors. He came to a t-junction, down which he could feel the faintest of drafts. He rested for a moment; the breeze was coming from the right. He examined the right branch with his hand to gauge if he could make the turn. It was going to be difficult.

He put his hands up into the gap and pushed forwards with his feet, jamming the bottom of his torso on the left wall and his ribs on the angle of the bend. He bent as much as he could in the middle and pushed with his feet. His chest stuck into the sharp corner of the turn which snagged on the button of his shirt. He pushed harder, trying to force himself through. The shirt tore and by wriggling as much as he could from side to side he slipped further round. The corner now pressed into his stomach. His chest burnt with pain but he was round.

He crawled forward, exploring further with his hand. The tunnel was now higher, a cavity running unevenly up a wall to a point above his reach. Surely now at least he was safe.

Both sides of the channel were wall and unless they came after him down the very same route, they would never find him. He started to see details of the course he was crawling down. Ahead, slightly to the right, he could see a shaft of light. He smiled to himself; the light was becoming brighter as he edged along. He could see that there was a small unobstructed aperture the size of which was hard to judge. His head reached it and he rested, looking out onto the derelict floor of an abandoned office. The smooth-edged gap, where an air vent must have been, seemed tantalizingly large.

He thought for a moment. He could go back and explore the other fork and come back and try to go through if he found no other escape. That would be exhausting. He could just lie there entombed, which would be pointless, or he could take a risk of getting stuck by trying to force himself through the tiny hole. He decided to give it a try.

The gap was a rectangular space with no sharp edges. It was just a little bigger in area than his head. He poked his face through and sniffed the fresh air. He ducked in again and pushed out his arms. With his head, arms and neck out, he braced himself on the outside of the wall, his shoulders lightly pushing against the inside sides of the space. He arched his shoulders in, then pushed. He needed a couple of inches, maybe just one.

He breathed out and pushed again, squeezing himself into the gap. If he got stuck now it would be almost impossible for him to breathe. He felt a hot flush on his face and he started to shake. His shoulders and chest moved slowly onwards, a hard constriction banding his torso. He gasped a little breath, his lungs beginning to burn. He panted out all his remaining breath and pushed again, moving with a tiny jolt onward until his ribs were suddenly clear.

Peter gasped sharply and began to cough. He lay still, half out of the wall. The dilapidated office space seemed a welcome place. Peter pulled himself out, slowly easing his waist through, losing his trousers in the process. He stood up, exhausted, and pulled them up from around his knees. He brushed himself down and straightened up. His chest bled from deep grazes, as did his head and arms.

He went to the window and looked out.

'Fuck,' he muttered. Across the field about a half a mile away was what looked like his old flying club. Someone had taken him to a disused part of it, an empty hanger where no one came by from one year to the next. He opened a window and climbed out. He could see the shuttered door he had heard earlier. He moved quickly around the building. There was no cover, just acres of flat ploughed fields. No trees, no hedges, just an unforgiving wasteland of tilled earth. His best route of escape was across the grass to the flying club offices. He stood against the wall of the building. If he ran he would get there faster, but he was not sure he had it in him. If he walked it might lose him the distance he would need to get there if he was spotted.

He started to walk, looking over his shoulder at the shuttered doors. He broke into a trot, realizing it was unlikely that anyone would be looking out of the small dirty window in the hangar part of the building. The lie of the airstrip was slightly downhill from this point and his jog soon broke into a run. Breathing soon became disrupted by the rhythm of his dash and the exhaustion of his limbs.

With three hundred yards to go, he saw a black Jaguar pull into the flying club's car park. It stopped sharply. He stopped running and looked. Two heavy figures got out. Peter looked around. They were between him and the club. Fifty yards to his right was a plane with someone in it. He turned and dashed to it. He saw the two figures jump back into the car and heard it start after him.

He leapt into the cockpit of the Cessna. A young woman looked up from a clipboard at him in shock.

'Get the fuck out,' he shouted at her, looking down for the keys. He started the engine running.

'What?'

'Get the fuck out.'

'But . . . '

He looked over his shoulder at the car speeding towards him. 'Shit, too late.' He hit the throttle.

The plane bounced along at a rapidly increasing speed and the car fell back as its occupants realized it couldn't stop him. The plane left the ground under its own acceleration as the realization dawned that he may as well have taxied it back to the club house as taken to the air.

The woman looked at him with a stunned expression. She swallowed heavily. 'What's going on?'

Peter looked over at the receding ground and put his harness on. 'It's a long story. To keep it short, I just escaped from some kidnappers. I hope you can land this thing.'

Her face went grey.

Peter registered her expression. 'Oh no,' he said.

'Oh yes,' she replied.

'Oh shit, you can't fly?'

She shook her head.

He looked down. 'Radio, what about radio?'

'The instructor's got the headset.'

'You're joking.' He looked out onto the patchwork of fields below. 'You've got to be joking.'

'No, why would I?'

'And you are sure you can't land?'

'It's my second lesson.'

'Oh God, I'm sorry.'

Peter banked the plane around, trying to locate the airfield again. 'I'll circle around, and see what comes up. I can fly, I've just never landed.' He looked at the dials. 'There's not much gas.' He saw something move near the ground. 'Oh, this may be interesting.'

'What is it?'

'A helicopter.'

'Maybe they can help us down?'

'Hopefully.' He looked at her. 'We need all the help we can get.'

'You look in a bad shape.'

He laughed crazily. 'I feel great; my blood must be pure adrenaline by now.'

The helicopter appeared beside them. She screeched and pulled her controls, yanking them into a loop.

Peter yelled with surprise, rolling them out as they hung upside down.

'They had a shotgun,' she shouted at him. 'He was pointing it at me.'

'Where are they?' said Peter looking around, thoroughly disorientated.

'Behind us.'

'Where?'

'Back there.'

'Okay, we are going to have to take a few risks.'

She nodded her head. 'I have a choice?'

He pushed forward on the stick, putting them into a dive. 'I'm going to fly up and down the motorway, maybe the police will notice, then I'm going to try and land somewhere flat. I've done four hours by the way and I play flight sims.'

She smiled weakly, bracing herself. 'Oh good, that's alright then.'

'I'm Peter,' he said, smiling at her as well as he could.

'Cindy.'

'Where are they now?'

She turned around in her seat. 'Back quite a way. In fact, they look like they are holding off.'

'Any idea which motorway this is?'

'M11, maybe . . . maybe M25.'

'Okay, I'm bringing her down to a couple of hundred feet. Let's attract some attention.'

'No. Land quickly and get it over with! I don't want to crash into a pylon.'

He looked at her. 'You sure?'

'Yes, let's find a big empty spot. We will do it together.'

Peter winced. 'Okay, you're the boss.'

'There,' she said, pointing to the right at a huge field. 'Land there!'

Peter throttled back. 'Going to come down real gentle and taxi it up to the gate.'

Cindy put the flaps out. 'We need these.'

'Oh yes, good idea.'

The ground approached as they both held their sticks, flying into the vast field of spring wheat.

'Down a bit, down a bit!' she prompted.

'Okay, okay,' he muttered.

'Nearly there.'

Suddenly the ground rushed up and there was a loud bang and jolt, then another and a lesser followed by the rattle of wheels.

'YES!'

'Wow,' she yelped.

Peter looked over his shoulder. 'Is our friendly chopper still back there?'

'Can't see it.'

'That was amazing, couldn't have done it without you.' He steered with his feet.

'What are you going to do now?' she asked.

'Get to a call box.'

'I'll come with you.'

'What?'

'My blood is pure adrenaline too.'

'No,' he snapped. 'You go the other way. The guys with the gun are after me, not you.'

'I'm not going out there on my own.'

Peter pulled the throttle out and pressed on the brakes. 'Are you a sucker for punishment?'

She turned up her nose in a grin. 'Maybe, let's go.'

He switched the engine off. 'Better get going then, captain.' As the noise of the prop died, it was replaced by another. He opened the door and looked up at the helicopter, five hundred or six hundred feet above. He jumped out and made for a gate in the hedge thirty yards ahead. He found that he was limping heavily and that Cindy was well ahead of him. She cleared the barrier with a vault and turned, watching him and the helicopter above.

'You alright?' she shouted.

He didn't answer. He climbed the fence awkwardly. 'What are they doing up there?' he puffed.

'Circling.'

'You don't have to do this,' he grunted, jumping the short way down.

'Chance of a lifetime.'

They jogged down the road towards what they thought was the nearest house. The chopper rotors thundered ominously behind them.

'What's he playing at?' he shouted.

'They're following us.'

'I would have never guessed.'

'Well?'

'I don't like it.'

'Car coming,' she called, starting to wave her hands.

A black Jaguar rounded the bend. Peter sprang across at her and pushed her into the hedge away from its path. The car screeched to a halt. They straightened up, the sound of the chopper growing suddenly much louder. The car blocked the road and two men jumped out. Peter and Cindy were surrounded, caught between the two burley figures in front, flanked by the high hedge and cut off by the helicopter poised behind them hovering thunderously, just above the line of their heads.

The two men approached. The larger one on the right waved his hand for them to come forward. 'Get in the car.'

Peter looked at Cindy, whose stance looked suddenly strange. 'Stand back; this is nothing to do with you!'

She leapt forward with a cry, poking the larger man in the eyes with straight fingers. Her right palm shot under the chin of the second, who fell backwards, prostrate. The first man was screaming, holding his face. Peter hit him hard on the crown of his head, feeling as he did so a shooting pain up his fist. The crouching figure fell forwards. The sound of the helicopter behind them changed.

'In the car.' Not looking back, he jumped awkwardly over the bonnet, past the open door and into the driver's seat. The keys were in the ignition and it started with a single turn. Cindy was instantly in the passenger seat.

'Wow' she yelped, 'wow, wow!'

He was reversing up the road, swerving unstably from side to side. 'Who are you?' he shouted trying not to plough into the hedge.

'No one.' There was a moment of awkward silence. 'They're up again, high,' she said, craning her head forwards under the rake of the windscreen. He reached a t-junction at the end of the lane, swung into it backwards and then sped on forwards.

'Where the fuck are we?'

'Don't know.'

He slowed down a little. 'Better find out.'

They flashed past a signpost. 'Nazing, 1 mile.'

'Where the hell's that?'

'I don't know. What are we going to do next?'

'We are going to drop you off at a police station.'

'I don't like the sound of that.'

He looked across at her. 'Who the hell are you?'

'Just me, why?'

'Why?' He shook his head. 'Why? I give up.'

'Sounds like a pretty stupid question to me.'

'Okay, okay, I'm heading into London. I've got to meet up with some police-type people who will help me.'

'What's it all about?' she asked.

'I'm Peter, I run a computer business. Any more than that and I'd be guessing.'

'Peter, you look pretty rough.'

He looked at her. 'Thanks. Considering, I'd say I'm doing pretty well.' They came to a junction.

'M25, Waltham Abbey, left.'

'Sounds good to me.' He pulled out.

'I think that helicopter's still back there somewhere, but I haven't seen it for a bit.'

They passed through Waltham Abbey. 'Last chance to get off.'

'No thanks.'

'Sure?'

'Absolutely.'

'Look, you did amazing back there, but you are at huge risk with me. Massive.'

She shook her head. 'I'll never get another chance of something like this happening to me again, will I?'

'And that's bad?'

'I do judo, karate, parachuting, diving, I even run marathons, but it's never real. You know, right on the real edge.'

Peter shook his head. 'You're mad. You could get killed.'

She bounced happily on her seat. 'Nothing like a bit of practical.'

'Just never say I didn't give you the option.'

'Don't worry, this is really living.'

They pulled onto the motorway. 'M25, M11 and into London,' he said.

'Put your foot down, Pete, this car's got twelve cylinders.'

'Jesus, you're totally barking,' he said, accelerating.

She laughed.

At 130 mph the Jaguar glided on the road, the light traffic seeming to evaporate before it. It hunkered down on the tight curves of the slip road onto the M11, taking the bends at sixty, like the carriage of a fairground ride. He powered out of the bend and accelerated back up to speed, reaching a magical equilibrium point when the route itself seemed to liquefy into a flowing, pulsating river of movement. Soon the motorway dwindled into feeder roads and terminated in the A12 where their progress was reduced to a crawl.

'So why would someone want to kidnap someone in computers? You a hacker or something like that?'

'I don't know and if I did, I'm not sure I'd say anyway.'

'Alright, be like that!' she goaded.

They crossed the Green Man roundabout and continued their slow passage through the outskirts. They pulled up on the front rank at a red light on Leytonstone High Road. A lorry pulled alongside then rolled forwards and across their path.

'Shit.'

There was a banging on the passenger door and a man pressed a sawn-off shotgun wrapped in newspaper against the window.

'Stay where you are,' said Peter. 'They want me.'

He put the car in park and left the engine running as he got out. The wagon started up again and rumbled on. The tall man signalled to him to move to the back of the car. He fixed the man's eyes and moved slowly. The next car back, a Granada, moved forward and the door swung violently open.

Cindy dived head first into the driver's seat; put the car into drive and pushed down on the acceleration pedal with her outstretched hand. The car lurched away.

The man ran forwards. 'Get in the car,' he screamed.

The passenger in the back was pointing a hand gun at Peter. As Peter made to get in, the tall man dashed forward and bundled him in. Peter snapped a glimpse of the Jaguar screeching unevenly into a side road. At least she had got away.

'What the fuck is this all about?' he shouted at them as the Granada sped quickly away.

'Make it easy on yourself and shut it.'

The man on the right stuck a gun in his side.

Peter wondered if he realized that if he shot him there he would also shoot his companion.

The driver in the front remained impassive and drove on at a calm pace through Leytonstone and into Stratford. It occurred to Peter that wherever they were taking him, they didn't care if he knew. That was ominous, very ominous.

The man with the revolver had a tense worried look, his face pock-marked, swollen and bright red. The tall man was a mean, vicious-looking character about Peter's own age with flat square features and tiny rat-like eyes set close together. Even in their respectable suits they looked like desperately dangerous people.

The passage through Stratford was unimpeded. Not a half chance, not a glimmer of an opportunity presented itself for any escape. If he could, he would jump from the car, whatever the speed, but it did not seem that he would get the chance.

'Whatever you're being paid, I'll double it.'

They remained impassive.

Peter scanned their expressions. 'What do you say?' They seemed to ignore him. 'Well, how much is this job worth to you, then? Come on, I'm sure I can make it worth your while to drop me off.'

'Not much point being rich if you don't get to spend it,' said the driver, looking into the mirror.

'Even less point dying poor.' Peter stared back. 'You people better be sure you're well connected.'

The driver looked away again. The car pulled off onto a slip road before the Bow flyover and headed for the Blackwell Tunnel. 'So where are you taking me?'

The tall man stuck the barrel of his paper-wrapped shotgun under Peter's chin and pressed it hard into his throat.

'Shut it! Just shut it!'

The driver spoke again. 'Just leave it out, alright? Co-operate and it'll save you some pain.'

Just before the tunnel they turned left, up a slip road. Turning right, the car headed down East India Dock Road, towards the City, then left into Docklands and down towards the embryonic office developments.

Peter tried to keep himself alert. They circled a great underground roundabout, reappearing into the light at another. As they went around it, Peter saw the sleek lines of a black Jaguar and realized as the Granada sped up that the driver had noticed it too.

'You better let me out here, she's with the Special Branch. It's only a matter of time before we'll be stopped.'

'Fuck,' muttered the driver, rounding a sharp corner to be confronted by a bus blocking the road. He pulled up sharply. There was a great jolt and a smashing sound as the Jaguar ploughed into the back. Peter shot forward into the empty front passenger seat. He grabbed the door handle and rolled out onto the road, dazed.

'You've just got to get up off the floor. Nothing else matters. Even if you fall again, just get up.'

'I won't get knocked down, don't you worry. He can't hit that hard.'

'Just remember, all right, get up, always get up.'

He stumbled to his feet. On the far side of the car he could see the worried man getting out and in the corner of his eye the driver stirring and a small crowd pouring off the bus. He turned away from the car and ran towards the crowd, his vision beginning to resolve.

The driver ran awkwardly after him. The worried man began to fire at the Jaguar that, having reversed back away, now charged towards him. There was a haze of screaming.

The windscreen holed and crazed. The twisted front end of the Jaguar smashed into the firing figure, crushing him into the car door and tearing it off its hinges.

Cindy jerked into reverse and swerved backwards, blood covering her blouse. She slumped onto her seat belt and the car careered out of control into a billboard.

Peter looked over his shoulder and saw the driver in pursuit. If the older man was still after him, he must have a gun and a very good reason. The straight road left him no cover and now he was starting to lose himself. His head swam, his mind drifted. A car blew its horn at him and swerved onto the pavement to miss running him down. The noise pulled him from his daze.

There was a driveway, to his right, leading up to what looked like an embankment. He swung right, looking back again to see his enemy still no closer. The drive ended at the river's edge and was flanked on both sides by high chain link fences. There was only one way to go, a ladder to the foreshore. He didn't hesitate. The tide was out and the swim across would, even in his sorry state, give him a better chance than a bullet.

He clambered, almost free falling down the rungs onto the reeking stony beach. Looking round for a fleeting moment, he grabbed a four foot stave from a pile of rotting iron. It was heavy but comforting. He ran down the beach towards the tip of the island, with the Greenwich Naval College on the far bank. There might be a way up, further along the shore; the swim would be a last resort.

He had made quite a lead on his chaser, who was now just a small figure following behind. Peter rounded a bend and looked with horror at the mud flats before him. Stray flotsam peppered the nebulous way ahead but it would take him careful minutes to pick his way across and he didn't have the necessary time. Flattening himself against a jutting concrete pier support he waited.

He began to hear the heavy cautious footsteps of the driver approaching, scrunching across the stones with an uneven tread. Whatever the reason they wanted him, it must be very special. Surely the whole place would be swarming with police soon. He wondered what had happened to Cindy. He prayed she had got away unhurt.

His mind snapped back to the present as the footsteps were on him. He jumped out and swung the stave at his hunter.

The driver flinched back, shielding his head with his hands. The bar struck his arms and sent him, with a pained yell, spinning back onto the shingle. The pistol flew into the air, landing with a hollow clatter on a sheet of corrugated iron lying on the mud thirty feet away. The driver scrambled up and tumbled towards his gun, grunting in pain and fear. Peter regained his balance and surged forward, only to pull back as the driver, lunging into the mud, sunk immediately to his knees and then with a struggle to his waist. He tried to turn towards solid land, but in the act of moving was already buried up to his chest in the grey, foul slime.

'Help me!' he squealed, his face distorted with terror.

'How?' He looked at the driver, now submerged to his chin.

The driver laughed crazily. 'I can't feel the ground. Oh God, oh God, please don't let me sink.'

There was a small ripple on the river and a tiny wave broke on the shingle a foot below. The filthy Thames tide was coming back. Peter looked around for something he could throw to him. As his eyes searched, he saw a black dot climbing down the ladder.

He looked down at the driver. 'You better hope your friend will help you, or you're fucked. Then again, maybe it's a policeman.'

Peter turned and ran to the next mud bank. If he could clear the eighty yard stretch, it was all stone beaches as far as he could see. He hopped from stone, to metal sheet, to tyre, to old door, picking his way unsteadily over the evil-smelling mire. The mud might be an inch deep or ten feet. He couldn't tell. The flotsam acted as his stepping stones, slowly sinking islands in a sea of fathomless slime.

He hobbled onto the beach and trotted awkwardly over a raised slipway and out of sight of the driver and the other figure. The tide seemed to be coming in faster. He scrambled over a broken stretch of concrete blocks towards another slipway where children stood and played by the murky water's edge. This must be a way off the foreshore.

He shook himself to hold back the light-headedness that swept over him again. Catching his breath, he looked across the water to Greenwich and its great Naval College. In his concussed state, the middle ground of the river was shrunken and the white stone carcasses loomed like cliffs.

The children stared aghast as he stumbled by and up the long ramp to the road. They began to follow him.

'Are you alright, mister?' said one of them in a broad cockney accent.

Peter stopped and looked at the kid. 'There's been an accident. Get to a phone and call the police. There is a man trapped in the mud back there.'

'Come on,' cried the little boy, waving his right arm in a sabre-brandishing gesture, 'let's go, there's been a massive accident.' He ran off, making a siren noise. 'Nah, nah, nah, nah.'

On the road was a sign stating 'Greenwich foot tunnel' and an arrow pointing along a lane. He floated through a wooded park to a domed building and drifted down a huge spiral staircase to a passageway far below. The tunnel rang to the sound of clicking heels and the distant distorted reverberations of chattering voices. He re-emerged half-conscious at the other side. In front of him was the towering clipper, Cutty Sark. He looked right to the Gypsy Moth yacht. He smiled, as standing beside the boat, looking bored, was a reassuring figure. He stumbled over to him. The police officer peered at Peter from underneath the brim of his helmet.

Peter's eyelids trembled. 'You don't look old enough.'

The policeman caught him as he fell.

———

The nurse didn't answer, she smiled and said nothing.

He felt rather silly sat in the small hospital bedroom all alone watching television. His head was bandaged, he felt pain but he didn't feel ill.

'I need a phone,' he had said before the nurse took his temperature, but she had just looked at him kindly, checked the thermometer and walked off.

Without warning the air seemed to change and he could sense someone was about to enter the room. Moments passed. There was the sound of movement at the door and Mojo-Smith entered.

Smith winced. 'You have been in the wars.' He closed the door behind him.

Peter switched the TV off.

'Cindy, the girl with me?'

'Intensive care, I'm afraid,' he said gravely.

'Oh,' he said sitting up a little. ' Bloody hell. Is she going to be okay?'

'I'm told she is very poorly.' Mojo-Smith tilted his head regretfully.

'Is she going to make it?'

'It's not for me to say. Is she one of your people?'

He slumped back. 'Accidental hitchhiker.'

Mojo-Smith looked puzzled. 'Really?' He shook his head. 'How peculiar.' He paused, taking a deep breath. 'What do you know about this furore?'

Peter sat up again. 'Absolutely nothing. I've racked my brains, but nothing clicks. I can't think they were sent from MonoLog. They don't feel like the sort of people they would use. It seems, well, too British. Apart from the Yanks, I don't actually have any dealings with anyone up to that kind of thing.'

'Not directly, you mean.'

Peter shrugged, making his head twinge. 'That's the problem, with my customer base, it could be almost any-one, for any reason and I'd know nothing about it.'

'Your oppo has been causing a fair amount of carnage too.'

'Oh shit,' Peter exclaimed. 'Is he okay?'

Mojo-Smith's face tightened into what might pass for a tortured smile. 'In rather better shape than you, I'm happy to say.'

'Thank God for that. What happened?'

'They wanted him to turn over your backups and let them into your office.'

'He doesn't have the backups.'

'They, it would seem, didn't know that.'

'And?'

Mojo-Smith looked at some distant building out across the Thames. 'Apparently age can be an advantage, particularly when the young underestimate.'

'Well?'

'He put the first into a coma with a brass poker and there he still remains. Then he proceeded to shoot the other dead with his friend's revolver. Quite an achievement, even for an ex-para. Decorated, your man, did you know that?'

'No, I didn't.'

'Quite a colourful career, one way and another.'

'I can imagine, but the main thing is, is he alright?'

'Cuts and bruises, nothing to mention compared to what the opposition received.'

'So what can you tell me about all this bloody mess?'

'I expected you might be eager for a few answers.'

'It will be a lot simpler than combing the system for clues. What can you tell me?'

Mojo-Smith walked across to the window that looked beyond the river onto the city. 'A little tale needs first to be told. It is a story of a man, his job and a slope; it's a study of incompatibilities and greed.'

He stood silent for a time. 'There was a criminal, a simple man, tired of going to prison. One day a realization struck him. There must be easier ways of making a living than stealing things of intrinsic value. If only he could steal things of no value, that somehow could be worth a great deal to others. A piece of jewellery might only gain him ten pounds, but to get it, he would have to break into a house with occupants and risk a long sentence. Although it might be priceless to the owners, the money he would receive did not reflect that.

'After years of,' Mojo-Smith grinned to himself, 'error and trial,' he was well known to the establishment; every mistake might cost him a long stretch in squalor. Then it occurred to him, perhaps paper would be better. He could break into an office and take their paper, or make copies. So long as he had a customer for the information, the pay might be very good and the risks rather low. So inspired, off he went to the first corporate security fair he could find. Lo and behold, he soon came across an old acquaintance from his years of incarceration, now a self-styled consultant. So, he became a new member of a little ring of office thieves, experts in commercial espionage. They were a proficient, professional group in constant demand.

'Then one day, they hit the big time.

'An agency, tired of using good men for such degrading work, decided to subcontract it out to people who are more suited to such petty activities. They were only little tasks, but nonetheless squalid and unattractive to a civil servant. The younger generation does not consider it fitting to their station. A good man, after all, does not join a service to become embroiled in such wretched things. What better solution than to pay professionals?'

'Are we talking about your organization?' asked Peter.

'No.' Mojo-Smith looked back to him with a sour glance. 'We are more cerebral and, if I may suggest, more practical.'

He looked away again. 'The professionals performed well, excelling themselves. They became a useful and oft-used tool. Then, as is common with human ingenuity, a good tool is used for other purposes. The agency approached them with work of another kind. Someone had become particularly awkward and he needed to be shown the error of his ways. An unpleasant duty but a well-rewarded one. Being men of the world and hardly frails, they duly obliged and augmented their work with such acts of violence. Then one day, an unfortunate individual died. Our band of freelancers were concerned, murder was surely another matter. But no, their commissioners considered it inevitable. The beating, as meant, was blamed on another competing group of extremists and the matter passed.

'So the work continued, a litany of burglary and beatings. Then, one day, out of the blue, they were offered an assassination. Without hesitation they took the job. They were now indeed playing in the big league. This kind of work paid excellent money, an order of a magnitude greater than anything they had earned before. What was more, surely they were now immune from the law itself. No one could possibly touch them. They were executioners, by decree.

'However, the supply of such work is not so great and its value is representative of its rarity. If only the supply was greater. Perhaps private enterprise might be the solution. A means of safe communications had been found to enable them to undertake an expansion of this trade so little seemed in their way.'

Peter looked pained, 'Ouch, that's me, isn't it?'

Mojo-Smith looked at him. 'Yes. Of course, the agency was practically powerless; not only had it lost many of its skills to an outside concern but it had no way of keeping the activities of its mercenaries in check. It had been a long, gentle incline to such a precarious state. It had had both no authority to undertake such activities, or to authorize a third party to act so on its behalf in this way. Worse, it had no means to contain or eliminate the resultant problem. Slowly the problem became known in a broader sphere.

'Heads rolled and my little department was assigned the task to monitor, report and even act if there was a simple, tidy solution to be had. Meanwhile,' he said deliberately, 'for one of the gang's number, the man who wanted to steal paper rather than objects, only the thought of sanction had made any of the violence forgivable. He no longer needed money and had chosen to wash his hands of the darker side of their business. Now that his partners had taken action to expand their trade in death, he could bear it no more. He argued with them to stop, they should curb their greed. As one might expect, his opinion did not receive a good reception. He soon feared for his own safety. He prepared some insurance, a package of information that would destroy them all if anything became of him.

'Indeed, he was right, and something did happen to him, but he was unprepared for what they would do to insure their own safety. So they learnt of an uploaded file on the very system upon which they were plying their trade. It seemed that their partner could not remember the password; perhaps the trauma was too great. He died before he could, or perhaps would, recall it. At all costs they needed to erase the file. Perhaps it might be disclosed or broadcast from its resting place. So they only had one course of action: eliminate the system and all backups.' He looked piercingly at Peter. 'Illuminating?'

'What are we going to do about it?'

Mojo-Smith moved to the end of the bed, deep in thought. 'What are we going to do about it? That is a good question. You could confront them or negotiate.'

'Does that YOU mean me or us?'

Smith lifted Peter's clipboard and looked at it. 'Oh, according to this, YOU will be out of here very soon.'

'You mean me then.'

'Well . . . us, I propose.' He waved a bony finger at Peter. 'You in particular. We in general.'

'So, do you want me to confront or negotiate?'

'I will leave that up to you. Although they are currently attached to an agency, we and others consider them to be very unwelcome.'

'What do you want me to do?'

'Whatever you need to do, to continue.'

'What is that?'

He looked sternly at Peter. 'That is for you.'

'What is THAT.'

'The solution to the problem.'

'Solution?'

'Solution.'

'Kill them, you mean?'

'Solve does not necessarily mean kill.'

'Don't you have properly trained people to solve this sort of thing?'

'That is in fact the problematic dichotomy. Where would one find such a man?'

'But you think I can do it?'

Mojo-Smith hung back the clipboard. 'You and your friends have already killed three of them and critically injured another two. There are only another four, with one of them just a simple runner. I would suggest that you have already solved the bulk of the problem.'

'So you would like me to sort out three killers and their boy.' Peter laughed. 'I must be delirious.'

'The boy is of no matter.'

'And you want me to be your solution?'

'Our solution; I seem to recall they are particularly fixated on you this moment.'

Peter snorted. 'I'm going to need your help.'

'Within the powers.'

'What powers?'

'THE powers,' stressed Mojo-Smith.

'I can't say I'm motivated.' He slipped down into the bed. 'How bad are these people?'

'In the normal sense of that concept, I would say quite evil.'

'And my system gave them a chance to expand.'

'Yes.'

'So this whole thing is partly my responsibility.'

'Perhaps.'

'And you really think I'm the best person to straighten it all out.'

'Yes.'

'So I've two problems to sort out.'

'Please elaborate,' said Smith, perplexed.

'Online Data is Pandora's box and it's open. Nothing will put it all back. If I hadn't have done it, someone else would. If I stop it, someone else will start a new one.'

'Most probably.'

'So if we get past stage one, you are going to need a way to control the system. That means someone in control of it, which means someone like you and me. But no one can know, or it's back to square one.'

Mojo-Smith interlaced his fingers and bent them back, cracking his knuckles. 'That is a scenario.'

'So I am going to have to work that one out too.'

'If you feel it necessary.'

He studied the dried up spy-master, but his mystique was impenetrable. 'And this is sanctioned right up to the top?'

Mojo-Smith shook his head. 'Nothing is sanctioned. Loose ends are tied, that is all. It is a silent authority, not a resounding one.'

'I'm probably a gullible idiot, but I trust you.'

'Very good then.'

———

George looked well, his smiling head popped around the door.

'Wotcha,' he said, barging in. 'Are they looking after you properly?'

He sat down by the bed and dropped a box of chocolates on Peter's lap. 'I've got things sorted. We are going to move the kit and redirect the lines. Got an office lined up in Docklands where the lift won't go, unless it's booked in advance.'

Peter chuckled. 'And how are you, George? You've been in the shit too, I hear.'

'Mustn't grumble. They weren't nothing compared to the Bosch. I like our friends. Rang the number, spoke with Q and they fixed up all the mess. I haven't had to say a dicky bird to the Old Bill. A couple of lads in a van turned up a little later and redecorated the house. Service with a smile.'

'That's good, so long as you're alright.'

'No problem. I've got a soccer team from Securicor staying at the office. It's a bit steep, but it's a good idea till the move. So are we officially OHMS?'

'Nope, we're just precious, to quote your friend Q.'

'Oh well, never mind, least we are not going to end up in pokey.'

'We would be so lucky.'

———

The bouquets of flowers Peter had sent had been distributed around the ward. Even with an oxygen mask covering most of her face, Cindy looked ashen.

'They say you're making great progress. I knew you would, someone as strong as you.'

She nodded slightly.

'I don't know if anyone has told you, but you almost certainly saved my life.' He held her hand gently. 'I don't have any big words to say thank you, but when you are better I'd like to get to know you.'

She nodded and squeezed his hand weakly.

———

Two security men stood on the landing above and looked down at him.

'I'm Peter Talbot.'

George rounded the next landing above them. 'It's alright lads. Hello boss, come on up.'

When he walked into the office he noticed his desk had been replaced by a large walnut reproduction and his chair was now a great leather monstrosity.

'How much did that cost?' he asked involuntarily.

'About two hours. I thought you needed something of stature to go along with your black eye.'

Peter sat into the chair which gave, then bounced softly. 'Nice.' He pulled out a slip of paper Mojo-Smith had given him and dialled a number under an address. 'Gordon Dewson, please.'

'I'm sorry you have a wrong number,' said a male voice.

'It's Peter Talbot. Can you get him to call me on 01 222 8787.' He hung up.

'A cuppa?'

'Superb idea!'

The phone rang; it was Dewson.

'You want to talk with me, so I gather,' said Peter.

'Sorry, I don't know where you get that idea.'

'I'll rephrase that. You whacked me and had me locked up in a hanger in Essex, so you obviously want me for something. Right?'

'I don't follow.'

'You need to talk to me, because I have something you want. You want it very badly, bad enough to go to great lengths. If you don't talk, you won't get what you want. Understand?'

There was a long silence. 'Why don't we meet up?'

'When?'

'What's your fax number?' asked Dewson.

'222 7878.'

'I'll fax you where and when.'

'Good.'

———

About an hour passed until the fax appeared. On it was a diagram of an industrial estate. They were to meet in an alley between two buildings, at midnight.

George looked over his shoulder. 'A nice spot for a chinwag, I think not.'

———

He sat on the bonnet of his car, the headlights streaming down the alley. The dark passage was open at both ends and was accessed between two old warehouses. There was a skip full of printers waste and scattered along its length were crates holding the rubbish generated by the light industry that surrounded them. It was raining, a glittering stream of tiny dots filling the car's beam. George sat in the driver's seat with the engine running.

In front of him, covered by a cardboard box, sat a Claymore mine. Mojo-Smith had given it to him on his visit to his office. When remotely detonated it would spray two thousand ball bearings in a 120 degree fan and would destroy everything, animate or inanimate, in its path.

A large car pulled in at the other end of the alley. From the shape of its lamps he could tell it was a 7 series BMW. It stopped and three people got out. They moved into the white light.

Peter took the control box resting on his lap. He touched the side of it with his index finger to check the position of the safety catch, which was on. In his other hand was a pistol.

'Dewson,' he shouted. 'Tell your men to get back in the car.'

'We haven't come to talk,' Dewson shouted back. 'Come with us.'

Lights of a vehicle splashed onto the walls behind the Mercedes. George blew the horn and the car jerked back. Peter jumped off the bonnet as it snatched itself from under him, rolling head over heels and onto his feet. He heard shots but felt nothing, dashing forward to the immediate cover of the skip.

He had miscalculated. He hadn't expected a full on attack. He thought they'd at least try and talk first.

There was the crash of a violent collision, with crunching metal and shattering glass. George had reversed into the flanking vehicle.

Peter snatched a blurred glance at the Mercedes. Its engine revved and its tyres screeched as it pushed back onto the rammed target. A flurry of bullets rattled the side of the skip as he ducked behind it. He wanted to press the button on the mine but he was now directly in its firing line. Peter leant out and fired a snatched shot. The BMW's headlights blinded him and he felt a bullet whistle by his ear as he snapped back into cover. With his back turned to them and pressed against the steel of the skip, he watched George jump out of the driving seat.

'Bastards,' shouted George, a flare of a machine pistol erupting in front of him. His left hand went out as if to grasp the phantom magazine of a Sten gun. Glass shattered behind Peter as he turned out of safety and fired two shots indiscriminately. Their attackers had taken cover. He ducked back again. The far side door of the van George had rammed moved and Peter opened up on its cabin, firing into it, where someone might be. There was a cry and the door swung sharply open.

George knelt behind a metal cage filled with rusty piping. They looked at each other across the alley. George was behind the firing line. Sobbing started to come from the van behind them.

He pushed the pistol into his pocket and took the safety off the detonator. Peter pointed at his chest and then up towards George. He held his palm up with fingers out stretched. Pulling his hand back then pushing it forwards again with one less finger he counted down: four, three, two . . .

George leant out and opened up. The returning fire rounded on him. Peter sprang forward along the line of the wall. He felt the wrenching feeling in his right side of a sudden jolt. His knees buckled under him and he toppled forwards. Had he passed the Claymore? He tried to get up but just flopped back onto the wet tarmac. He groaned in agony and then, with a final effort, pressed the button.

There was a thunderous explosion, a great quake that shook the world. The air clapped them like giant hands; glass and debris bit their bodies in a vicious stoning. Behind them lay desolation, a burning torn wilderness of wet brick and burning metal.

Peter lay still. George jumped up and ran. He dropped to the ground and rolled Peter onto his back.

Peter coughed. 'I think they caught me,' he said, finding it hard to breath.

'You lie still,' said George, rolling him onto his side and crossing his legs. He pulled Peter's arm out, and rested his head on it. 'Don't move or it's no tea for you.'

'No tea?' He coughed, blood dribbling from the side of his mouth. He shivered. 'Do a runner with the money, George,' he whispered.

'Come on boss, leave it out. You hold on.' He laid his coat over him.

'You can get out.'

'You stay put, I'm getting help.'

'Just take . . . ' he coughed again.

George jumped up and ran as fast as he could to the car. He dived into the driving seat and reached for the phone. The yard lit up around him as car after car screeched in, blue lights flashing.

George dropped his Uzi and ran towards the police cars, waving his arms over his head. 'Ambulance, get a fucking ambulance.'

———

The Talbots sat on the front row of the chapel with George directly behind them. It was a small service, congregated by relatives that only got together at times of bereavement. Usually it would be a gathering to remember one of their own generation, not one so young. The Talbots were shocked, silently stricken with grief. Peter had everything; youth, health and success. A kind policeman had visited them and explained how his car had left the road on a tight bend and crashed into a tree. He had died instantly. He had such a fast car for someone so young.

A number of Americans were there and had offered them their condolences.

It was to be a cremation. Peter hadn't had a preference; he wasn't old enough to have even thought of such things.

After the service, George mingled with the small crowd of mourners. He walked over to a pale young woman in a wheelchair who was crying quietly to herself. A nurse had a comforting hand on her shoulder.

'Hello Miss, I'm George. You must be Cindy. Peter talked about you, you're some lady.'

Cindy sniffed. 'It's all these drugs they're giving me. They make me weepy.'

'Don't worry yourself, he's safe now.'

'Yes, I suppose so.'

Sandy nudged George on the arm. 'Hi, can I have a moment of your time?' They walked through a colonnade onto a gravel drive and across to a bench by some rose-bushes. She looked fetching in a mustard yellow and black suit. 'What lovely flowers,' she commented.

'Plenty of blood and bone, I bet,' smirked George darkly.

Sandy turned up her nose. 'Ooh, gross.'

'So what can I do for you?'

'Well, George, you must understand that even after such a tragedy, work must go on.'

George sat across the bench and interlaced his fat fingers. 'Indubitably.'

'Firstly I need to know, can you run Online Data, until we find a replacement for Peter?'

'As long as you need. I do all the system housekeeping and the maintenance, Peter handed all the day to day stuff over to me a long while back.'

Sandy smiled, cat-like. 'That's good, that's real good.'

'Fifty grand good?' enquired George.

Sandy hesitated. 'I would have to clear that.'

'That's fine. You see, I can run the shop single-handed. On the other hand, you might want to send someone high-powered over from HQ. Much more lucre though.

I would have to teach them the ropes and they'd probably need to keep me on anyway.'

'Sure, that could be true.' Sandy nodded. 'So you feel you want to stick around?'

'Why don't you stay for a few days and check me over? Monkey see, monkey do.'

Sandy pinched George's cheek. 'I might just do that.'

———

It had taken Cindy four months to feel good again. Recovery had been a slow process as she had wasted away in bed.

As soon as she could she had begun moving about, but it had been a long struggle to get to the point where she could go a whole day without needing to rest. Even so she hadn't regained her full strength but at least she felt in full command of her faculties. She sat back in her Peugeot 205 and waited.

It was a cold Saturday morning and her blanket didn't quite keep out the chill. A door slammed and drew her attention. Out of a nice new semi-detached house walked George. He opened his garage and reversed his Volvo onto the road.

Cindy started her car and threw the blanket aside, setting off after him. Soon they were on the M25 heading towards the Dartford tunnel. George was driving embarrassingly slowly and she found it extremely hard to stay far enough away, on the deserted carriage, to feel unobtrusive. She followed him from behind a lorry as they passed into the tunnel, staying at the toll until he was way ahead of her once more. He turned off onto the A2 and continued his stately progress.

The Volvo pulled off the motorway at Sittingbourne and drove cross-country. Down the winding lanes it was increasingly hard for her to follow without being seen. Obviously the old man wasn't concentrating or perhaps he was just toying with her. Cindy rounded a bend just in time to see the tail of the Volvo disappear down a wooded track. She stopped and waited a couple of minutes before turning into it. She rolled the car down the twisting uneven path for a quarter of a mile and then, amongst the trees she saw the outline of a building.

She cut the engine and got out to approach on foot. Working out her way ahead quickly, she moved using as much cover as she could. Obscured by the wood stood a large 1930's residence, set engulfed within the shady gloom of the trees. It looked as if it could have been plucked out of some fairy story, had it not been for the cheap red brick construction. She darted from trunk to trunk, closing in on the house. George's car was parked out front, empty. Everything lay silent. She made a dash for a shed set back from the left elevation. Peeping around, she could see no movement behind the windows.

She ran up to the main wall and looked in through the window. The lounge was empty, furnished in a tasteless but solid fifties style. On the floor sat a laser printer connected up to a computer. There were various gadgets and wires spread across the floor in a web. She moved down the wall to the back of the building, turning her head round the corner to sneak a glance.

She shrieked with surprise.

'What are you doing here?' said Peter.

She darted forwards and kissed him. 'I knew it, I knew it.' She danced with joy. 'I knew it couldn't be.'

George stood behind him. 'Bloody hell, she must have followed me.'

'You gave it away, George,' cried Cindy, 'long ago. You said he was safe.'

'I meant safe in Jesus,' protested George.

Peter gave him a dirty look. 'Great, bloody gr-rate.'

'You realize now I've found you, I'm going to keep you to your promise.'

'We can always feed you to the crocodiles,' said George, snapping his hand together like a jaw. 'Did you bring any with you? We've run out.'

Peter smiled turning to George. 'You better nip back home and get that stuff you left behind. I've got to interrogate our prisoner.'

George saluted, 'Right you are. Anything you want me to pick up while I'm on my way?'

'Tomorrow's papers would be good.'

'Okey-dokey,' said George clicking his heels.

He took Cindy's hand. 'Let me show you my hideout.'

The End

Also available: The Hacker Chronicles
Part 2: Logon for Crime.